Abiqua

a John Bitter novel • 2

ROD COLLINS

BRIGHT WORKS PRESS

Abiqua

A JOHN BITTER NOVEL • 2

Bright Works Press
Redmond, OR 97756
www.brightworkspress.com

Print ISBN: 978-09965394-7-0
Library of Congress Control Number: 2020909595

This is a work of fiction. The events in this story are purely the author's imagination, but several historical characters were "borrowed" for this story. The Oregon towns and topography the characters traveled can still be visited today.

Cover photo: ©weerachai/Adobe Images
Map: Courtesy of the National Archives & Records Administration
Cover and interior design, editing, and production
Long On Books
www.longonbooks.com

Printed in the United States of America

TO

Charles Augustus Troop,
grandfather and great storyteller

1862-1865

S TUNG BY A BROKEN ENGAGEMENT, JOHN Bitter turns his Willamette Valley farm over to his brother Luke and heads east to see what the fuss between the states is about.

Three years later, a discharged Civil War veteran with the rank of Captain, he heads home across the Oregon Trail with his beautiful redhead wife, Morgan, two adopted sons, Ethan, age ten and Mikey, almost age six, and an entourage of friends: Ezra Shipley, a freedman and his wife Ruth and son Davey; Liam O'Grady, a Confederate prisoner turned galvanized Yankee; Owl, a Cherokee turned Cheyenne medicine man and Owl's adopted son, Thomas, the lone survivor of an Indian raid against his family's wagon train; Woman, Owl's young wife; and Tom Beecher, Indian scout and one of the richest men in Oregon.

Bitter plans to just ride his big black horse, Rockford, home across the Oregon Trail, tagging along with military patrols for safety. But the Good Lord and Morgan have different ideas about his return to Oregon. As the old saying goes, "If you want to make God laugh, tell him your plans."

Abiqua

"Be careful what you wish for."

Kidnapped

PETER FRANKLIN WOKE TO THE INSISTENT voice of his wife, Clarissa. She was saying, "Wake up, Peter! Wake up! She's gone." Clarissa shook his shoulder until he stirred.

Oregon State Representative Peter Franklin rolled onto his back, rubbed his eyes with a knuckle, and blinked sleep away. "What are you talking about, woman?"

"Anna. She's run away." She thrust a scrap of paper at him. "She left a note on the kitchen table. And her carpet bag is missing."

Representative Franklin flipped the blanket aside and sat up, skinny bare legs dangling from the high bed. He lit the bedside lamp with a match and reached for the note.

Reading glasses perched on his nose, he squinted, held the note under the lamp and read aloud,

"Dear Mother and Father, I am going to the gold fields with Billy Bradford. We are to be married. I know you don't approve of Billy, but he is my one true love. I'll love you always. Anna."

"Good Lord. Bradford is an idiot child. If he was standing here, I'd shoot the sonofabitch."

Clarissa Franklin wiped at her tears with the sleeve of her high-necked cotton night dress and said, "She just turned fifteen, Peter. She doesn't know her own mind."

He looked up at his wife of twenty years and thought, *What mind? She takes after you, Clarissa. Dumb as an ox.* But he didn't say it aloud. Instead, he said, "Clarissa, she didn't run away. She was kidnapped."

"No, she wasn't, Peter. She ran away."

Peter put his glasses and the note on his bedside table and stood up, his knobby knees open to the cold air below his nightshirt. He wrapped his arms around his diminutive wife and pulled her head against his chest. He patted her back and said, "Now, listen Clarissa. What happened is she was kidnapped. Do you understand?"

She shook her head. "No."

"I'm going to hire the Pinkerton Agency to bring her back. In the meantime, if anyone should ask where Anna has gone, you say she is visiting her grandmother in Portland. If word gets out she ran off with Billy Bradford, we'll be the laughing stock of Salem society. It could hurt me politically. No," he said more to himself than to Clarissa, "we keep this quiet, but if word does get out, we'll say she has been kid-napped and we are working to get her back."

He picked up his pocket watch from the nightstand and noted the time: 6:00 a.m. "Right. Clarissa, tell Harvey to hitch Midnight and Mercury to the buggy while I get dressed. And get that lazy cook out of bed. I'll want a hot cup of coffee before I leave."

"They're asleep, Peter."

"Well," he said as he walked barefoot to his closet, "they hadn't better be for very long. Get 'em up, Clarissa. Time's a wasting."

He watched his wife walk out of the bedroom and scurry down the hallway to the landing. While he dressed, he considered as he often did, the reason for his marriage to Clarissa. She wasn't what you would call pretty, but her ready smile and her pleasant ways obscured her lack of conversational skills…for which she often substituted a nod and a tentative smile. Most people thought she was a good listener and a pleasant companion. And Peter Franklin liked good listeners. That her family was wealthy hadn't discouraged his pursuit, either.

He sighed and turned to getting dressed.

A quick cup of coffee and Franklin was out the back door to the brick carriage house and his waiting team. Harvey, who lived in a small apartment over the carriage house and worked as Franklin's general handyman and groundskeeper, offered to drive. Peter Franklin shook his head. "I'll drive this morning, Harvey."

He said, "Hup," flicked the reins and guided the matching team of blacks down the red brick drive and onto rutted Mission Street. The buggy tilted and then settled into the wagon ruts, a curl of dust spiraling behind each wheel. *We've got to do something about these streets.*

A two-story brick building near the river on Ferry Street housed the Pinkerton Detective Agency. It also served as domicile for Nelson Goff who managed the office and was employed as secretary to John Bitter. Their relationship was awkward at best. Goff, who thought himself something of a sleuth, could not see why Mark Anthony, the managing agent for the Pacific Northwest Division of the Pinkertons, kept paying Bitter. As far as Goff could tell, Bitter had done nothing in the past few months to deserve payment of any kind.

An early riser, Goff looked up and then set his morning cup of coffee on the desk when Franklin reined his buggy to a stop in front of the office. Goff knew Representative Franklin by sight and wondered what business he might have for the agency. Nelson made it his business to be in attendance when the Oregon State Senate or the Oregon State House of Representatives was in session. He thought it made good sense to know the major players in state politics.

Franklin wrapped the lines around the brake handle and stepped to the flagstone walk that kept the dust at bay. He took a deep breath, straightened his coat tails, and pulled his black linen vest down in a vain attempt to hide a growing belly. He strode to the door, surprised when it opened before he could knock.

Goff pulled the door open and said, "Representative Franklin. Welcome. Won't you come in? I'm Nelson Goff, secretary to Agent John Bitter."

And ambitious, I think. Franklin held out his hand. "Yes. Nice to meet you, Nelson."

Goff gave no indication he was aware Franklin had used his first name, a casual dismissal if you thought like that. "Please have a seat. Agent Bitter is away at the moment, so perhaps I can help?"

Franklin remained standing. For a moment he studied the slender blond man, noted his impeccable dress, polished shoes, neatly combed hair and thought, *Why don't I trust you?*

"It's highly confidential. I'd rather speak to…Bitter? Is that your agent's name?"

"Yes. John Bitter of Abiqua Creek."

"You don't suppose he's home?"

"Yes. He's very good about letting me know his whereabouts. Perhaps I can take a message?"

"I don't think so. Have you been to his farm?"

Goff hid his disappointment and said, "Yes, sir. I have."

"Good. I'll need directions."

Satisfied he could find Bitter's farm, Franklin turned and walked out the door without bothering to say thank you to Nelson. He stepped into the buggy, unwrapped the reins from the brake handle and turned the horses for home.

He nodded and said, "Yes. A picnic basket and a nice ride with Clarissa to Abiqua Creek. We can stay overnight at the traveler's hotel in Silverton. Make it an outing. Maybe drive to Silver Creek Falls tomorrow. I've been wanting to see that. Maybe do a little politicking."

He slapped the reins. "Hup, now boys. We have things to do."

Abiqua Creek

Barefoot, britches rolled to his knees, twelve-year-old Ethan Bitter filled another bucket with red apples from the low-hanging limbs of the two apple trees in the family orchard. He grinned when his seven-year-old brother Mikey put his nearly empty bucket down and watched their big gray barn cat slip through the tall grass. A meadowlark sang in the hedgerow growing along the fence separating the small orchard from the dusty county road.

"What's he saying, Mikey?"

Mikey shook his head, a strand of yellow hair falling over his forehead, "Well, brother, birds don't say much. They just do bird things. But that cat is thinking he'd like to eat that meadowlark."

"Mikey, I think you just make things up sometimes."

"Not true, brother. Some animals are smart. The smart ones can talk if you listen."

"Well, you better listen to this. You pick that bucket back up. Mama wants a full bin of apples so we can squeeze some cider for winter."

Lucifer, Morgan's black mammoth mule feeding in the lower pasture started braying, the sound carrying for a mile or more up and down the creek. "Okay, Mikey. What's Lucifer saying?"

Mikey shook his head in disgust. "He's says somebody is coming up the county road."

"Well, tell Lucifer to stop braying. He hurts my ears."

After a five-mile trip through the rolling hills east of Silverton, Franklin found a hard-packed dirt track on the west side of a small stream he assumed was Abiqua Creek. He breathed a sigh of relief when he spotted a hand-painted sign on a board tacked to an oak tree. It fit the directions provided by Goff, so he turned south on the road until he saw a neatly kept farm with solid looking fences and a small orchard.

When Franklin turned his team into the lane separating the orchard from the lower pasture, the big, black mule charged the fence, lips pulled back. He came sliding to a halt two feet shy of the split rail fence, and Franklin's team spooked and broke into a gallop. Pulling hard on the reins with one hand and pulling on the brake with the other, he brought the horses to a stop near the gate to the orchard.

Ethan set his bucket in the grass and shook his head in disgust. "Don't worry, mister," he hollered. "He just does that for fun. He won't come through the fence." *Unless he wants to,* Ethan thought.

Lucifer was so tall it was hard for Ethan to get up on the big mule unless he was saddled. Inspired by necessity, Ethan taught him to jump gates and fences. So far, no one had caught them in the act.

Ethan walked through the grass to the orchard gate and waited.

Franklin eyeballed the black mule and then turned to study Ethan. "What's that critter's name, boy?"

"Lucifer."

"An appropriate name it seems. Is he dangerous?"

"Not unless a grown man tries to ride him. Far as we know, he's only killed one man, but that man was fixing to hurt Mama."

"Killed him?"

Ethan nodded, but didn't elaborate.

Franklin raised his eyebrows and glanced at his wife who looked a bit bewildered. "Well, I'm sure as heck not going to try him. Is this the John Bitter farm?"

"Yessir. I'm Ethan Bitter, and that's my brother Mikey," he said, pointing toward the orchard.

"Your daddy at home?"

"Yessir. He's in the woodlot with Mister Shipley. They're cutting firewood. The wind blew an old bam tree down. Cottonwood is not great firewood, but Pa, he don't…doesn't…like to waste things."

"Well I'm State Representative Peter Franklin and this is Missus Franklin. I'd sure like to talk to your daddy. Is Missus Bitter home? I'm hoping my wife could sit with her while he and I talk."

"I think Mama would like a little company. Baby sister Sarah kept her up last night." He looked at Mikey and pointed to the box on the tailgate of the family wagon, the same wagon which brought them across the Oregon trail the year before. "You finish filling the box, Mikey. I'll be right back to help."

The sound of harness bells brought Morgan Bitter to the front porch, little redheaded Sarah cradled in her arms. The child was finally asleep after a croupy night. Morgan walked the baby to the bedroom and gently tucked her in bed. She took off her apron and smoothed her cotton flour dress before walking back to the front porch.

Ethan ran barefoot down the lane. "Ma, he shouted, "it's State Representative Franklin and his wife come calling." He bounced up the steps and said, "Mister Franklin wants to talk to Pa. He hopes you can entertain Missus Franklin while I show him how to find the woodlot."

Peter Franklin helped his wife down from the carriage and said, "I'll be back shortly."

He tipped his hat to Morgan and said, "Thank you for entertaining Missus Franklin. I need a word in private with your husband."

He climbed back in the buggy and said to Ethan, "Lead on, son."

Ethan jogged down the wagon tracks leading to the woodlot, Franklin's buggy close behind.

Woman to Woman

MORGAN STEPPED DOWN FROM THE PORCH and held out her hand. "Welcome. Come on up. I'm Morgan Bitter, John's wife. Let's sit on the porch. It's cooler and I don't want to wake the baby. She had a hard night. Croup."

Clarissa nodded and said, "I'm Clarissa. Nice to meet you. My Anna was a croupy baby. It was enough to wear me out. Did you get any sleep?"

Morgan smiled and shook her head. "Not much. At least not last night. Would you like some cold apple cider? It's fresh pressed."

Clarissa nodded. "That sounds lovely." She sat down on a cane-backed chair next to a small wooden table.

When Morgan returned with two water cooled glasses of cider, Clarissa said, "Your red hair is so lovely. I'm jealous. I'm afraid mine is thinning. I'd love to have a full head of hair again."

Morgan nodded, but said nothing. She sat in the other cane back and shooed an intruding yellow jacket away.

Clarissa sipped the sweet cider, sighed, and then said, "That's good. Thank you." She looked at the meadow, the orchard where Mikey was slowly filling the apple bin, and then said, "My husband thinks I'm stupid, so he never shares anything important with me. But I'm a good listener, and I pick up enough information to know what's going on."

"So...you know why he wants to see John?"

"Yes." Clarissa skootched her chair an inch closer to the table. In a confidential tone, she began to tell Morgan the story of her marriage to Peter Franklin, the birth of Anna, and the failed effort to have more children.

"I know Peter wanted a son, but we just never seemed to have another child. As a consequence, he pretty much ignored Anna. And me. Politics has become his mistress. Anna feels unloved by her father, so she has looked to other men...boys really...for love."

She took another sip of cider and said, "Damn him." And then she looked embarrassed.

"I'm sorry. I really don't know what came over me. I have so few people to talk with since my older sister died."

Morgan nodded. "I do understand. If it wasn't for my friend Ruth, I think I'd be lonely, too. My family is still in Missouri. Although there is hope my brother Harley and his wife will be here before winter." She paused. "I'd like that."

～

Franklin followed Ethan down the wagon track through the walnut trees. The grove was the work of John Bitter, planted before he turned soldier and headed east to see the ruckus caused by Southern Secession. He hadn't known he'd be gone for more than three years.

At the sound of harness bells, Ezra Shipley leaned his splitting maul against the big cottonwood round he was turning into firewood. "Somebody coming, John." The big man, arms like tree trunks from days at the forge, wiped the trickle of sweat from his cheeks. "You sure picked a warm day to make firewood."

At six feet, John Bitter was leaner than Ezra, and two inches shorter. John was lightning quick with his hands, a quirk of nature he had done nothing to earn. But when he and Ezra shared work on their adjoining farms, Bitter was always surprised by how strong Ezra had become. "I sure wouldn't want him mad at me," he told Morgan. "He's turned into a mountain of a man. I'll bet he can lift a horse and put shoes on each hoof without ever setting the horse down."

And that wasn't the only change. Ezra had a confidence and an open way of dealing with people that belied his former status as a plantation slave. "Freedman," he'd say on occasion right out of the blue. Or, "God bless Abraham Lincoln and the Union Army." Sometimes he added, "God bless John Bitter. A better friend never lived."

When the buggy entered the walnut grove, Ezra said, "Who do you suppose that is?"

"I don't recognize him, but given the leather buggy top and the silk hat, I'd say he probably thinks of himself as important."

"Nice team," Ezra added.

Franklin pulled to a stop and stared at the two men. Stripped to the waist they were a contrast––the bulked muscles of a black man, erect and tall versus the lean, whipcord muscles of the white man beside him. Both were shiny with sweat.

"Pa," Ethan said, "this is State Representative Franklin. Says he wants a word with you."

Franklin wrapped the lines around the brake and stepped down. He laid his hat on the buggy seat and wiped a nervous hand through his thinning gray hair. "Thank you for showing me the way, Ethan." He fumbled a quarter from a trouser pocket and held it out. "Here."

As hungry for money as any country boy, Ethan never-the-less felt insulted." He shook his head. "Nope. This is our farm. We are hospitable here."

Confused, Franklin put the quarter back in his pocket. He shrugged and looked at Bitter. "I need your help."

On the Road Again

FROM THE PORCH OF THEIR LOG home on Abiqua Creek, Missus Morgan Bitter, lips pursed in disapproval, little redheaded Sarah hooked to her left hip, shook a finger at her husband and said, "When you get back, you need to decide what's more important. Family or working for the Pinkertons."

Eyes big, Ethan Bitter and his little brother Mikey watched this rare quarrel between their adoptive parents. Even Rusty, their big red hound sensed the trouble in the air.

John Bitter, Pinkerton Agent for Oregon, slid his Henry repeating rifle into the rifle scabbard, swung into the saddle and smiled at his wife. His mouth got the best of him when he said, "I've been told redheads are feisty, especially pretty ones. I just can't resist feisty red-headed women."

She said, "Don't you try to sweet talk me, John Bitter," but a smile brushed her lips. She did her best to hide the smile, and said, "You make this a fast trip."

"Yep. I'll go get the Franklin girl and get back as soon as I can. I'm taking the Barlow Trail. I'm hoping to reach Sherar's bridge before she does. Her daddy said she left a note about going to the gold fields in Canyon City."

"You do that. And stay safe."

Bitter winked at the boys and said, "Try to stay on her good side while I'm gone. And tend to your chores. I'll be back before the walnut harvest."

He waved and turned Rockford, the meanest, blackest horse a man could ever own, down the lane to the Abiqua road. Windy, Bitter's choice for a pack mule, tugged at the lead rope, but Rockford hardly noticed. He just kept pulling the reluctant mule up the lane. Rusty trotted alongside his friend Rockford. Why the big horse and the hound got on so well was a mystery Bitter was still trying to plumb.

Less than a year had passed since the Bitters ended their long trek across the Oregon Trail, but Rockford, Rusty and John Bitter were all happy to be on the move again. After the first mile, even the ever-flatulent Windy had his head up and his ears pointed forward, eyes looking down the road.

Day Three

ROCKFORD SWIVELED HIS EARS FORWARD AND stamped a hoof, staring at the dark willows between camp and the Zig Zag River. Rusty growled, and the pack mule jerked his head up. John Bitter rose from the log in front of his small evening campfire and slipped into the shadows at the base of a rock overhang. He eased his revolver from the holster and waited. Night was only about twenty minutes away, and he knew his clothing would blend with the dark basalt.

Rockford tugged at his picket rope and snuffed.

"Hello, the camp," someone said from beyond the willows.

Bitter waited. The intruder finally said, "Is that you, John Bitter?"

"Who wants to know?"

"It's me. Owl. I've come to help you find the girl. I stopped by your farm and Morgan told me what you are doing."

"Come on in."

Old Owl led Horse and a spotted pack horse up to the fire, ground hitched the animals, and said, "Is that bacon? I'm hungry. Took me two days to catch up. You set a mean pace, John Bitter."

Bitter looked at his old friend, a broad brimmed yellow hat perched on his head, decorated with the tail feather from a red-tailed hawk, gray braids tied with leather thongs, spring still in his step, eyes bright with amusement. Bitter thought, *He always looks like he's playing a great joke on the world.*

"I thought you were teaching school to the Calapooya kids at French Prairie."

Owl grinned and said, "School is out, and Woman is driving me crazy. I think I'll go back to the Cherokee. Be a teacher or a medicine man again."

"And leave Woman?"

"She likes our friend Liam O'Grady." He chuckled and said, "Might divorce me." He moved to the pack horse, untied his pack, and slipped it to the ground with a grunt. "Too much gear for an Indian."

"What about the Cheyenne? Would they take you back?"

"Maybe, but that life is over. Makes me sad. I don't want to watch the end of the wild ones."

"Not sure I blame you."

With Horse unsaddled and his pack horse picketed, Owl dug a tin cup from a saddle bag and dusted it off against his denim britches. He pulled up a round block of wood, a makeshift stool used by earlier campers, sat down with a sigh, and held the cup out. "Coffee smells good."

The metal handle of the coffee pot warm through the rag he used as a makeshift potholder, Bitter filled Owl's cup and then refilled his own. He set the smoke-blackened pot back on a rock next to the fire to simmer, and then he waited. He knew Owl would get around to telling him why he was here.

Rusty pushed his wet nose in against Owl's knees and sniffed, knowing Owl's scent from days following the Oregon Trail from the high plains to Wheatland Ferry on the Willamette River.

Owl absent mindedly scratched behind Rusty's ears, sipped his coffee, and then said, "Your friend O'Grady built a nice tavern." He paused and then added, "Us Indians should never drink. Not raised to it. Makes for bad medicine. But Liam has enough business from white people, if you can call the Métis white people. They look like white people."

Owl took another sip of coffee and then said, "I'm told the Métis came from a place called France. But now they been gone so long they are changed. They aren't Frenchmen any longer."

"Good people," Bitter said.

Owl grinned. "Until they get drunk. Then they are just like us Indians. Might pull a knife on a friend."

Bitter shook his head. "The Métis and the Indians don't have a corner on that. Drunk whites are liable to do the same."

Owl nodded. His teeth flashed in the firelight and he half grinned. "This coffee is pretty bitter, John Bitter. You wouldn't have any whiskey to sweeten it up?"

Bitter laughed and said, "You haven't changed a bit, have you?"

Owl smiled and said, "I'm older. And Tom Beecher and I saw the ocean. Had ourselves a drink. The ocean is big. Very big. Made me feel like I was standing on the edge of forever."

Surprised, Bitter stared in admiration. He pulled a whiskey bottle from the saddle bags straddling the log and handed it to the old man. "Owl, you amaze me. At times you are downright profound."

"I think I know what that means. It's a white man's word for thinker. Or maybe for big medicine. Profound. I'll think I'll keep that one."

Bitter nodded and suppressed a chuckle. "You got a plate? The bacon looks done, and Morgan packed me some good soda biscuits with butter, and some sweet dried apples."

As the fire faded to coals, Bitter made his bed between the log and the overhanging bluff. If it rained, he stood a chance of staying dry. Rusty curled up next to the dying fire. Bitter knew Rusty and Rockford were all the sentinels he needed.

His new lever action Henry beside him, Owl crawled into his bed between his two horses, trusting their instincts to give him warning if anyone tried to sneak up on the camp. From the dark, he said, "Three bad men are following you, John Bitter. They want your horse and your mule."

John shook his head. "And you waited to tell me this?"

"They were getting drunk the last time I saw them, so I turned their horses loose. We'll be gone in the morning before they find their horses…if they can. When I was coming up the trail, I heard them shooting pistols. So, I sneaked up and watched. They were trying to break an empty whiskey bottle."

Owl waited a few seconds and then laughed. "They are very bad shots. I was going to leave them alone until one said he wanted your black horse. Then I knew they were thieves."

Bitter waited in silence until Owl said, "Indians hate thieves. Unless they steal from the white man. Or from other tribes. Anyway, I thought, Owl, if you shoot them, there could be trouble you don't want. So, I just drove their horses off."

"Thank you, Owl. I owe you…again."

"You talk like a white man. I just did it for fun."

Bitter stayed quiet, hands under his head, looked through the tops of the cedar trees at the clear night sky, saw the wink of a falling star and let his mind drift back to time spent on the Oregon Trail, and to an encounter with a renegade Mormon named Butler. That particular cuss planned to wait until the cavalry patrol escorting the Bitter and Shipley wagons turned for home, and then he planned to kill the men to have the women.

What Butler got instead was his throat cut and his own knife shoved in his belly. Scared the crap out of the two men who had shared Butler's tent when they woke to find him dead.

Bitter knew Owl had done it, but none of the soldiers could find Owl's tracks, and Bitter never said a word about the note Owl left, written in his plain missionary school script. Bitter memorized it over time.

John Bitter. Woman and I go back to the Cheyenne leaving son Thomas with you. The white world is too mixed up. I can't tell who the enemy is. My new son should be Indian, not a white Indian like Thomas will be. I will miss son Thomas, but he should be a white man, not a Indian white man. Take care for him, John Bitter. The horse is for Thomas. The evil one won't bother you anymore. Owl

Bitter thought, *I owe you my life and the lives of Morgan and the boys. And maybe I owe you a second time.*

He listened to the murmur of the river and drifted off to sleep.

Summit

BITTER WOKE TO CHILL MORNING AIR and the smell of wood smoke. He pushed up on one elbow and looked over the top of the log he'd slept behind in time to see Owl feed a handful of dry twigs to a burning pile of fir needles.

Owl saw Bitter was awake and said, "Why do you care about the girl?"

Bitter shook his head and said, "She's young and gullible."

"Gullible. Another big, white man's word. I don't know that one."

Bitter sat his butt on the log, turned his boots upside down to remove any errant critters and slipped the cold boots over his cotton socks. "Well, it means she is easily fooled…or easy to trick. And her daddy wants her back."

"What if she doesn't want to come back with you? What if she is married by the time you find her?"

"Well…if so, I'll just have to let it be."

"Was she stolen?"

"In one sense she was. She let herself be talked into doing something pretty foolish." He started rolling up his blankets.

He looked upriver, eyeballing the trail. "From what I've been told, we should climb out of here and cross the pass by noon. I'm anxious to see that Tygh Valley country. I keep thinking I might start a horse ranch someplace around there."

Owl grumped. "A ranch is too much work."

A fine mist and a cold wind chased Owl and Bitter up Laurel Hill. It was rocky, slippery and steep. The animals were sucking wind by the time they reached the top. An errant puff of wind blew the clouds apart and Owl stared at the huge mass of Mount Hood, its bones showing in most places, but still wearing a cap of last winter's snow. He nodded and said, "Nice mountain. Good spirits live here, I think."

The trail on top wound through the timber to Collins Lake, an acre of ice-cold water in a deep crater hemmed by willow thickets and a grassy meadow. Bitter pulled Rockford to a halt and stepped down. "Let's noon here."

Rusty lapped water from the lake and then plopped down on a hump of sun-warmed bear grass and rested. As strong as he was, it was still a tough climb.

While Bitter watered and picketed the animals on the coarse mountain grass, Owl gathered small wood and started a fire in a circle of smoke-blackened rocks. A series of ripples marred the glassy surface of the lake as a school of bright silver trout rose to eat the morning bug hatch. Bitter grinned and said, "If Ethan was here, we'd be eating fresh trout for lunch."

Owl struck a wooden match on the rough surface of a rock, cupped it in his hand, and then fed the flame to the small pile of fir needles and bark he used for starter. He watched the flames, and satisfied with the fire said, "Have you heard from Thomas?"

John's mind jumped back to the Little Blue River on the Oregon Trail and the first time he saw Owl and Thomas, a young white boy Owl had adopted. Those two were in rough shape because Owl had been chased out of the Cheyenne tribe when the chief's wife died. Owl's medicine hadn't been enough to save the poor woman.

After Owl killed Butler and took off, John and Morgan, Mikey and Ethan looked after Thomas until a family claiming to be relatives showed up at the Abiqua farm…with a deputy sheriff in tow.

John shook his head. "No, and I didn't like the looks of the people who claimed him. I have a suspicion they just see him as free labor. I hope he'll be okay."

Owl nodded. "If you wait, he will be back."

John scooped the coffee pot full of lake water and asked, "Biscuits and bacon again?"

By late afternoon, they crossed the White River, a rocky tumbling stream fed by a glacier tucked high on the slopes of Mount Hood.

"Milk water," Owl said. "Never saw any before."

John dismounted, grinned and picked up a fist sized rock. "Watch this." He tossed the rock in the swift water.

Owl shook his head. "That is strong medicine. The rock floats. Never seen that before. Good trick. What do you call this rock?"

John picked up another chunk of rock and handed it to Owl. "We call it pummy, but I·think the scientific name is pumice."

Owl turned the yellow rock over in his hand and then dismounted. "I want some of these. In case I have to go back to be a medicine man."

U.S. Marshal

AN HOUR AFTER FORDING THE WHITE River, they spotted a mule train about eight hundred yards downhill, coming up through an open stand of timber. Bitter stepped down and fished his French field glasses from a saddle bag.

He focused on an open lane in the timber and watched until he was certain he had seen the entire train. "I count eleven pack animals, and six armed men. They have rifles across their saddles, and they are looking nervous. Something is going on." And then he spotted what looked to be a body tied across the saddle on a big bay horse. "I think they've had trouble."

Owl stepped down off Horse and opened a saddle bag. He pulled out a flat package wrapped in canvas, tied with a leather thong. He tapped John on the shoulder and said, "You might need this. I hear some of the Wasco Indians are causing trouble for the ore trains, the ones bringing gold from Canyon City."

John lowered the field glasses and looked at Owl. "How do you hear these things?"

"Tavern talk. In O'Grady's."

Curious, Bitter unwrapped the package and found an official looking envelope with his name on it. He raised his eyebrows and looked at Owl. "And you waited to tell me?"

"I had orders from Tom Beecher to wait for the right time." He pointed in the direction of the mule train. "This might be it. Could keep us from being shot as outlaws…or as Indians."

Inside was a letter appointing John Bitter a U.S. Marshal. It was signed by Federal Court Judge Matthew Paul Deady. A bright silver star was lodged in one corner of the envelope with U.S. Marshal stamped on the rim of the silver circle holding a star.

"I never asked for this," John said in an accusatory tone.

"You can thank Tom Beecher. He talked the Governor into asking Judge Deady to make you a marshal. Beecher said you might find a use for it. Might need to arrest someone. And…it might keep me from being shot by white men who don't know I'm a Christian Cherokee."

John frowned. "Unless I shoot you first."

He sighed and shook his head, but he unbuttoned his canvas jacket and reluctantly pinned the star to the pocket of his faded blue denim shirt. When he took his hand away, the jacket slipped back into place, hiding the star. *No sense in showing a badge unless I have to,* he thought. He folded the letter from Judge Deady and stuffed it into his shirt pocket, in behind the badge.

He tied the pack mule's lead rope to the saddle horn, backed Rockford off the narrow road and ground hitched him. "We might as well wait here."

Owl led Horse a few yards off the narrow winding road, tied the reins to a pine sapling and pulled his Henry lever action rifle from the saddle scabbard. He took cover behind a big rust-colored pine tree. "Maybe you can tell them I'm your Indian scout, so they won't shoot me."

"I'll do my best."

John took the makings from his jacket pocket and carefully shaped a roll-your-own. He thumbed a match, lit the cigarette and took a puff, letting the nicotine settle his nerves. If the men in the pack train had trouble earlier, they might be a touch nervous…might be inclined to shoot first and talk later. That Owl was Indian might also aggravate them. He blew the match out, pinched the head to kill the heat, dropped it in the dirt, and ground it with the toe of his boot.

Rusty barked a challenge at the pack string until Bitter said, "Quiet, Rusty. Knock it off."

The rider in the lead was a small wiry man with a drooping brown moustache. He pulled a big stocking footed bay horse to a stop about thirty yards from Bitter and then just sat there, rifle across the saddle, nervously eyeing the timber, trying to see if he was about to be ambushed.

Bitter stepped to the edge of the road and called out, "Looks like you've had trouble."

The man nodded slightly, but he didn't answer.

Bitter said, "We mean you no trouble. Headed for Canyon City on business."

"What business?"

"Personal."

A second rider, lean and wiry like the first, probably a brother, rode up and stopped a big buckskin horse a little off to the side. He held a rifle propped upright on his thigh. "Who's hiding in the trees?"

Bitter said, "My friend Owl. Didn't want you to shoot him for an Indian."

"Owl, huh? Sounds Indian to me."

Owl shouted from behind the tree, "Just an old man! A Christian Cherokee!"

"You sure you ain't a Wasco?"

"Pretty sure," Owl answered back.

"Come on out where I can see you."

Bitter pulled his jacket open to let the star show and said, "No. Stay where you are, Owl. And you boys step down. I'm U.S. Marshal John Bitter. Maybe we should talk. What happened to you boys?"

The two riders looked at each other. The leader gave a short nod, a bit reassured by the badge, but wary, nonetheless. "You stay here,

Melvin. I'll go talk." He swung down from the saddle and ground hitched the horse.

Digby

RIFLE IN HIS LEFT HAND, EYES sweeping the timber, he walked steadily toward Bitter.

He's either bullheaded or extremely confident, Bitter thought. *Well, here goes.* He started walking toward the man.

They stopped about six feet apart, appraising, sensing, trying to feel if the other was dangerous. Finally, the small man with the drooping moustache said, "How do I know you really are a U.S. Marshal? Anybody can pin on a badge."

"Good question. Go easy and I'll show you my letter of appointment." Bitter pulled the folded paper with Judge Deady's signature from his shirt pocket and stepped close enough to hand it over.

The small man read slowly, working hard to make out all the words. Finally, he puffed up his cheeks and then exhaled, a long , slow breath that signaled relief there would be no trouble from John Bitter and Owl.

He handed the letter back and then hollered, "Come on up, Mel. This gent is legit." He turned back to Bitter and shook his head. "Judge Deady, huh? You have some mighty big friends, Marshal Bitter. How long you been a U.S. Marshal?"

Bitter shook his head. "I don't know. Up until about five minutes ago, I didn't even know I was one. I guess Owl's been packing this letter…and the badge…around until he thought it might be useful. Owl is friends with Tom Beecher."

"I know Beecher. I scouted with him for the Army a couple years back. You'd never know he was filthy rich if you was around him. Just plain old Tom Beecher, rascal and Indian scout."

"Sounds about right. I'd have to add manipulator to that. He is determined to mess with my life."

The rider grinned and held out his hand. "Call me Digby. Never did like being called Barnabas or Barney. Just use my last name. Yep, I'd say you know Tom. Just does things his way and expects the rest of us to follow along."

The handshake was signal enough for Owl that peace was made. He led the big bay gelding he called Horse and the small spotted pack horse out to the road, and then watched the other rider gather up the reins of Digby's horse and lead him to where Digby and Bitter were waiting.

Bitter pointed and said, "This is my friend, Owl. He is indeed a Christian Cherokee. Teaches school at French Prairie. And he's a pretty good doctor."

Digby stuck out his hand and said, "Nice to meet you Mister Owl. Call me Digby. That runt over there is my brother Melvin."

Bitter asked, "And who's over the saddle?"

"Sad to say, he's cousin George…named after President Washington."

"And he died how?"

"Four white men jumped us…or tried to. Come riding out of the brush, guns out, yelling like Comanches. I don't know what they was thinking. Maybe cause we was scattered they thought they could take us one by one."

He shook his head. "Didn't work that way. Mel hasn't missed a shot since he was born, so he dumped one with his rifle before they hit the road. The other three started in shooting. Came riding right at us. That was when George was hit. I think I hit one, but he stuck to the saddle and rode off. The other two just turned and hightailed it."

Brother Mel dismounted and held out his hand. And then he said, "They were riding good stock…a buckskin, two bays, and one of the prettiest spotted horses you ever saw. Rose-colored, it was. I'll be looking for that horse. Mean to kill the rider if I can."

Bitter didn't say anything, but he decided he wouldn't want the Digby brothers mad at him. Highly capable of carrying out that plan was how he thought of them.

"Where's the dead outlaw?"

"Well, we just sort of propped him up against a tree alongside the road. Mel took a big slab of cedar bark and carved 'Jacob Short, Outlaw' on it and propped it up alongside the body. Thought it might just make other outlaws stop and think. He had a wallet with a card in it said Jacob Short. We figured that must be his name. And he had a twenty-dollar gold piece. We took it and his gun belt and pistol. Figure to give it to Samantha, George's wife. His boots were worn out or we'd have taken them as well."

"And the other men with you?"

"Hired hands, and I'd say pretty nervous right about now."

Bitter nodded, and then said, "I'm assuming you are carrying gold from the Canyon City mines."

Digby said, "Yep."

"And how do I know you didn't steal it?"

Digby grinned, his moustache rising a bit. "Good question." He walked to his horse and rummaged through his saddle bag before he said, "Yep. Here it is."

He handed a paper to Bitter who unfolded it and read it over. Bitter nodded and handed it back. "Looks official to me, seal and all. Now, I have one more question. Did you see a young woman, say about fifteen years old, dark hair with a young man…say about nineteen or so?

Digby nodded. "Might have. There was a young couple riding on the Bake Oven road. Didn't stop to talk, and he looked mighty nervous. Kept looking back like he was afraid someone was chasing him."

"When was that?"

"Yesterday."

"Good. Thanks."

Owl stepped closer and held out a bottle of amber liquor. "I'm glad you didn't shoot me for an Indian. That calls for a drink."

Rockford's ears were pointed straight ahead when Bitter pulled him to a halt a few feet from the outlaw corpse propped against a big pine tree. The bullet hole in his forehead was hard to miss. The letters on the sign were crude, but clear enough.

Rusty sniffed at the corpse and growled, the hackles on the back of his neck rising.

"My sentiments exactly, Rusty."

Owl rode Horse up beside him and said, "We gonna bury him?"

"I don't know. What do you think?"

"Well, maybe we should let the devil bury this one."

"Not very Christian."

"No."

Bitter kneed the big horse and started on down the road toward Tygh Valley, Windy tugging the lead rope, like he was trying to say he had enough packing for one day.

Hard Men

Bitter thought Tygh Valley was just about perfect for a horse ranch. Timber on the slopes to the west, good water from the river, and deep rye grass in the meadows…just about everything a man could ask for.

He glanced back at Owl and said, "Why don't you pick us a campsite. I want to get a look at the valley before dark."

"You gonna wear that horse out."

"Won't go very far. Just want to ride out to the middle a ways, see what I can see." He walked Rockford across the river on a shallow riffle and followed a wide game trail through a willow thicket. *Elk trail, maybe?*

A short ride of two-hundred yards was all he needed to see a small creek coming off the tall open ridge to the north, a line of cottonwoods marking the channel. Mount Hood to the west made a beautiful backdrop. He nodded. "Yep, Rockford, I like it. Pretty as a picture. I think we might just be back before Fall. Build a cabin, a small barn and a corral. Put up some hay to winter the stock."

A light column of smoke a half mile down the creek caught his eye. "I wonder who's camping downriver from us?"

The sun slid behind Mt. Hood before Bitter spotted Owl's campfire. He smelled coffee and realized he was tired and hungry after all. Owl had coffee on to boil, and a skillet of bacon sizzling over the fire by the time Bitter and Rockford got back to camp.

Bitter swung down and uncinched the saddle.

Owl watched and said, "You spot something?

Bitter nodded. "Got us some company a half mile downstream. As soon as I have a bite and cup of coffee, I'm going to scout them. See who's there. Something doesn't feel right."

"Why?"

"No animals in the meadow. I'd graze mine there…planned on it. But maybe not now. No. Whoever it is wants to stay out of sight. Hadn't been for a trickle of smoke, I wouldn't know anyone was sharing the valley with us."

❧

A CRESCENT MOON WAS EDGING UP over the horizon, and the crickets were filling the soft air with their raspy songs when he called, "Owl. It's me. I'm coming in."

"What did you find, John Bitter?"

"A half dozen hard-looking men. Got close enough to hear them talking about raiding the next gold train. And I think they know we're here. Spotted me looking over the meadow earlier. Said something about paying me a visit after I bedded down." He sounded frustrated when he said, "That blasted Rockford is too handsome. Somebody is always wanting to steal him."

"You have enough trouble to be an Indian."

"Trouble comes with living, Owl. You know that." He paused, nodded to himself. "Let's build the fire up, and then move the animals back a ways. Maybe arrange our bedrolls to look like we're sleeping here."

"Shoot them?"

"Not unless we have to. But I want to them to think twice before raiding my camp again."

"If you kill them, you won't have to worry."

Bitter chuckled. "That's kind of bloodthirsty, isn't it?"

"But certain," Owl said.

"I don't know. That's a tough looking bunch. Might be a chore to handle all of them at once."

Owl laughed, "You want me to play Indian? Sneak up and turn their horses loose."

"No. Let them come to us." Bitter put Rockford's saddle up against a big cottonwood, untied his bedroll and heaped up some leaves to make it like somebody was sleeping under the blankets. As final touch, he placed his hat on the saddle horn.

"What do you think?"

Owl looked over from the dummy bed he was making and nodded. "Might fool a white man."

"Might…in the dark." Bitter put a couple dry limbs on the fire and then led Rockford and the pack animal through a willow thicket and into the dark. Rusty looked the fire over like he was trying to figure out what was going on, and then padded after his friend Rockford.

Owl led his horses through the thicket. "Good moon coming up. We can see to shoot."

Marshal John Bitter

After an hour of listening to the crickets and watching the bats feed on mosquitoes, Bitter was getting restless, but when Rusty gave a low rumbling growl. Bitter patted his head. "Quiet, Rusty."

Owl whispered, "They have their pistols out. Gonna shoot our blankets," and then the night erupted with muzzles flashes and the sound of pounding guns.

The shooting stopped and Owl chuckled. "Their guns are empty, John Bitter."

Rifle butt to his shoulder, Bitter stepped into the firelight. "All right. Put your hands up." A thin man wearing a dirty canvas shirt continued to reload. He said, "You can't kill us all."

Bitter said, "No, but I can kill you for certain. I hate killing people, but I will. Drop the pistol on the ground."

Owl's voice from behind caused a stir. "You look pretty plain to me, all lit up by the fire. Two to six is good. But you emptied your guns. So, it's two to none." And then he laughed.

A big man wearing a cowhide vest jumped his horse at Bitter and got himself slapped to the ground by a rifle barrel. And then Owl was firing, and the thin man's pistol fell at the edge of the fire just before he tumbled from the saddle with Owl's fatal bullet rattling around in his rib cage. The other four men had their hands raised, and one said over and over, "Don't shoot. Don't shoot."

Bitter barked, "Get off those horses, on this side so I can see you, and keep your hands in the air."

The man Bitter knocked from the saddle stirred and opened his eyes to stare into the white teeth of a snarling red hound. He was reaching for the knife in his boot when Bitter smacked him with his rifle barrel again. The man sighed and slid into troubled sleep. Bitter didn't know if he had smacked him hard enough to kill him, and frankly he didn't care.

Bitter held the four outlaws at gun point while Owl disarmed them and tossed their guns against the log supporting Bitter's saddle. "Now," Bitter said, "take off your boots, and strip."

One of the men whined about the skeeters. A shot from Bitter's rifle kicked dust next to the man's ankle and he stopped his whining. When they were all naked, Bitter tossed their clothes on the fire.

Owl found two knives hiding in the boots. "Nice knives, Marshal Bitter. I think I'll keep them. Pay for my new blanket."

"Marshal? We didn't know you was no Marshal. We meant no harm. Knew you wasn't in the blankets. Just having some fun."

Bitter just shook his head and said, "That's a pretty good story. My friends are going to get a kick out of that one. Now here's what we are going to do. We keep your horses and your weapons. We burn your clothes and your boots. And then you can go. But if I ever see any of you again, I'll shoot on sight. Got that?"

A heavy-set man, his face obscured by a large black beard, growled, "You can't do that. We'll starve or get killed by the Indians."

"You should have thought about that before you tried to kill us."

Bitter pointed at the dead man. "You want his scalp, Chief?"

Owl said, "No. Blood makes my stomach sick."

Bitter had the men strip their unconscious partner and then added his boots and his clothes to the fire. Owl collected one more knife.

"Okay," Bitter said, "That's it. You take your dead partner, and your knot-headed friend and get out of here. Out across the meadow. Don't go to your camp, because that's where we'll be."

"You ain't arresting us?"

"I don't have time, or I would. Now get."

The outlaws fell and stumbled over the rocks in the bed of White River and dropped the unconscious man in the water. He came up spewing river water and cussing. But he calmed right down when his companions explained their predicament.

"We'll get you," he shouted at Bitter and Owl.

Owl said quietly, "It's not too late to shoot them. You should do it now."

"You could be right." He watched the white bodies of the naked men, stark in the moonlight, start across the big meadow until they grew harder to spot. "I think, old friend, we should saddle up and move on down river."

They had no desire to chase the lone wayward outlaw horse in the middle of the night, so they tied the remaining five horses on lead ropes, gathered the pistols, and rode down river in the moonlight. The faint glow of the coals in the fire pit led them to the outlaw camp, and to two pack horses.

While Owl loaded the outlaw's food supplies on the pack horses, Bitter built a huge bonfire and burned the canvas tents and bedrolls. When they were smoldering ruins, Bitter said, "That'll do it."

∾

FROM A DISTANCE OF ABOUT three hundred yards, five naked men, pale bodies washed by moonlight, watched the bonfire consume their tents, packs and clothing. Alfred Swift, the biggest of the outlaws, rubbed the knot on his head, felt the sticky blood on his fingers, and then growled, "I'm gonna kill those sonsabitches."

Another of the outlaws, a small man called Ace, snorted and said, "With what, Alf?" We ain't got nothin' to work with."

Swift looked at Ace with disgust. "They took five horses. My horse is still out there. And my extra pistol is in the saddle bags. We'll find the horse in the morning and figure it out from there. In the meantime, I aim to get close to that fire to warm up. We'll scrounge what we can."

Chance Encounter

Bitter was too tired to appreciate the silver beauty of the riverbank cottonwoods lit by the crescent moon. Dead beat, nearly asleep in the saddle, Bitter was startled when Rockford stumbled. Rockford had never stumbled, not once in battle during the Civil War, and not once in the long trek across the Oregon Trail. *Pushing too hard,* Bitter thought. *Either that or Rockford is getting older.*

He pulled Rockford to a halt and felt the mule bump into the big black horse. "Owl," he called, "let's rest right here until daylight."

They unsaddled, dropped the packs from the four pack animals and picketed all the horses. Bitter rolled out his bedroll, ruefully poked a finger through a hole in his blanket made by a .44 slug, and then stretched out. Owl laid out his own bedroll. After a minute or so he said, "Never just wound an enemy, John Bitter. Those men, they will come hunting us. You'll have to kill them next time."

Bitter took a deep breath and said, "I hope not."

⁓

The sound of hungry horses cropping the wild grass took him back to the long trek on the Oregon Trail, to the time he and Ezra Shipley waited on a moonlit night much like the Tygh Valley moon, waiting for about forty or fifty Wildhorse Cheyenne warriors to ride over the open hills of the plains, chasing the Bitter-Shipley wagons. The plan was simple: lead the Indians into the waiting rifles of a cavalry patrol.

Ezra had told him to rest while he kept watch. Bone-weary, a grateful John Bitter had simply laid down in the prairie grass and slept while

Rockford grazed close by. Three hours later Ezra woke him and said, "John, you best be awake now. Our Indian friends are headed this way."

At the four-hundred-yard mark, Ezra had touched off his .52 caliber Sharps rifle, watched as the big slug punched an Indian off his horse, and then had said, "I sure hate killing people." The two men had mounted up and run for their lives, stopping occasionally to take a shot at the mass of Indians in hot pursuit, and then finally led the Cheyenne up over a hill and into the waiting line of Sergeant Callaghan's troopers and a nasty Gatling gun. Ironically, after three years of Civil War battles without so much as a scratch, the fight with the Wildhorse Cheyenne left Bitter with an Indian bullet in his thigh.

He put the memory aside and drifted off to sleep.

⌇

Daylight found Owl and Bitter headed downriver to Sherar's Bridge, pronounced by most people as Shear's Bridge, the main crossing of the Deschutes River on The Dalles-Canyon City military road. Breakfast had been dry biscuits and a drink of water from their canteens. Owl grumbled about not having any bacon or coffee, but Bitter ignored him.

As they led the string of horses past a low basalt bluff and down the rocky road to the bridge, Bitter caught sight of a company of blue clad troopers in front of the log store. They looked about ready to mount up. "Owl, is that Captain Bidwell?"

"Looks like it. Not many white men that big."

Bitter laughed and said, "I wonder where he finds horses strong enough to carry him?" Without waiting for an answer, he gigged the horses into a trot.

Bitter's whistle turned Bidwell in the saddle. "Sergeant Benteen," Bidwell barked, "my field glasses, if you please."

Without a word, the sergeant fished the glasses from his saddle bag and handed them to Bidwell. Benteen's creased and sunbaked face told the story of years under the sun. If asked his age, he refused to answer. But troopers in his platoon guessed him to be somewhere between sixty and one hundred. Nonetheless, he was a comfort to the green troopers. They had confidence in the old Civil War veteran and Indian fighter. As the saying went, "He'd been to see the elephant."

"Uh huh," Bidwell said. "I thought I recognized that black horse." He turned in his saddle and said to the waiting troopers, "Gentlemen, prepare to meet John Bitter, former captain of the Union Army and a veteran of the Civil War."

When Bitter pulled Rockford to a halt next to Bidwell's big horse, he reached across the saddle and extended his hand. Bidwell grinned and said, "Mister Owl, you're keeping bad company again."

Owl nodded. "But lucky."

Bidwell eyeballed the five saddled horses following Bitter and Owl's four pack animals, and then asked, "Where did you get the horses?"

Bitter shrugged, "Well, we sort of confiscated them from a bunch of would-be outlaws. Tried to kill us, but we scotched that."

Owl thumped Horse in the ribs and eased up alongside Bitter. "If you see five naked white men, don't believe anything they say."

Bitter laughed and said, "We felt compelled to relieve them of clothes, weapons, horses and grub."

"How many?"

"Five survivors and one deceased."

Bidwell nodded. "Two to six, huh? Did you sneak up on them?"

Bitter shook his head. "Nope, they tried to sneak up on us. Shot up our camp, and when their pistols were empty, we sort of let them know it wouldn't be smart to try anything."

"I want to hear this story. Sergeant Benteen, we'll rest here."

Catching Up

BITTER AND OWL GROUND-HITCHED THEIR ANIMALS and followed Bidwell into the store. The ceilings were so low Bidwell had duck to keep from bumping his head, but the smell of coffee staying warm on a wood cookstove invited them in. A back room was secured by a wooden door. A rough-cut plank shelf ran the length of the back wall. Flour, coffee, beans, blankets, britches, shirts, ammunition, and whiskey were on display on shelves behind the counter.

Owl spotted a jar of striped candy sticks. He walked over, read the sign. "Two for a nickel." He dug a five-cent piece from his pocket and opened the jar for his two sticks. He put both in his shirt pocket…for later.

A lean, middle-aged woman, gray streaked black hair in a bun, her gray cotton dress protected by a red floral apron, turned from the stove, smiled and asked, "Coffee?"

Bitter said, "You bet. And whatever else you have for breakfast."

"How about eggs with biscuits and gravy?" she said.

Owl asked, "Any bacon?"

She shook her head. "No, but I can add a slice of ham." She looked at old Owl and then at Bitter. "Is he tame? We've been having a lot of trouble from the Indians lately. Drove off my husband's best saddle horse two nights ago. He and the boys are tracking them down."

Owl pursed his lips in disgust. "I am a Christian Cherokee," he huffed. "And a teacher."

"And my friend," Bitter added.

"Okay, okay. No offense," the woman said, and then stuck out her hand to Bitter. "I'm Jane. My husband built the bridge, and I run the store."

"John Bitter," he said. "This is Owl."

She nodded and pointed to a rough plank table and two benches. "Have a seat."

She set three tin cups on the table and poured hot coffee. Bitter took a sip and thought it a lot better than the metallic tasting canteen water he'd drunk earlier that morning.

Bidwell, sipped his coffee and asked, "How is that beautiful wife of yours?"

Bitter said, "Well, Morgan's just fine. A little peeved that I'm gone so much, I think. But she has little Sarah to keep her spirits up. And the boys are big enough to be a help on the farm."

"What about Thomas. Did he ever hook up with kin folks?"

Bitter frowned. "He did, but I don't think highly of the matter. Some people showed up at the farm, along with a deputy sheriff…and a court order. Just summarily hauled him away. Caught me totally by surprise."

Owl said, "He'll be back, John Bitter. He won't stay if they make him a slave."

Bidwell looked surprised. "Slave?"

Bitter nodded. "Free labor for sure. These are hill people with a different way of looking at youngsters."

"And Ethan and Mikey?"

Bitter laughed. "Growing like weeds. Ethan is quite the hunter, and Mikey still says animals talk to him. Tell him things."

He paused and then added, "The heck of it is, he's almost always right. Might miss the number of kittens the barn cat is carrying, but that's about all. Kinda spooky."

Owl smiled and said, "He could be Indian."

"Mister Owl," Bidwell said, and held out his hand. "And how is that beautiful woman you married? Woman I think you called her."

"Gonna divorce me. Likes Liam O'Grady. I think I'll find my things stacked by the door when I get back." And then he chuckled. "Never take a younger wife, Captain. They want to tell a man what to do."

Bitter grinned and looked at the big man. "What about you, Captain?"

"Well, I'm still a Captain. Surprising. When the war between the States ended, there just wasn't a need for so many officers. And a lot of those who weren't discharged were busted in rank. I know of one colonel who wound up being a second lieutenant."

He paused and then added, "I'm thinking it's time to retire and do some prospecting."

"And your wife?"

Bidwell turned slightly, the bench creaking under his weight, and stared out the door at the dusty yard. Finally, he looked at Bitter and said, "She died shortly after I escorted your wagon party to The Dalles. The doctor said it was pneumonia. She had been poorly after our last boy was born. Just never got well."

"Sorry," Bitter said.

Bidwell took a deep breath and gave Bitter a sad smile. "Me, too. I sometimes feel guilty I wasn't home more."

Bitter nodded. "I feel the same at times."

"What are you doing here, John Bitter?"

"Looking for a young woman. Fifteen years old. Her name is Anna Franklin. Ran off with her boyfriend. Her daddy doesn't want the town to know, so he hired the Pinkertons to find her and bring her back. I drew the short straw, so here I am."

"And you are still a Pinkerton."

Bitter nodded.

"Where do you think she went?"

"She left a note that said she was going to the Canyon City gold fields with a William Bradford. Going to marry him."

"Why didn't her daddy just go to the sheriff?"

"As Agent Mark Anthony says, pride keeps the Pinkertons in business."

Mrs. Sherar set three plates of steaming food on the table and table talk ceased while three hungry men dug in.

Finished, Bidwell wiped biscuit crumbs from his drooping moustache, stood up, stretched and said, "Well, we just came from The Dalles. We did not see a couple traveling together. Just teamsters and wagons."

Bitter said, "I think they have about a two-day lead on us." He tipped his hat back to look up at the six-foot-seven-inch Bidwell and said, "What is the Army doing here, Captain?"

"We," Bidwell said, glancing out the door at his troopers, some sitting on the porch of the store talking in low tones, "have been assigned to pacify the Dalles-to-Canyon City road as well as the Barlow Trail, and to protect the ore trains."

"I see. Well, when you get up to the timber on the Barlow Trail, you might look for a dead outlaw. The Digby brothers left him leaning up against a tree."

Horse Trade

BITTER AND OWL WATCHED BIDWELL EXAMINE the horses. He picked up their hooves, ran his hand over their withers, pulled their lips back to look at their teeth, and patted the saddles. Satisfied, he turned and nodded.

"I am authorized to pay up to seventy dollars a head. Four of your horses look to be sound. The little red mare may be sound, but she's a bit small for a cavalry horse. I'll give you two-hundred-eighty dollars for the other four."

"For money or for army script?" Bitter asked cynically.

Bidwell frowned and looked a bit peeved. "You do know I could just confiscate them. Maybe they were stolen from the Army."

Bitter crossed his arms and said nothing.

Finally, Bidwell shrugged and said, "Will gold work?"

Bitter smiled and let his arms settle to his sides. "Gold always works."

Bidwell sighed, and then said, "Sergeant Benteen, bring me my saddle bags."

As Bidwell counted out fourteen twenty-dollar gold pieces, Bitter added, "And fifty dollars for each saddle."

"I have army saddles," Bidwell countered.

"And a sorry lot they are, Captain. Ass crackers. Kill horses and men, they do."

Bidwell smiled and shook his head. "You drive a hard bargain."

"Not really. I just don't have time right now to fiddle with outlaws and captured horses, or I'd keep the horses to stock my own horse herd."

Bidwell didn't say anything more. He just counted out ten more twenty-dollar gold pieces.

"Sergeant Benteen. Swap these mounts for the four poorest of the stock."

"Gladly, sir."

Benteen rattled off four names in a booming voice that seemed a prerequisite for being an army sergeant. "Private Donovan, Private Pearl, Private Ross, Private Jones. Pick your new mount and swap your gear."

Bitter took the coins, handed half to Owl and slipped the rest in his saddle bags. "Now, about that receipt."

"What about the outlaw's guns. Would you sell those?"

Bitter thought it over for a few seconds and then nodded. "Owl gets the best of those. You can have the rest for twenty dollars."

Bidwell fished another gold piece from his pocket. "Deal."

◇

Daylight convinced the outlaws Bitter and Owl had done a good job of destroying their camp. The only things that might be of value were the scraps of clothing left on the edge of the fire and an old butcher knife. The wood handle was gone, but the blade still looked usable.

Albert Swift walked the sandy trail upriver in the direction his horse had gone the night before. He was sore footed, but the sandy trail made for soft going. He heard his horse nicker before he saw its dark head poke through a willow thicket. A herd animal, the horse was sociable, and with the daylight, he went back to the camp looking for the other horses.

Swift held out his hand, palm up as though it held the sugar cube. He fed the big horse a treat each morning. He was a hard man, a killer and a thief, but he took good care of his horse.

The big buckskin gelding stepped out of the willows and walked eagerly to Swift for his sugar cube. The outlaw said, "Come on, boy. Come here, Buck." And then he had the reins in hand. He expelled a big sigh of relief and fished for his spare britches and the spare shirt in the saddle bags. He had no belt and no shoes. Just another set of socks. But he had an extra revolver with the five rounds in the cylinder—and a dozen extra loads. It was a start.

He dressed and then mounted up and rode back to the fire. "Well, I'll be damned," Ace said. "You found him."

Billy Wilder, the youngest of the gang said, "Now what?"

Swift, the son of a Baptist minister who got that part of the Good Book about sparing the rod and spoiling the child without understanding what was really meant, had endured his share of misery, misery which led him to hate all Christians. In a rage when his preacher daddy had tried to whip him again, fifteen-year-old Albert knocked his daddy down with a big fist and then beat his daddy's head to a pulp with a handy rock.

When his rage cooled, he looked at the bloody mess that was once his preacher father and knew he was in trouble. Nothing but a noose would satisfy the local sheriff. Knowing it, however, did not tarnish the satisfaction of what he had done to "that sonofabitch" as he thought of his daddy.

So, he took his daddy's best horse, his daddy's rifle and ammunition, a sack of canned goods, and, turning a deaf ear to his mother's wailing, rode away from the Arkansas farm he called home. He wound up in Missouri where he joined a guerrilla company. It was a good fit. He learned to rob and kill, and he enjoyed it. The end of the civil war ended any legitimacy his robbing and killing spree might have had and marked him an outlaw.

"Now we wait for travelers. We need horses, clothing, food, guns, and money. But most of all I need to kill that marshal and his Indian friend."

Bake Oven

RUSTY GROWLED AND CHASED A FOUR-FOOT rattlesnake slithering across the road. When the dog barked and waded into the tall grass after the snake, Bitter called him back. "Dog. You get bit, and I'll catch hell when we get home. Get back here." It was the third rattlesnake they had seen in the last four miles.

Owl said, "I don't think we should camp down here tonight, John Bitter. Too many snakes."

Bitter nodded and said, "I'm told there's a spring a few miles up the Bake Oven road. We'll look that over."

"Bake Oven. How does a road get a name like that? Hot sun?"

Bitter laughed. "No. It does get hot in the summer. But as the story goes, a baker planned to set up an oven and bake bread for the miners in Canyon City. His wagon broke down, and when the Indians chased his horses off, he just set up his oven and went to baking bread right there, right along this section of road. Sold his bread to teamsters and other travelers."

"I hope he's still there," Owl said. "I like fresh baked bread with my bacon."

The road switch-backed up away from the Deschutes, heading east. They climbed a thousand feet or so and then followed a long, rolling ridge running roughly west to east. Bitter grabbed at his hat to keep it from blowing away in a strong wind that worked hard to bend the stiff stalks of miles and miles of yellow bunch grass. A small herd of wild horses a half mile away lifted their heads, ears forward, suspicious of the two riders and their string of pack animals. And then the lead stallion snorted, stamped a foot and the small herd turned and trotted over the crest of the hill and out of sight.

Bitter pulled to a halt and stepped down. "Let's give the animals a rest."

Owl nodded and pointed back to the west. "Fine view from up here."

The snow-capped peak of Mt. Hood in the west, a fringe of dark green timber dressing the lower slopes, Mt. Adams on the north side of the Columbia, the symmetrical white cone of Mt. Saint Helens further down river, and in the northwest, the tip of Mt. Rainier, a faint point on the horizon, painted a picture no man could resist. A man just had to stop and stare if he had any feelings whatsoever.

Bitter dug his field glasses from his saddle bag and scanned the tall Cascade mountains, and then handed them to Owl. "Will you look at that. Quite a sight, my old friend."

Old friend, Owl thought. *I like that.*

They didn't see the circling turkey buzzards until they topped the rise of a big bald hill. Below, a fringe of green grass marked a half-acre seep supporting a scraggly willow tree half gone to dead limbs.

Bitter pulled Rockford to a stop and stepped down from the saddle, keeping the big horse between him and the circling buzzards. He didn't want to be a skyline target for anyone waiting by the seep to ambush unwary travelers.

He pulled his field glasses from the saddle bag, the same glasses he carried through three years of the Civil War, leaned over the saddle, adjusted the focus, and studied the draw sheltering the small spring. Except for the yellow bunch grass, it didn't seem there was enough cover to hide a rabbit, but he was taking no chances. He hadn't lived through the Civil War by being careless.

I guess someone could lie in the grass and surprise unwary travelers, but where would they keep their horses?

Old Owl eased Horse up beside Rockford. "Something's dead down here, John Bitter."

"Yep. I see the rump of a horse, but I can't tell if it's dead or taking a nap. That willow tree is in the way.

Owl nodded. I think I see it." He watched the buzzards skim the ground without landing. "And I think something is keeping those buzzards from their lunch."

"A human being?"

Owl grinned, "Or a white man."

John just shook his head and let it go. He knew most Indian tribes referred to themselves as "the people" or as "the human beings."

Owl wrinkled his brown forehead in thought and then said, "Horses and people go together sometimes. I think we can get a better look if we ride around the spring a ways."

Bitter saw the puff of smoke before he heard the shot. He watched as the startled buzzards flapped their way to a broader, higher circle, but they didn't leave.

"Somebody's down there for sure." He looked at Owl and nodded. "I like your idea." He slipped the strap to the field glasses over his neck and mounted. "Let's go see if we can get a better look."

Two minutes of riding gave them an open view of the small spring. Bitter glassed the draw again and nodded. "Yep. A saddled horse is down on its side. Looks dead. And a small person is just lying on the ground…a woman maybe. Holding a big pistol. What do you think? You want ride down there, Owl, and take a look?"

Owl smiled and shook his head, his dark eyes crinkled in amusement. His long gray braids swayed in the wind. "No. You lead the way, John Bitter."

Bitter kept his right hand raised as he eased Rockford, the little red mare, and the two pack animals on his string down off the side of the big hill. When he was within fifty yards of the spring, he shouted, "Hello. We come in peace. Are you alright?"

Startled, a young, dark haired woman rolled to her left and pointed the big pistol in the general direction of Bitter and Owl.

Bitter kept Rockford walking and said, "Easy miss. We mean you no harm."

The woman studied the lean rider, and like so many before and so many after, she decided John Bitter was trustworthy.

In a weak voice, she said, "Come on in."

Owl's Medicine

BITTER SWUNG DOWN, GROUND HITCHED ROCKFORD, and walked over to the girl. He could see where she had dug in the damp sand to free her left leg from the weight of the dead horse. It was obvious the leg was broken. It was also obvious she was in a lot of pain. And a long, shallow gash across her left cheek had bled down the side of her face. The blood was dry and black looking.

Damaged and unkempt she might be, but the abundance of dark, auburn hair and her gray green eyes graced a clear complexion and told him that underneath the blood and the dirt was a very pretty young woman.

"Hi," he said. "Looks like you've had some trouble."

She nodded weakly but managed a hint of a smile. "You might say that."

"Are you Anna Franklin?"

She looked surprised. "How did you know?"

"Your daddy sent me to find you."

"Good old Daddy." She said. She let her head fall back into the grass and closed her eyes as tears started down her cheeks. "That greedy bastard," she muttered. "He wanted to sell me to a fat, greasy old man. Call it marriage if you want, but it was just like selling a mare. Buy the mare and seal the bargain."

She opened her eyes and when she saw Owl bending over her, his long braids nearly touching her face. She was startled and tried pick her pistol up. Bitter put a foot on it and said, "No, Miss Franklin. He's with me. And he's a pretty good doctor."

Bitter took the revolver, spun the cylinder and then shoved the pistol in his belt. "I'll give this back when Owl has you fixed up. Besides, it's empty."

She gave up and just seemed to sink into the grass. She wiped the tears away, and then she laughed. "Empty, huh? And to think I was saving the last round for myself."

"Not a good plan." Bitter paused and said, "Now then, this old man is called Owl. He's an educated Christian Cherokee, a pretty good medicine man and an even better doctor. With your permission, he's going to set your leg and tend to the cut on your cheek. Is that okay?"

She nodded and said, "I'd like a drink of water."

At Owl's orders, Bitter pinned Anna's shoulders while he stretched her leg and popped the bones back in place. She cried out, but once the bones were properly aligned, she looked at Owl and said, "Thank you. It hurts, but I don't think it hurts as bad as it did."

"It will, but I'll make you some willow tea for the pain." He walked to where Horse was ground hitched, fished a tin tobacco can from a saddle bag and held it up. "This is salve for the scratch. Help you heal."

Owl took a deep breath, looked at Bitter and said, "I think we will camp here. Give her a chance to rest a bit. Make some soup, maybe. Pitch my tent, make her a good bed. She's young. The young heal pretty fast."

He looked at the dead limbs on the willow tree and held his hand about eighteen inches apart. "Go cut two branches about his long, John Bitter. We need to splint and bind the leg. And I'll need a green limb for the bark. And we need to get a fire going. I'll need to boil some water for the tea. Put some sugar and whiskey in it. Help her sleep."

As Bitter walked off, Owl rocked back on his heels, looked at Anna and asked, "What happened here? John Bitter tells me you travel with a man named William Bradford."

She looked away, a trace of tears in the corner of her gray blue eyes. "Was. I don't think I want to talk about it."

Owl looked off in the distance, not making eye contact. Finally, he said, "Embarrassed, huh? Us Indians get embarrassed sometimes, too. Nothing to feel bad about." He stopped, cocked his head sideway and added, "Look, Miss Anna, you can trust John Bitter. He's a U.S. Marshal. Might arrest Bradford if he knew what happened."

Bitter walked back dragging a twenty-foot piece of dead willow for firewood and a four- foot green limb about an inch in diameter. "If I knew what?"

Owl looked serious for about the only time Bitter could remember. "I think this Bradford did something bad, but Miss Anna won't say."

Bitter was at a loss. Gun fights, war patrols, horses, men, farming… were all things he knew about. But he knew next to nothing about talking to young women. Finally, he said, "Did he…uh…mess with you?"

Anna looked like she was going to laugh. "Why, Marshal, you are blushing." And then she added, "Billy…Billy Bradford said he was going to marry me as soon as we got to the gold fields. But he got to drinking last night. We were camped right here. And he got very fresh. Said he was tired of waiting, and he was going to…uh…have his way. When I objected, he slapped me across the face." She touched her cheek. "I think that's where I got the cut. He wears a ring with an eagle crest. Anyway, I got scared and grabbed his gun. I tried to shoot him. I think I creased him some place. Anyway, he backed away and was saddling the horse. Kept saying he was just going to leave me here and I could die for all he cared.

"I just watched. I mean, he had always been polite. But when he started to lead my horse away, I shot at him again. I'm afraid I'm not much of a shot. I killed my poor horse instead which reared back and knocked me down. And then I was on the ground, and the horse was lying on my leg, and Billy was just riding away." A small tear fought with her self-control. She blinked the tear away and said in disgust, "To think I was in love with him."

Bitter and Owl waited while she regained her composure. "Anyway, I think the stirrup is what broke my leg. And this morning the buzzards showed up. I don't know what I'd have done if you hadn't come along." She paused and then said, "Thank you. I think you saved my life."

As night fell, Owl's small wall tent was up, the flap open so Anna could see the glow of the fire from the bed Bitter and Owl had made up for her…with blankets shot full of bullet holes. The horses had been picketed on the sparse grass of the seep, and Anna had choked down a cup of Owl's sour tea. Bitter had no sugar, so Owl had reluctantly offered one of his striped candy sticks to the tart brew.

Later, when he saw his patient had fallen asleep, he said quietly to his young friend, "A little coffee and a little whiskey is called for, John Bitter."

Bought and Sold

S OMEONE HAD TIED THE FLAP OF the tent shut after she had fallen asleep, but the thin canvas failed to completely block the sunlight. She smelled wood smoke, tasted the odor of cooking bacon, and heard the quiet voices of her rescuers. *Morning*, she thought.

She needed to relieve herself and wondered how in the world she would accomplish that. She saw the tent flap wiggle and heard the scrape of a calloused hand on the canvas. She threw the wool blanket off and tried to sit up, but the pain grabbed her, and she cried out.

Bitter pulled the tent flaps open to let in the sunlight, a worried frown on his face. "Are you okay?"

She shook her head…and then nearly laughed. "No. I have a broken leg…set by an Indian…my fiancé just left me to die, and I have to…" She failed to find a lady like way of saying she had to pee.

Bitter nodded his understanding. "Can I help you get up? You can get behind the tent for privacy. I don't know how to help beyond that." He handed her a four-foot staff he had cut from a willow limb about two inches thick. "Here. Use this."

He held out his hand and helped her pull herself up, hobbling on the good leg. She grimaced but didn't cry out. "Got it," she said. She took a tentative step and almost went down.

Bitter shook his head and then just picked her up and carried out of the tent and around behind it. He set her gently down on her good leg, handed her the staff and said, "Call me when you're ready."

He walked back to the small fire, picked up a tin cup and poured coffee. Owl sat on his saddle, looking amused, but the scowl on Bitter's face discouraged any comment.

Finally, Bitter took a deep breath and said quietly so Anna couldn't hear, "I was paid to take her back to her daddy, but I can't do that."

"Why not?"

Bitter told Owl what she had said about her father.

"We could take her back to the store by the bridge. Maybe that nice Jane lady will look after her."

Bitter nodded. "Might even be an army doctor come by if Anna stays there."

"What are you going to tell her father? He paid you to find her."

"I might just have to lie and say I couldn't find her."

"Won't work. He'll find out."

"I'll think of something."

He heard Anna call, "Mister Bitter. I could use some help now."

Anna, splinted leg stretched out from the saddle she was sitting on, chewed hungrily on a bacon and biscuit sandwich washed down with warm coffee. Owl nodded his approval. "Hunger means healing."

Without a word, she reached for another biscuit from the tin plate Bitter had set beside her. Rusty, a drool hanging from one cheek, moved closer and lifted a paw, begging for a bite. "What? You want my breakfast? Can't have it, dog."

Bitter turned from where he knelt close to the fire cooking bacon. He grinned and said, "Rusty will be your friend for life if you feed him." He picked a warm biscuit from the plate near the fire and tossed it to her. "Feed him this one."

Owl said, "We got company, John Bitter." He pointed to the hill that carried the wagon road. At five-hundred yards or more, it was impossible to make out the features of the driver, but it was clear two men, one mounted on a gray horse and one driving the wagon were stopped on the road.

Bitter lifted his field glasses from the saddle bag. He adjusted the focus and watched the rider on the gray horse turn and head downhill toward their camp on the short grass of the seep.

"I wonder what he wants?"

Bitter watched through the glasses until he could make out the butt of a rifle in a saddle scabbard and a pistol holster. "Doesn't look too friendly, Owl."

Owl nodded, took off his yellow hat and placed it carefully on his saddle horn, and then pulled his lever action Henry from the saddle scabbard.

"What's with the hat?"

"I don't want someone to shoot it full of holes."

Bitter shook his head. "That doesn't make sense, Owl. If somebody shot your hat full of holes, you'd have a head full of holes, and then you wouldn't need a hat."

Jaw set in defiance of Bitter's logic, Owl said, "Might get in a tussle with someone. Don't want any dirt or blood on my hat."

Stubble faced, dressed in a black cotton shirt, a dirty striped railroaders cap on his head, a lean rider pulled the gray horse to a stop about twenty yards from the camp. His right hand rested near his pistol holster. "Hello the camp. Can I come in?"

"If you're peaceful."

Rusty's low growl alerted Owl who saw what Rusty was looking at. And it wasn't the rider. In a near whisper, he said, "Got another man trying to sneak up on us, John Bitter. Using the willow tree for cover."

"You got him?"

"Yes. Glad I took off my hat."

Bitter's draw was so quick the rider wasn't sure he had actually seen it. All he could see was the big bore of the pistol aimed right at his head. The rider's eyes switched nervously from Bitter to Owl and then to Anna. He held his arms wide, hands empty. He said, "No need for trouble. We just come to claim our property."

"You don't have any property here."

The rider pointed at Anna and said, "The whore. We paid good money for her. Gave a gent back up the road fifty dollars for her. He said she was too much trouble. Showed us his arm where she had shot him. But we figured we could whip her into shape."

"No. You were cheated. She's no one's property. And she's no whore." The rider's eyes got wide at the sight of the badge when Bitter pulled the flap of his jacket back with his left hand. "I've been sent to take her home."

Anna nearly jumped out of her hide when Owl touched off a round, the sound rolling up the draw. A limb on the willow hung from a scrap of bark, swung back and forth and then dropped to the ground. Owl shouted, "I didn't miss, mister. The next one will be between your eyes."

A muted, "Don't shoot," told Bitter the trouble might be over. He shouted, "This is Marshal Bitter. Raise your hands and come on in. If you don't, I'm going to let Owl shoot you and take your scalp."

A Fine Morning

A SMALL, DECREPIT-LOOKING FIGURE IN A TATTERED gray coat, greasy blond hair poking through a big hole in the side of his brimmed hat, rose from the grass at the base of the willow, hands empty, arms outstretched. He was almost tiny, maybe five foot two, and gaunt, like maybe he was starved down to bone and gristle. At fifteen he was more child than man.

"Please don't shoot, mister. Don't shoot."

"Why not?" Bitter shouted, his voice choked with anger. "You come sneaking up on my camp trying to bushwhack us."

"We meant no harm," the boy whined.

"The hell you didn't. You get over by your partner." He looked at the rider and said, "And you get off that horse before I shoot you off."

Encouraged by dark bore of Owl's rifle, the boy scurried across the short grass fed by the seep, Rusty growling and nipping at his heels. When the rider started to step off his horse, Bitter said, "Step off on this side. I want to see you. No tricks."

The rider stepped down and stared at Bitter, his dark brown eyes hard and flat. "Now what?"

"Now you unbuckle your gun belt and let it drop to the ground."

Owl said, "Just shoot them. You don't need any more enemies." Owl pulled a big, razor sharp knife from the sheath on his belt. "Of course, we could just cut them like a horse. Make geldings out them."

The boy keeled over in a dead faint.

Bitter knew Owl was bluffing, or thought he knew, although he was not always one-hundred percent sure. "No. I'm thinking we fine these slave buyers about fifty dollars each, keep their guns and send them on their way."

"You can't do that," the lean rider protested. "We need our guns. The Indians are raiding this road. Besides, we already paid fifty dollars."

Bitter nodded toward the big hill where the freight wagon was parked. "Do you have extra ammunition in your wagon?"

"Yep. We do."

"Okay then, pay the fine and I'll give you your guns back…empty. All you need to do is make it back to your wagon without getting caught by any wild Indians."

All the blond headed boy had in his ragged britches was a dollar and some change, but the lean rider had close to sixty dollars. Bitter settled for the boy's dollar and for fifty dollars from his partner.

While Owl covered the two men with his rifle, Bitter pulled the rider's rifle from the scabbard and levered all the rounds from the weapon. Then he picked up the still-unconscious boy by his collar and his belt and threw him across the saddle of the gray horse. He looked at the rider, handed him his empty rifle, his empty revolver and his gun belt, the loops empty of rounds, and said, "Mount up."

They watched until the horse and riders reached the freight wagon. Bitter walked over to Anna and handed her fifty-one dollars. She nodded without saying thanks, and then Bitter said, "Let's get out of here."

Anna said, "Not before I clean up." She held up her hands, dirt under her nails from digging her leg out from under the dead horse, a smudge of dirt on her left cheek. She pointed to the dead horse and said, "I'd like my carpet bag, please."

Bitter untied her carpet bag and carried it to her. He watched as she opened the bag and searched the contents. She pulled a washcloth from the bag and said, "Would you wet this in the spring?"

Owl was busy picking up the ammunition Bitter had shucked from the gun belt and the two guns.

For a short minute, she just stared at the cold, wet rag Bitter handed her, and at her small bar of scented soap, suddenly overwhelmed at how much her life had changed in the last seventy two hours…from fiancé on her way to Canyon City and marriage…to betrayed and sold for a whore…to say nothing of going from daughter to bargaining chip. She took a deep breath and then worked a bit of soap into one corner of the rag, her determination asserting itself again. *Just like when I decided to not be bargained away as a wife for a greasy old man.*

Owl got busy rolling up the tent while Bitter led the horses to the spring. While they drank, he searched the grass where the boy had been hiding behind the willow. He hadn't even tried to hide the small double-barreled derringer. Just tossed it in the grass. Bitter checked and it was loaded. At .44 caliber it was a heavy load. It was good for only two shots, but it was a lot better than nothing. He stuffed it in his coat pocket and led the horses back to the fire.

Thirty minutes later, canteens filled with water from the spring, they topped the big rolling hill and headed down the dusty, rocky road, a cavalcade of four pack animals, and three riders mounted on saddled horses, Bitter on Rockford, Owl on the bay he called Horse, and Anna on the small red mare.

The pain in her leg kept rhythm with the pace of the horse's walk, but it was of little consequence compared to the pain in her heart. She hadn't cried when Owl set the leg and she was determined not to cry now, but she felt like it.

Bitter stopped the horses on the crest of a long rolling ridge, stepped down and pointed at a wisp of dust a full mile down the road. "We best wait a bit. I think that's dust from the teamster's wagon. I imagine the tall one has reloaded his pistol and his rifle by now."

Safe Harbor

A SEVENTEEN-YEAR-OLD BOY, BROAD SHOULDERS PAINTING A clear picture of the man he was to become, hurried into the store. "Ma, we got company. One of them is Indian. I'll get my rifle."

Jane Sherar walked to the door, shaded her eyes against the sun. "Nothing to get fussed about, Orin. I recognize the horses. The black belongs to Marshal Bitter, and the bay to his old Indian friend, Owl. But I don't know the woman. Must be the girl they were looking for. No bonnet," she idly observed. "Gonna get sunburned for sure."

She watched her younger son collect the toll and listened as the horse hooves drummed a hollow song on the planks of the wooden bridge. Bitter looked the yard over as they neared the store and was relieved to see no sign of the teamster's wagon.

Jane Sherar waited on the porch until the small cavalcade pulled up to the hitching rail. "Found her I see."

Bitter nodded and stepped down. "At that first seep a couple miles the other side of the summit. She has a broken leg. Owl set it. I think he did a good job, but she won't be up to traveling for a while. Too painful. Any chance she can stay here until she heals up?"

Jane nodded and then said, "Orin, you and Ben move to the barn loft. I'm going to put this girl in your room for a while."

Orin looked Anna over and decided if he had to give up his bed, it might as well be to an auburn-haired girl. A very pretty auburn-haired girl. One with beautiful gray-green eyes. He smiled and nodded to Anna. "Yes, ma'am. I'll tend to it."

In spite of her pain, Anna smiled back, and said, "Thank you. I'm Anna Franklin."

He took his hat off, blushed and said, "I'm Orin Sherar. Pleased to meet you."

Bitter helped Anna out of the saddle. She nearly fell when he set he on the ground, so he just picked her up and said, "Where do you want her, Missus Sherar?"

Settled in Orin's bedroom, Anna drank a cup of beef broth, chased by a cup of Owl's willow bark tea…generously dosed with sugar and whiskey. Feeling safe from harm, Anna relaxed, closed her eyes and drifted off to sleep.

Jane Sherar quietly closed the bedroom door and turned to Owl and Bitter, who were drinking coffee at the table. "I think she'll be fine. Just needs some sleep and time to heal. What happened to her?"

Bitter shared what he thought was proper, and Jane Sherar nodded. "Does this scallywag have a name?"

"William Bradford."

"We'll keep an eye out for him. He won't be welcome here. And he has no need to know Anna is staying with us."

Bitter nodded. "Good." He dug in a pants pocket and pulled out two twenty-dollar gold pieces. "Take this. For her room and board."

Jane nodded, tucked the money in her apron pocket, and asked, "What comes next?"

"I don't know. I may have to come back and take her home. Or I might just lie and say I couldn't find her."

She smiled and looked at Owl. "Is he a good liar?"

Owl shook his head. "He doesn't know how."

Bitter frowned. "Lying has never been my style, but I might have to give it my best shot. I'll think on it as we ride."

She nodded. "I'm sure you'll do the right thing."

Ambush

By late afternoon, Owl and Bitter were eyeballing the crossing on the White River and not liking it much. Over the roar of the river, Owl said, "The river's up. Looks a lot deeper than last time."

"And a lot faster," Bitter said. "Must be the snow melt."

He shrugged and added, "Well, if we want to go home this way, we still have to ford it. Why don't you take the red mare across? She's not as tall as Horse. You might have to help her. And, then I'll bring the pack horses across."

Owl wrapped the mare's lead rope around the saddle horn and gigged Horse in the ribs. He kept the small mare on the downriver side of Horse and just waded the river. Bitter held his breath when the mare stumbled, but her hooves found purchase, and then Owl and Horse pulled her ashore.

Bitter shook his head and waved at Owl. He took a deep breath, scooped Rusty up and stepped into the saddle. Rusty struggled to get loose but Bitter patted the dog's head. "It'll be okay, Rusty. You calm down."

When the big dog stopped struggling, Bitter wrapped the lead rope from the pack string around the saddle horn and kneed Rockford into the river. About halfway across, Rockford stepped in a hole in the rocks and almost went down just as a pistol bullet knocked Bitter from the saddle. The roar of the river muffled the shot, but Owl saw the small cloud of powder smoke and jerked his rifle from the saddle scabbard. He fired at the smoke, levered a second round into the rifle chamber and waited for something to shoot at.

He saw Bitter drifting face up in the river. Rusty had one sleeve in his jaws and was paddling hard for the riverbank on Owl's side of the river. And then Bitter and the dog were around the corner and out of sight. Owl thought he could hear a man shouting, "You got him, Alf! You got him!"

The whip of a bullet galvanized Owl, and he put Horse into a dead run up the Barlow Road in the direction of the Mount Hood summit, the red mare in pursuit. He looked back and saw Rockford pulling the pack string up out of the river and into a gallop up the trail behind Horse.

He felt bad for leaving Bitter, but another explosion of bark from a pine tree convinced him he could do nothing now but run for it. *At least two shooters*, he thought.

⁓

T HE SHOCK OF THE COLD river brought Bitter to a semi-conscious state. Later he would remember Rusty pulling him into a back-eddy pool. And when he fully regained his senses, he was sheltered behind a big buckskin log sticking out of a log jam. A rough canopy of drift logs gave shelter. The sand beneath was dry. *I must have crawled in here*, he thought, and then he drifted into a troubled sleep.

Owl ran Horse for a half mile, the red mare, Rockford and the pack animals close behind. As the darkness settled, he slowed Horse to a walk and looked for an opening in the timber…some place that would let him move a safe distance from the trail. A small stream, Clear Creek maybe, showed elk tracks on a trail of sorts through a fringe of willows. Without hesitation, Owl turned Horse into the willows and followed the dim trail. He rode a few yards and stopped. For once Rockford behaved himself and didn't try to bite or kick the old Indian.

It took Owl some time to hide the tracks of the horses, but he sifted dirt into the depressions the heavy animals made in the damp soil as best he could. Satisfied no one could follow him, at least not in the dark, he rode up the narrow trail until the ground opened out into a small meadow.

Sadly, he said, "I'll hunt for John Bitter's body in the morning. Take him home for burial."

Rusty

A TINY SHAFT OF SUNLIGHT LIT BITTER'S face, and he woke with a start. He was shaking with the cold, a pain hammering his skull. He rolled on his back, gingerly probing the shallow gash down the side of his head. Other than the headache, and fingers sticky from coagulating blood, he didn't think he was hurt too bad. Just cold, hungry and thirsty. And then he remembered Rockford stepping into a hole in the riverbed. "That might have saved my life," he said aloud.

Over the noise of the river, Bitter thought he heard a man voice say, "Did you hear something? I swear I heard someone talking."

"No, I didn't hear anything. Damn river makes a lot of noise."

"Well, he's probably downriver someplace. Just keep looking."

I recognize those voices. Two of the outlaws who shot up our camp. Maybe Owl had the right idea after all. If we'd shot them, I wouldn't be in this fix. He automatically reached for his pistol, but all he found was an empty holster. *Must have lost it in the river. What now? I've still got my knife, and my dry matches. I'll wait until those guys leave and see if I can get a fire going.*

He waited a good ten minutes before deciding the outlaws had gone. A whisper of sound had him pulling his knife from the sheath, and then Rusty was there, a fat rock chuck in his jaws.

He got to his hand and knees, patted Rusty on the head and then crawled further into the log jam, looking for dry material for a fire. Rusty picked up the rock chuck and followed.

His hands shook so hard he dropped the first match in the sand, but concentration, aided and abetted by desperation, helped him strike the second match on a dry flat stone. Carefully, he fed the flame to a small pile of dry leaves and small limbs. He knew there was risk in building a fire, a chance the smell of smoke would give him away, but a soft breeze pulled the smoke upriver, away from his hiding place, and the men had gone downriver. There was greater risk if he didn't get warmed up…soon.

As the fire caught, he sat as close to the heat as he dared. When his wet jacket started steaming, he stripped it off and hung it on the broken limb of a buckskin log to dry. The lump in the jacket pocket brought greater relief than the warmth of the fire. "The derringer, Rusty. I forgot about it." He pulled it from the jacket pocket, wiped at it with damp fingers and popped it open. Bright brass cartridges gave him hope the gun would still fire. "It isn't much of a gun," he whispered to Rusty, "but up close it should do the job."

The fire burned down to coals, and Bitter went about the business of cleaning the rock chuck. Between the warmth of the fire, a bit of charred meat and a cold drink of river water, he started feeling better about his chances of survival. He stretched out on the dry sand and let the coals warm his back. Then, he drifted off to sleep again.

◆

BEFORE DAYLIGHT OWL LED THE horses one at a time to the small stream in the meadow for water, and then tied them to a picket line run between two lodgepole trees. He saddled Horse and said, 'I hope we get back before they starve to death. Or a mountain lion finds them."

He chewed on a piece of jerky while he rode, the Henry rifle across his thighs, ready to hand. "I'll find you, John Bitter, and take you home. And then I'll hunt those outlaws down and kill every one of them. We should have shot them while we could."

He was about a hundred yards from the ford when he caught the scent of woodsmoke, and then Rusty was barking and running up the trail toward Owl and Horse.

"Where is he, Rusty?"

Looking back to make sure Owl was following, Rusty barked and started back down the trail. Owl put the buckskin into a lope. As he neared the ford, Rusty took to the open timber and trotted parallel to the river. When he reached the log jam, he stopped and looked back to make sure Owl had followed, and then he ducked through a crack in the pile and out of sight.

Owl stepped off Horse and got down on his hands and knees to see where Rusty had gone. "Too small for an old man," he grumbled to no one in particular. He put his yellow hat on the saddle horn, looked at the milky, fast- moving glacier melt, and said, "No help for it."

Holding his pistol in one hand to keep it dry, he stepped into the cold, fast moving water. The river was waist deep and he had to hang on to the log to keep from being swept downstream, but the water pressure eased on the back side of the log, and then he was looking at John Bitter's hideout.

Owl waded up out of the water and crawled on his hand and knees under the canopy of the log jam. Rusty licked at his face.

He sat down next to the fire, and Rusty sat next to Bitter. Owl could see Bitter's chest move with his breathing, and he could see the long gash down the side of Bitter's head where a bullet had clipped his skull. Owl folded his hands in prayer, and said, "I give thanks to the Great Spirit that he is alive. I wouldn't want to tell Morgan I didn't take care of him."

He smiled at the sight of the half-eaten rock chuck and nodded. "Rusty, you are a good dog."

Owl puzzled over some way to get John Bitter out of the log jam without getting him wet. He studied the canopy of small limbs overhead and shook his head. "Even if I break through, I don't know if John Bitter will have the strength to climb out of here. No. I'll tie a rope to Horse and a rope around John Bitter. Keep the river from washing him away. I hate to get him wet again, but I don't see another way."

Bitter rolled over, the derringer in his hand. "Who's there?"

Owl reached over and pushed the gun away. "It's me, Owl. Don't shoot me."

Bitter put the gun down and sat up. "How did you find me?"

"The dog went hunting for me. Led me back."

Bitter nodded. "I think he pulled me out of the river and into this place. Good thing, too. They were hunting me this morning, but you can't see in here from the riverbank."

Owl said, "Did you see them?"

Bitter shook his head. "No. But I did hear their voices. Sounded like two of them, and they sounded like the men who shot up our camp."

Owl said, "Good thing they didn't find you. I crawled in here and you never even stirred. If I'd been a wild Indian instead of a Christian Cherokee, I could have taken your scalp."

Bitter gave Owl a tiny smile and then grimaced as a pain lanced through his head. "I think a bullet already took some of it."

"I'll get you out of here and fix some coffee. That will help."

Bitter looked at the canopy overhead and then back at the boiling river. "I guess I'll get wet again."

Owl waded into the river and worked his way around the log. When he made the trip back to Bitter, he had the end of a rope in his hand. "The other end is tied to the saddle horn on Horse. If you can, just hold the line when you get around the log. Horse will pull you from the river.

The cold water started Bitter's shakes again, and when Horse pulled him out of the river, he was close to exhaustion. Owl boosted Bitter up into the saddle, and then led Horse through the open timber back to the trail, eyes alert for danger. "I smelled your smoke. Didn't you worry about that?"

Bitter nodded. "Yes, but they went downriver, and the smoke went upriver."

"Lucky."

"Maybe. Where are the rest of our animals?"

"I've got them picketed in a meadow about a mile up the trail. I hope no one has found them. And I hope your Windy mule doesn't get to braying. Bring in a cougar or something."

"There's a happy thought."

Pacifying the Road

T HEY WERE NEARLY TO OWL'S SIDE trail when eight mounted troopers, led by grizzled Sergeant Benteen, came trotting around a bend in the road. Owl stopped and waited.

Benteen pulled to a stop, looked at Bitter slumped in the saddle, a bloody bandanna tied around his head, and said, "Mister Owl. Looks like you've had trouble."

"Jumped by at least two men at the ford. A bullet knocked John Bitter off his horse and into the river." He pointed at Rusty. "The dog pulled him ashore, and I found him this morning."

Bitter pulled himself from the half sleep he'd fallen into and raised his head. "Same men," he slurred with effort, "who shot up our camp. If my horse ha…hadn't shtepped in a hole, I'd be dead." His head dropped and he drifted closer to the darkness edging up on him.

Benteen pulled a flat plug of chewing tobacco from his shirt, folded back the waxed paper and bit off a chew. He wrapped the tobacco back up and stuffed it in his pocket before saying, "Well, we are charged with pacifying the road. Finding these bushwhackers might be a good way to start. Any idea where they went?"

Bitter fought off his drowsiness and said, "Downriver from the ford. They were hunting for me. I heard one of them say he wanted my clothes. Got to be one of those we left naked. Naked in the wilderness. Like Adam without his Eve." He chuckled and then winced as a sharp pain shot through his head.

Benteen nodded. He turned and said, "Private Brown. Take a message to Captain Bidwell at Government Camp. Tell him to send the doc with the ambulance. And tell him we are in pursuit of some renegades who tried to kill Owl and Bitter."

Private Brown snapped a salute and said, "Yes, Sergeant. On my way." Brown turned his horse, the black Bidwell bought from Owl and Bitter, and gigged him into a lope back up the road in the direction of the summit.

"Where's your pack animals?"

Owl nodded up the narrow side trail the elk had cut through the alder and willows. "In a little meadow up the creek."

"Why don't you go get them and start for Government Camp. It'll be a few hours before Doc gets here."

Owl said, "I'll find a good spot to wait. Make some coffee for John Bitter. Let him rest a bit."

Benteen said, "About two miles up the road, there's an open meadow that might do."

Benteen spit tobacco juice at some white plumed bear grass growing in the shade of the timber and turned to look at his troops. "I know Captain Bitter was mustered out at the end of the war. But he's still one of ours. I want the bastard who shot him. Check your weapons. I want every carbine and every revolver loaded. We are going to do our best to apprehend these hombres. If it's the same bunch, there's five of them. And they are meaner than hell."

He spit again, wiped his chin with the sleeve of his uniform shirt, and said, "I hope to take them alive, but if they shoot, don't hesitate to shoot back. They aren't hardly worth the powder anyway. And I don't want any of us to get shot."

He looked each one of them in eye, scouting for signs of reluctance, but all he could see were set jaws and a glint of anger in every man's eyes. "Okay. Corporal Winston, when we get to the ford, take three men and cross the river. I'll keep the others with me, and we'll make a wide sweep downriver until we catch up to these bastards. Keep your eyes open and stay alert."

That said, Benteen pulled his carbine from his saddle boot, checked to see a round was chambered, and laid it across his thighs, ready for use. He turned and led the troop past Owl and Bitter.

They watched the soldiers pass, and then Owl led Horse up the dim elk trail to the meadow where the other animals were picketed.

"I'm thinking we should make coffee now. Eat some bacon and biscuits. And then ride to where Benteen wants us to wait. What do you think, John Bitter?"

Bitter nodded without saying anything, hanging on to the saddle horn to keep from falling off Horse.

‿

HE WAS LYING BACK AGAINST his saddle, a blanket around his shoulders, and another around his legs, sipping a scalding hot cup of coffee. He watched Owl slice green willow bark into a pot of boiling water and said, "You don't expect me to drink that, do you?"

Owl just nodded and said, "I drink it for my aches and pains. So, I know it works." Then he smiled and added, "A little sugar and some whiskey helps too."

‿

BENTEEN LED HIS SQUAD FROM the front, like he always did, so he was the first to spot a man walking upriver, and, except for a long-tailed shirt, naked…a pistol in his hand. Benteen signaled a halt, pointed at two troopers and pointed left toward the river, and then pointed at the other one to sweep wide and execute a pincer movement.

He cocked the carbine, set the butt on his right thigh and gigged his horse forward.

The barefoot man was paying more attention to his sore feet than where he was going. When Benteen was about twenty feet away, he pulled his horse to a stop, made a quick check of the timber to see if the man was alone, raised his carbine to his shoulder, and then hollered, "Hands in the air!"

Ace, Swift's sidekick, was so startled he nearly dropped his pistol when he cocked the hammer. He didn't make it. Benteen shot him in the chest and watched the bullet slam him backwards against a tree. The sergeant heard a half dozen rifle shots echo through the timber and then fade into tense silence.

Benteen stepped off his horse and retrieved the dead man's revolver. He let the hammer down and then slid it into a saddle bag. He heard one of his troopers shouting, "Sergeant! We got 'em."

Benteen's squad gathered at the ford and waited while Corporal Winston's squad dragged two naked men across the icy river, each wearing a noose.

Benteen spit tobacco juice again and said, "See anything else?"

Winston said, "Yes. We found a dead man. Somebody had shot him earlier. All bled out. And we chased these two. I don't get it, Sarge. What are they doing here?"

"Good question. Maybe you should ask them. If they don't talk, just drag them back across the river again. And ask them where the fifth man got off to."

§

BITTER PAUSED BETWEEN SIPS OF the vile tasting tea, head turned to listen. "Did you hear that?"

Owl looked across the low burning fire. "Hear what?"

"Sounded like gunshots. Quite a few."

Owl shook his head. "I didn't hear anything." He tossed the coffee dregs from his tin cup into the fire and stood up. "You ready to move again?"

Bitter nodded. "Yep. Let's go before I fall asleep. I'm having trouble keeping my eyes open."

"Probably from being in the cold water for so long. We'll get you bedded down when we find Benteen's meadow."

Thirty minutes later, Owl led the pack horses and the little red mare into the meadow Benteen told him about, Rockford and Rusty close behind.

Bitter loosened the saddle girth and pulled the saddle off Rockford, sat down on it and promptly passed out without a clue as to what had just happened. He was still unconscious when Benteen led the troops to the meadow, two sore-footed outlaws tagging along behind, each with a noose tied around his neck. Their bare feet left blood on the rocks. The troopers didn't care.

Sergeant Benteen pulled his horse to a stop and looked at Bitter stretched out on the ground, his head propped against the saddle, a blanket around his shoulders, put there by Owl, and then barked, "Private Jones, you ride the biggest horse, so we'll put Captain Bitter in the saddle, and you ride double. Keep him in the saddle." He looked at Owl and pointed to the prisoners. "How do you feel about putting these hombres on your pack horses? Or maybe the smaller man can ride the red mare, and the other can ride Bitter's black."

Owl nodded. "Use the pack horses. No one can ride Rockford except John Bitter. At least no one has ever been able to. That big horse is too mean."

Two hours later, Bitter was tucked into an army ambulance and headed for Government Camp. He woke briefly when the wheels of the ambulance found a hole in the rocky road and dropped a good six inches. Consciousness lasted a short minute and then he was back asleep.

Beef Stew

Short, bustling Major Strickland, U.S. Army Medical Corps leaned over the narrow cot and squinted through a big magnifying glass into the eyes of an unconscious John Bitter.

"I wish," he said to Owl, "I could see into the human skull. I think the brain swells sometimes from wounds like this one, and a man doesn't regain consciousness until the swelling goes down. My problem is not knowing for sure.

"Best we can do is make sure he drinks enough water and keep him comfortable. Mother Nature and his own constitution will have to do the healing. I've given him a dose of laudanum to keep him still."

Owl nodded. "Once a Cheyenne family brought me a young man who was kicked in the head by his horse. That one was asleep for a week. I wanted to drill a hole in his skull and drain the water off, but his family said no. He died."

"Might have died anyway," Major Strickland said.

"Maybe." Owl raised his eyebrows and smiled. " At least I didn't get blamed for killing him."

Strickland unwound the cloth around Bitter's head. He looked at the groove in Bitter's scalp and said, "Hmm. Well, while he is out, I'll stitch his scalp. Much easier if he is unconscious."

$\backsim$

Two days later Bitter pushed through the laudanum induced fog to discover someone in a white frock coat pulling at his left eyelid. He pushed the hand away and saw the man smile.

"Good! Good! I'm Doctor Strickland, U.S. Medical Corps. You've been out for a couple of days, but it looks like you are on the road to recovery."

Bitter took a deep breath and said, "On the road to home is where I'd like to be."

"I'd say by this time next week, you'll be able to ride. Now…how about something to eat?" As Doctor Strickland turned and walked out of the tent, Bitter heard him call, "Mister Owl. Your friend is awake."

Bitter scrubbed sleep from his eyes and muttered aloud, "Fight through three years of the Civil War without a scratch, and then some Wildhorse Cheyenne puts a hole in my leg on the way home. And now an outlaw shoots me in the head. Maybe Morgan is right. Maybe I should just stick to farming."

And then he grinned. "No. Not a farmer. A horse breeder maybe, and that takes money to get started. The Pinkertons pay well. I'd best keep doing what I'm doing."

He pushed the rough wool blanket away and swung his feet to the floor of the tent just as Owl pushed through the tent flap, a bowl of beef stew in his hand.

"You look better, John Bitter."

Bitter touched the cloth wound around his head and said, "That's a little tender."

Owl nodded. "The doctor stitched you up. Might be sore for a few days."

"I'm grateful, but, where are we?"

"You don't remember?"

"Not much. I know somebody shot me. It's all a blur after that."

"Well," Owl said, "they call this Government Camp. Must be because this is where Bidwell chose to camp. The doctor brought you here in a wagon."

Bitter reached for the stew and said, "Right now, I'm hungry as a horse."

"Good. Means you are healing up."

Rusty pushed through the flap of the tent and then sat in front of Bitter, eyeballing the bowl of stew. Bitter reached out and patted the dog, and then memory came flooding back and he remembered Rusty pulling him from the river. He set the bowl on the floor of the tent and said, "Rusty, you saved my life."

Rusty stood up, a drool hanging from his lower lip, his tail wagging, until Bitter laughed and said, "Go ahead, dog. Eat up."

Unfinished Business

JOHN BITTER, FRESHLY SHAVED, A THIN bandage hiding under a floppy forage cap, compliments of Captain Bidwell, swung up in the saddle, ready for the expected tussle with Rockford. The big horse skipped the crow hopping fuss that generally preceded any forward progress, and Bitter decided the horse must sense his rider was not up to snuff. *Mikey would know what Rockford was doing,* he thought. He looked at the sky, smelled the rain just waiting in the clouds to get him wet.

Captain Bidwell stepped over and held out his hand. "Ride safely home, John."

Bitter shook hands. "Thank you. And thank Doctor Strickland for me."

Bidwell nodded. "I will when he gets back. He's gone to Sherar's Bridge to tend to Miss Franklin's broken leg."

Owl looked miffed to hear his medical help for Anna dismissed, but he held his peace. *At least the Army doctor seems to know his business.*

"I've meant to ask," Bitter said, "what you did with the two outlaws you captured."

"Followers, John Bitter. Just followers. So, I gave them a choice. Enlist in the U.S. Army or be hung. They are now in the loving hands of Sergeant Benteen."

Bitter chuckled and then gave Bidwell a salute. He gigged Rockford into motion. "Stay well, Captain."

The road was wide enough to ride side by side, and Bitter slowed to let Owl catch up. "Nice morning," Owl. I'm sure glad to be moving again."

Owl nodded. "How's your head?"

"Sore."

"Does it ache?"

"Some, but I think a week's rest was more than enough."

"Horse is happy to be on the trail. Frisky. Nearly bucked me off this morning."

He looked at Owl, reins in hand, a lead rope for three pack horses tied to his saddle horn, his yellow hat firmly settled on his head, gray braids tied with strips of leather. Bitter grinned and said, "Owl, when are you going to give that horse a real name? Maybe something like Jake, or maybe Buck. Come to think of it, he strikes me as a horse named Buck. We'll sit by the fire in our old age and talk about the wild rides you made on old Buck."

Owl glanced sideways at Bitter, and then looked away. "Don't make fun, John Bitter. Names matter more than you white men think. And Horse does have a name. It's Horse."

"Like Woman's name is Woman?"

"I told you her Cheyenne name. It means the dark shine of a magpie's wing, but you can't speak it right. I keep it simple for white men. I call her Woman."

"And if you get a dog?"

Owl grinned. "I will name him Dog. Good name for a dog. Easy to remember."

Bitter smiled, took another wrap around his saddle horn with the lead-rope tied to his mule Windy, his young soul happy at the thought of home, and happy to just be alive. Rusty trotted alongside Rockford, and Bitter wondered again at the strange bond between Rockford and Rusty.

His memory opened the flood gates and he was back in Missouri again, camped on the slough where he first spotted Ethan Sharp, a boy who, along with his little brother Mikey, soon became his adopted son.

He remembered his fear when five-year-old Mikey walked in front of Rockford, the meanest horse a man could find. He had held his breath, and then the big horse had nudged the little boy with his nose to get a whiff of his little boy scent. Mikey pulled a handful of grass to feed the horse, and the horse nudged him again, sending him giggling and falling backward. And then the big red dog was standing over Mikey, hackles raised, defending the boy, crouched to attack.

What followed was still a mystery to John Bitter. Rockford had put his nose close to the dog and then went back to cropping grass. Rusty had moved in closer and touched noses with the horse. Rusty and Rockford had been friends ever since, but he still didn't know why.

With their pack animals strung out, the little red mare bringing up the rear, Owl and Bitter rode past Collins Lake where a few trout were busy making rings on the still surface as they fed on the morning bug hatch. Three cautious hours down Laurel Hill and ten miles later, they paid the toll keeper at the Barlow Road Tollgate and picked up the pace.

"I hope Morgan has some biscuits for us when we get there, John Bitter. And bacon," Owl said.

"I'd settle for anything right now.

They rode in silence for another mile, and then Owl gigged Horse and pulled his pack string alongside Bitter again. "What are you going to do about that outlaw?"

"The one that shot me?"

"Yes. When he hears you are alive, he'll come after you. That one is a hater and a killer. You shamed him. Twice. Once when you knocked him off his horse, and again when you took his clothes and burned his camp."

"How will he know I'm still alive? He thinks he killed me."

"Word will get out. Soldiers drink and drinkers talk. You should find him. Use your badge. Arrest him."

"And if he resists?"

"Shoot him, like you should have when they shot our blankets."

"That's a little blood thirsty, Owl."

"Some men are no good. Need to be sent on to the next life. You don't want him following you home."

"No. I guess I don't."

They rode another mile before Bitter broke the silence. "I hate the notion, but I think you got it right. Unless somebody shoots him before I find him, I have it to do." He pulled the worn forage cap Bidwell had given him and held it at arm's length, staring at the short bill and the faded blue color. "Besides, he owes me a new hat."

Home

WHEN BITTER TURNED ROCKFORD DOWN THE lane between the big pasture and the orchard, he caught a glimpse of a barefoot boy, blond hair bouncing, running toward the cabin. He heard Mikey yelling, "Mama! Mama! Pa is back!"

The big black mule grazing in the lower pasture picked his head up, stared, pulled his upper lip back, and then charged the fence, galloping right at the pack string. The pack string and Horse shied, but Rockford just looked at Lucifer as if to say, "That the best you got?" Lucifer slid to a stop and then, job done, turned and trotted back across the pasture. Bitter laughed. "Somebody is going to shoot that old mule someday."

He gigged Rockford with his heels and led the cavalcade down the lane between the lower pasture and the orchard. He noted the pears, peaches and plums set on the trees and thought the harvest would be good come fall. *I see somebody has made a cutting of hay in the upper pasture. I wonder who did that?*

Morgan stepped out on the covered porch, a hand shading her eyes. She patted her hair into place, untied her red checked apron and folded it over a cane-backed chair next to a small round table. She would never admit it to John, but it was her sipping table where she sat each evening to sip her cider and watch the lane for her husband. Her temper flared for a brief few second at his absence, and then tears blurred her vision at the sight of her husband riding down the lane.

Mikey slipped his hand into Morgan's and squeezed. "I told you he was coming back soon."

"Yes, you did Mikey. And I'm glad."

Rusty bounded ahead of the cavalcade, bounced up on the porch, and, paws on Mikey's shoulders, knocked him down. Mikey giggled and pushed the big dog away. "No licking, Rusty."

The string of horses behind Bitter and Owl piqued Morgan's interest, especially the small red mare. There had to be a story behind that.

Leave it to John, she thought. She could hear her close friend Ruth Shipley saying, "He gathers himself a flock, just like Jesus." Only that time, Ruth was referring to a small Indian boy riding a stumble foot mare, and his grandmother, a small woman named Blue Flower riding double on Rockford, arms wrapped around Bitter's waist.

When Bitter pulled Rockford to halt near the front steps, he stepped out of the saddle and was nearly knocked down by the rush of Morgan into his arms. She hugged him, kissed him and then stepped back to survey his face. She saw fatigue and something else.

"Are you all right, John?"

Owl answered for him. "No. He got himself shot."

Alarmed, Morgan said, "Shot?' She looked him up and down, and then demanded, "Where?"

Bitter pulled the faded forage hat from his head so she could see the bandage. He pointed, gave her a lopsided grin and said, "Right there. Sort of almost missed me. Good thing I've got a hard head, huh?"

He pulled her close again, gave her a squeeze and whispered, "It was a close thing, Morgan. I owe Owl and Rusty my life."

She pulled back. "Well, let's get the horses and Windy put away and then you can tell me about it. I'd really like to know where you got the Red Mare and the two pack horses. I recognize Owl's pack horse, but not the others."

He picked up the reins and started to lead Rockford toward the barn. Morgan said, "No. You sit here on the porch. We will take care of the stock. And then we need to talk. Listen for Sarah while I'm gone. I just put her down for a nap."

He skootched his butt up on the edge of the porch and watched them lead Rockford and the pack animals to the barn and strip them of gear, dump cracked corn in the feed trough, and shoo the stock into the pasture behind the barn. Rockford found a dusty place to roll and Windy the mule sniffed at the corn and walked down to the creek for a drink of cool water.

"You are unflappable, Windy," Bitter said aloud. And then he chuckled at the memory of buying the mules from Black Jack Jefferson back in Missouri. He could still hear Black Jack singing gospel songs down along the river.

When Black Jack offered Bitter a taste of moonshine, he had asked, "How do you work that out…I mean gospel songs and moonshine?"

To which Black Jack had answered, "No problem. Each is a joy given to us by the Good Lord. It's sinful to disrespect the good things our Lord Jesus and his Father provides."

Bitter had grinned and then bought Windy and three other strong mules to pull his wagon from Saint Joseph, Missouri, to his farm on Abiqua Creek in Oregon's Willamette Valley.

A small cry cleared his mind of memories and he stepped up the porch and into the cabin. He walked to the cradle and looked down at his infant daughter, bright red hair and blue eyes making her the spitting image of her mother.

He smiled and picked her up, sniffed and said, "Yep…I know what happened. I don't like crap in my pants either."

At the sound of his voice, and in the comfort of his arms, she calmed, and when he gently stroked her cheek with a rough index finger, he was rewarded with a smile. Morgan stepped quietly into the cabin in time to hear him say, "Yep…I reckon we'll keep you after all."

"I think that's a fine idea, John Bitter. And next time, I think we'll have a boy."

He turned and looked startled. "You aren't…"

"Yes. You're going to be a papa again."

He held Sarah with one arm and hugged Morgan with his other. "Oh, my, Morgan, my love."

He and Owl shared the kitchen table with Mikey while Morgan heated coffee and sliced potatoes in her big cast iron skillet. Bitter asked, "Where's Ethan?" He caught the quick glance Mikey shot in Morgan's direction.

She nodded and Mikey said, "You see, Pa, Thomas's kin were here yesterday…three mean men looking for Thomas." His chin quivered and he blinked back tears.

Bitter asked gently, "Did they scare you?"

And then Mikey was in Bitter's arms, sobbing. When he finally calmed down, Mikey said, "They looked like the men who took our mama back in Missouri."

"Raiders," Bitter spat. "Sorry I wasn't here. You go ahead with your story."

Mikey wiped tears with the back of his hand, slid off Bitter's lap, and took a deep breath. "Anyway, they had that same deputy sheriff with them. The one who came and got Thomas. When they wanted to search the house, Mama pointed her pistol at them and told them to leave." He grinned. "Really made them mad."

Bitter couldn't help himself. He laughed.

Mikey added, "And they did search the barn even though Mama told them not to."

Morgan turned from the stove, a stubborn look on her face. "Trespassers! Every one of them. I'd have shot the sour-faced one, the elder of that bunch, but I didn't think I should also shoot the deputy."

"And that explains where Ethan is?"

"Yep. He has a hideout up the creek near Abiqua Falls. That's where Thomas is. Brother took him a bunch of food and some blankets."

Morgan added, "Ethan will be home in the morning."

Owl nodded. "Ethan is a good boy. Could be an Indian. Gonna be a warrior."

Bitter nodded. "You might be right." He looked at Morgan. "Which horse did he take? I know he didn't ride Lucifer."

"That Josey horse."

"Owl, old friend. You think you can track his horse?"

"Depends."

Morgan shook her head. "No. You leave it be for now. He'll be fine tonight. Look at you both. Worn out. And tired people make mistakes. Leave it until morning. Besides, Thomas and Ethan are having an adventure."

Bitter shook his head. "Like the trip across the Oregon Trail wasn't adventure enough?"

Morgan said, "They didn't ask for that one."

Bitter looked at Owl who shrugged and said, "The tracks will be there in the morning."

✍

ITTER AND MORGAN SAT AT the sipping table on the front porch long after Bitter had tucked Mikey in his bed in the loft above the kitchen.

Owl kept company for a while, his skinny butt perched on the edge of the porch. He drank a second cup of coffee laced with sugar and whiskey and then said, "We'll take care of tomorrow's business tomorrow. I'm for bed." They watched him disappear into the barn.

Morgan reached out and took John's hand. "A good friend." And then she added, "And he smells a whole lot better than the first time we saw him."

Bitter smiled. "Yep. You know, as I count it, he saved my life three times now. Once on the Little Blue coming west when he warned us about the Wild Horse Cheyenne. Once when he killed that Mormon fella…Butler. Was that his name?"

Morgan nodded. "Yes. Butler. But why do you think he killed Butler?"

"Why did he, or why do I think he did?"

"Why do you think he did."

"He left me a note saying the bad Mormon wouldn't be bothering us any more. Sort of a confession."

"And you never showed it to the Army. Or to me."

"Nope. Put me in a bind. Can't turn on someone who just saved your life and the lives of your family. And since you didn't know about it, you didn't have to lie."

She squeezed his hand again and added, "Did you ever notice that he always calls you John Bitter? Never just Bitter and never just John. Always John Bitter."

He nodded. "He told me once that names are important to Indians. I know they are to him."

Bitter rolled a smoke, twisted the ends of the paper and lit it with a match. "And he saved me this time, too. If he hadn't come back for me, I think the cold of the river would have killed me. Rusty pulled me out of the water, but Owl got me out of the log jam. I'm not sure I could have done it alone."

"Tell me. What happened?"

When he finished the story, Morgan looked pensive, watched a bat flying in the near dark, working at the business of feeding on insects, and then said, "Do you think it's over? With the outlaw, I mean."

"Owl doesn't think so."

"I don't either. What are you going to do?"

"Well, when this business with Thomas is cleared up, I guess I'll pin on my U.S. Marshal badge and hunt him down."

"What about the girl, Anna?"

"I think I'll tell the truth. The way young Sherar was looking at her…and Anna at him…she could be married before her daddy finds her."

"What are you going to tell him?"

"I'll tell him I found her. She is injured, but safe. And she has no intention of coming home. And I guess the Pinkerton Agency will refund his money."

"Won't work."

"Probably not."

"Her daddy will go after her."

"I might not tell him where she is. Won't have to lie that way."

Morgan stood up and pulled at his hand. "I think the skeeters are getting to me. Let's go in."

Brigands

BITTER FINISHED HIS BREAKFAST AND PUSHED back from the table. "That was pretty tasty, Morgan. And I think Owl got enough bacon for once."

She laughed. "I don't know how anyone as thin as he is can put away so much food at one sitting."

Little Sarah, sitting in an ornate hardwood high chair, a gift from her Uncle Luke, looked up from her food and imitated her mother's laugh. Mikey forced a laugh, too, and Bitter thought Mikey might be a little jealous of Sarah, but he let it pass.

He smiled. "She's going to be a charmer, just like her mother."

"I recall you accusing me of having an Irish temper."

"That, too. Part of the charm. Well, I wonder when Ethan will get back? I'm thinking Thomas would be safer right here with us. And I intend to talk to brother Luke's lawyer. See what we can do about adopting Thomas away from his kin."

Morgan nodded. "I think that's a dandy idea. Ethan said Thomas was starved down to bone and gristle."

"I think Owl and I will take a little ride. By the way, who cut the hay in the upper pasture?"

"Ezra and a couple of men I hired. I gave half the hay to Ezra."

"Good. I'll stop and see him on our way up the creek."

He stepped out on the porch, coffee cup in hand, intending to sit at Morgan's sipping table when the slap of a slug tore into the door frame. He dropped the coffee cup, jumped back into the cabin and slammed the door just as another slug punched through the tough wood.

"Get Sarah into the back room," he shouted as he wrapped his pistol belt around his waist and grabbed his lever action Henry from the pegs over the mantle. He fit the bar in place, locking the front door, and then hurried to the back of the cabin. He pushed the hinged window open and scanned the woodlot behind the cabin. When he didn't spot anyone, he dropped to the ground and hurried around to the side of the cabin.

A man's voice called out, his accent marking him Southern. "We know he's in there. So, y'all send Tommy on out. He's our kin and we're be takin' him home. Send him out or we'll burn your house down. Ain't no John law to stop us today. He's our property and we want him back."

A quick peek told him three hard-looking characters were dismounted and standing at the edge of yard. The Dicksons. How they had missed him with the first shot, he would never know. Providence, maybe. *Mean and stupid*, he thought, *and they don't know Owl is in the barn. No wonder the South lost.*

He stepped out and started a slow walk toward the men at an angle to pull gunfire away from his family. He held his rifle in his left hand, his right hand brushing the butt of his pistol

"You boys are in a lot of trouble," he said. "You tangled with the wrong people. You come in here without warning and scare my wife and my children. You threaten to burn my house. You shoot at me. You are cowardly bullies is what you are. We had enough of that during the war." As he talked his anger grew. He was boiling mad. "This ends now!"

"You can't get all three of us," the elder said. He spat on the ground, wiped a dribble of tobacco juice from his gray beard, and turned the rifle in his hand in Bitter's direction.

"Maybe not, but count yourself among the dead, no matter what happens."

"Ah, Pa," one of the younger men said, "he's all bluff." And with that he reached for his pistol. Bitter didn't hesitate. He pulled his pistol and shot the one called Pa right in the chest, shifted aim and then shot the younger one just as Owl's rifle barked and the middle one folded up in the roadway.

"Checkmate," Bitter said.

Bitter's bullet had shattered the younger man's right arm. He cussed Bitter and tried to shift his pistol to his left hand. Bitter walked toward him, pistol ready. He kept saying, "Don't do it. I don't want to shoot you."

Just as the bearded young man finally got a grip on the pistol, Bitter kicked it out of his hand. "Damn. How dumb can a man be? You looking to die?"

"I'll kill you. You shot my Pa."

"Yes, I did, and I'm sorry I didn't kill you, too." He waited a few seconds and then added, "I'll bet you rode with the guerrillas during the war, didn't you?"

The pain of his busted arm was beginning to awaken, but he said defensively, "We was duly authorized by the Confederate States of America to wage war against the North and against Union sympathizers."

"Which meant anyone who had something you wanted. Including women and children. You are without conscience. Evil through and through."

Owl walked up, rifle in the crook of his arm. "Shoot him John. He'll only bring you trouble."

Bitter said, "I would surely like to, but I can't bring myself to shoot an unarmed man."

"Give me a gun. I'll show you."

Owl walked to the pistol laying in the dust and picked it up. Without a word he handed it to the wounded man.

The man took the pistol left-handed, thumbed the hammer back, and turned toward Bitter. "Now we'll see."

Bitter's shot ruined the man's left hand and sent the pistol flying into the dusty yard. The wounded man whimpered and looked stupidly at the shattered hand. "You shot me again."

Bitter took a deep breath to steady the tremble in his hands, and then looked at Owl. "Is that whole family full of damned fools?"

"They aren't the only ones. You're gonna patch him up and send him home, aren't you." It was more statement than question.

"I have to patch him up. It's the only honorable thing I can do."

Owl just shook his head. "Well, he won't be shooting at you for quite a while."

Pistol Shots

SIX MORNINGS EACH WEEK, EZRA ROLLED out of bed at the crack of dawn, milked their cow, Queeny, wondering the whole time why he still owned her, and then ate breakfast while his diminutive wife Ruth packed him a lunch. A quick kiss for Ruth, a pat on Davey's head, and out the kitchen door to the barn marked the routine of another day. Regular as sunrise, he hurried each morning to the barn and saddled Lucky for the six-mile ride to the blacksmith shop in Silverton.

He rode tall in the saddle, eyes alert, a .44 colt revolver in his holster. So far there hadn't been any physical threats, but he nonetheless sensed the hostility of the southern sympathizers living in the town of Silverton. Even though the war was over, and even though the slaves had been emancipated, a lot of the early settlers just didn't want any black people living the fine state of Oregon. *Like the war was the fault of black people*, Ezra thought.

Fresh from their trip across the Oregon Trail, Bitter had introduced him to Doc Hardy, the local blacksmith. At first Hardy was skeptical about taking on a black man, but the steel in Bitter's eyes when Hardy hesitated to say "yes" convinced Doc it was worth a try. A few months later Ezra overheard Doc telling Ozzie Oster, owner of the Silverton Saloon that Ezra had an uncanny knack for working metal.

The sound of gunshots from the direction of the Bitter place drifted across the farm fields and through the orchards. "Pistol work, Lucky. That sounds like trouble." He kicked the big bay in the ribs and urged him into a ground-eating gallop down the county road.

He rode with the reins in his left hand, his pistol in his right, ready for trouble. The echo of one more shot carried over the sound of pounding hooves. "Yep. Pistol work. And trouble for sure."

He slowed Lucky to a walk and rode past three horses cropping grass alongside the lane to Bitter's orchard. He noted the shabby saddles and the rough-patched reins. One horse had its neck stretched over the fence trying hard to get to the ungrazed orchard grass. "Okay, then, Lucky. Three people. Men most likely."

The sight of Bitter and Owl standing a short distance from two men sprawled on the ground and a third man plopped on his butt in the dust, blood running down his arm, eased his worry for his good friend John Bitter. But Ezra still didn't holster his pistol.

"I see you're back home, John. And it looks like you brought trouble with you."

"Ezra," Bitter said by way of greeting.

"Howdy, Owl. Looks like you two have been busy."

Owl shook his head. "These are Thomas's relatives. Dumb as buffalo chips. Shot at John Bitter coming out the door. Bad mistake."

Ezra dismounted and shook his head. "The miss or the shot?"

Owl grinned and said, "Both."

Ezra looked at Bitter, pointed at the bandage around his head and asked, "Recent?"

"No. About two weeks ago."

"This bunch?"

"No. This bunch brought a deputy sheriff with them yesterday… looking for Thomas. We hadn't gotten back yet, but Morgan ran them off at gunpoint." He stared at the bodies staining the dust of the yard with blood. "These three came back without the law. They said that if we didn't send Thomas out, they would burn the house. Riled me, it did."

Ezra holstered his pistol and noted dryly, "I'd say it did."

"Well, dang it, Ezra, I warned them off, but one of them pulled a pistol. I just didn't have much choice."

"What now?"

"I'm going to patch this one up, I'm going to arrest him, and then I'm going to take him to Sheriff Buckholtz so he can put this one in his nice new jail. I'll swear out a complaint. I want him tried for attempted murder, for shooting at an officer of the law and for terrorizing innocent women and children."

"Can Pinkertons arrest people?"

Owl chuckled and said, "He is now a U.S. Marshal. Means he can arrest bad people."

Ezra frowned and said, "How did that happen?"

"Beecher is interfering with my life again," Bitter said.

Ezra almost laughed and then said, "Will this mean trouble with the rest of the clan?"

"I don't know. These three are the only ones I ever saw."

The wounded man snarled and said, "Uncle Samuel will be coming after you. My Pa is his brother."

"Just shut the hell up."

Hearing familiar voices, Morgan cautiously opened the door and peeked out. At the sight of the bodies, she took a deep breath and sighed. "Oh, Lord, John Bitter. What happened?"

"Let's get this guy's wounds plugged so he doesn't bleed to death, and I'll explain." He looked at the man and said, "Get your skinny ass over to the porch and sit." Then he looked at Owl. "Feel like playing doctor again?"

Owl shook his head in disgust before saying, "I guess."

Jail Bird

JOHN BITTER TIED THE DICKSON DEAD each over the saddle of a horse, tied the wrists of the youngest Dickson to the saddle horn and told Ezra and Owl to keep a watch. "If he tries to ride off, you have my permission to shoot him." He hurried to the back bedroom of the cabin and took his U.S. Marshal badge from a small wooden chest hiding under the bed.

He pinned the badge to his left shirt pocket, slipped on his denim jacket to hide the shiny star, folded the letter appointing him a U.S. Marshal, and slid it into the front shirt pocket of his jacket. *Just in case*, he thought.

Morgan and Mikey were still working off the adrenalin encouraged by the gunshots and the sight of the dead. Little Sarah seemed unaffected by the ruckus, but she reached out from Morgan's arms toward her father. Bitter held her, put her on his shoulder and patted her gently on the back. "Sure sorry, Morgan. I don't know what we did to deserve this."

Morgan slipped her arm around his back and leaned against his shoulder. "Nothing. Sometimes trouble comes knocking even when you are simply doing the right thing."

"Like taking in Thomas, I guess. Who would have thought?"

Mikey stared at both of them until Bitter handed Morgan the sleepy baby and knelt down. He took Mikey in his arms and said, "Mikey, you are a brave boy. You've had some hard times, but I'm thinking this should end any fuss with Thomas's family.

"I'm going to take the one I wounded, and the two dead men to Salem to the sheriff's office." He pulled his jacket back and showed Mikey the U.S. Marshal badge. "I'm a U.S. Marshal now and I'm going to charge him with attempted murder. That should see he gets a long jail sentence. And, I hope, wrap this up so we can get on with our lives."

Mikey stared at Bitter before saying, "Promise?"

"I can only promise to do what I just said. As for the others in that family, I can only hope this ends it." He gave Mikey a hug, stood up and kissed Morgan, and said, "I should be back before dark."

As he swung into the saddle, Bitter turned and looked at Owl. "You up to tracking Ethan and Thomas down?"

Owl nodded. "I'll bring them home."

Ezra said, "If you ease along for a bit, I'll catch up. I need to let Ruth know what the shooting was about."

⌇

THE FOUR-HOUR RIDE TO SALEM gave Bitter time to consider the recent dust-up. He knew he was right to not kill Hezekiah Dickson, but he reasoned the trouble with the Dickson's was liable to continue. *Might have continued even if I had shot him*, he thought, *but at least I can argue self-defense instead of murder.*

At the Pudding River bridge, Bitter paid the toll keeper a dollar–twenty-five cents for each horse–and muttered, "Kinda steep, don't you think?"

The young man gave Bitter a blank stare, glanced at the nearly vertical twenty-foot banks of the river and then said, "I reckon you could swim across if you wanted to."

Bitter frowned and let it drop. He gigged Rockford and pulled Hezekiah's horse, and the two horses tied on behind with lead ropes across the hollow sounding bridge.

Hezekiah spotted an outhouse just off the road on the west side of the river. "I want to get down. I need to pee."

Bitter shook his head. "No. You just sit right there. I'm not going to unbutton your britches for you. You'll dry before we get to the Sheriff's office."

"Humiliating," Hezekiah muttered.

"Nothing is more humiliating than death," Bitter growled, "which is what you were fixing to serve me and my family. Don't get me riled again. I'm might be tempted to take three corpses to the sheriff. Nope. You just sit the saddle, boy, unless you want to ride draped over it."

⁓

IN SALEM, BITTER TIED THE horses to a wrought iron hitching rail in front of a fairly new two-story brick building serving as sheriff's office and county jail. He noted Hezekiah was looking a bit sick, pain and grief written on his face. "Stay here, boy. No sense in running. I'd just shoot you again."

Bitter walked up three concrete steps and pushed through the door into an open area that served as office for the sheriff. Bitter walked over to a man sitting behind a desk and said, "I'm Marshal John Bitter. I've got a prisoner for you."

A lean, hard-eyed man with a black mustache, a badge pinned to his vest, Sheriff Buckholtz sat behind the desk and frowned. "I never heard of any marshal named John Bitter."

"I'm not surprised," Bitter said dryly. "I'm kinda new to the job."

"Got any documents saying you were appointed?"

Without a word, Bitter fished the letter from his jacket pocket, unfolded it and handed it across the desk to Buckholtz. "I brought this along."

Buckholtz studied the letter for a long minute and glanced back up at U.S. Marshal John Bitter. "You must have some powerful friends, Marshal. Have a chair. Now what can I do for you?"

Bitter sat down before saying, "You can take two corpses off my hands, and put my prisoner in your jail. I'm charging him with at-tempted murder and for attacking an officer of the law…me…and for attacking my family. The father shot at me this morning and threatened to burn my house. I killed him and the older brother. And I put a bullet in the young one."

One of Bitter's decisions made during the long ride was to keep Owl out of it. *I'll take the blame for shooting the other one, too*, he thought.

"What is the prisoner's name?"

"Hezekiah Dickson. Says the graybeard hanging over the saddle is his father Abner Dickson, and the other corpse is his brother Jacob. I have no idea where they live…or lived as the case may be."

Sheriff Buckholtz pushed his chair back, stood up and held out his hand. "Well, nice to meet you, Marshal Bitter…I think. Let's go see what you brought." Buckholtz hollered down a short hallway, "William, get out here. We got company."

When Deputy Sheriff Will Harp had Hezekiah tucked safely in Sheriff Buckholtz's brick jail, and when the corpses had been assigned to the local undertaker, Buckholtz offered Bitter a cup of coffee and said, "Let's take care of the paperwork. And then I'd like to hear how you became a U.S. Marshal."

Friends

ETHAN USED THE POINT OF HIS skinning knife, a gift from Mark Anthony, to turn dollar-sized venison steaks in the sizzling skillet. He laughed at the sound of Thomas's growling stomach. "Be done in a minute, Thomas."

"I sure hope so. Haven't been this hungry since old Owl and I got kicked out of the Wildhorse Cheyenne camp. We didn't eat much for a week or two."

"I remember thinking you were a skeleton when I first saw you," Ethan said. He eyeballed the steak and then scattered a pinch of salt over the meat. "I think it's done." He slid the tender venison backstrap onto two tin plates and set the skillet aside. "There you go. Just right."

They were camped up off of Abiqua Creek about a half mile downstream from Abiqua Falls. Ethan hadn't wanted to camp too near the falls because, he had told Thomas, "The water makes so much noise we can't hear the bad guys sneaking up on us."

Camp consisted of a stained, weathered piece of canvas about ten feet square pegged to the top of a big downed cedar tree, corners propped up by two long willow poles, a shelf of cedar bark for a bed and a ring of big river rocks for a fire pit. A second downed cedar tree blocked the wind on the upstream side of camp. Both Thomas and Ethan liked their hideout because it couldn't be seen unless you walked the length of one of the cedar logs.

Josey, tied to a tree in the open timber beyond their camp, posed a bit of a problem. The fir and cedar timber crowding the stream just didn't leave much room for meadow grass. Ethan's temporary fix was a nose bag and some cracked corn, but he knew the she would need to graze before too long.

He dabbed at the bacon grease in the skillet with a dried biscuit, and without looking at Thomas said, "You know we can't stay here forever."

"I know that, but I'm not going back to those people. They are meaner than snakes."

"Whip you?"

Thomas's eyes flared in anger. He pulled his shirt up and turned his back to Ethan, showing a nasty pattern of scars. "Sometimes just for nothing, nothing at all. All they wanted me for was to work. And when I asked about people we knew back home, they never even heard of 'em.

"Ethan, I don't think they are really my kin. They just heard about me somehow and decided I could be their free labor." He pulled his shirt down and turned back to the fire.

"What's their names?"

"Last name is Dickson. I never heard that name growing up either."

"Well," Ethan said, "Pa will know what to do. I think we should catch a stringer of fish from that big pool and then go home." He looked at the deer carcass hanging from a big limb of a fir tree between the camp and the creek. "That meat won't keep forever."

Thomas was envious of the deer and of Ethan's little .30 caliber Clemens rifle. "How many deer have you shot, Ethan?"

"Well…the first one was the buck I killed in Star Valley when we were coming across the Oregon Trail. And I shot four more since we got home. Pa won't let me shoot more than we need to eat at one time, but he lets me do all the hunting…most of the time."

A voice above them, someone hidden by the tarp, spoke in Cheyenne. "You got any more of that meat, Thomas? I'm hungry."

Ethan didn't understand the string of words, but "Thomas" is "Thomas" in any language. He looked across the fire and said, "Owl?"

Thomas nodded and grinned. "Yes, old man, we have more meat."

Owl walked into sight and then sat his butt on the log and slid to the ground. "Pretty good camp."

"How did you find us?"

"Tracked that Josey horse upstream. And then I smelled woodsmoke. Figured that was you. Followed the smell right to your camp. That cedar smoke is sweet smelling."

Ethan looked disgusted. "Not much of a hideout, I guess."

Owl fished a piece of venison from the skillet and said, "A comfortable camp, but you can't see the enemy coming. Got to be someplace where you can see them without being seen."

"Where's Pa? I know you went looking. Did you find him?"

Owl took a bite of the tender backstrap, chewed and swallowed before saying, "He's a U.S. Marshal now. Arrested one of Thomas's kin…after we shot two others. Took the young one to jail. Gonna try him for attempted murder. You got a pot? I'll make some coffee."

Thomas asked, "Did you kill the other two?"

"Yes. John Bitter shot the old man, the one with a gray beard. I shot another man. He was a head taller than the young one. Bitter shot that young one in the arm, and then shot a pistol out of his hand. Ruined it."

"The pistol or the hand?" Thomas asked.

Owl laughed. "Both."

Thomas nodded. "The old man is head of the clan. They call him Abner. The middle one, the one you shot is either Paul or Jacob. The younger one is Hezekiah. He's the meanest of the bunch. Beat on me with a leather belt almost every day."

Ethan said, "Show him, Thomas."

Thomas turned his back and hitched his dirty, blood stained cotton shirt up so Owl could see his back. The scars crisscrossed in a maze of misery. A couple of the fresher welts still wept a little blood.

Owl's eye narrowed. He didn't utter a word for a full minute. Then he said, "Get down to the creek and let the water clean your back, Thomas. I'll go get Horse and my medicine bag. Dress those wounds. And then get you home." He paused before adding, "John Bitter and Morgan will adopt you. Get you away from those people."

Thomas, who had endured each whipping without uttering a sound, suddenly found tears in his eyes at the thought of being free of the Dickson clan, and of being the adopted son of John and Morgan Bitter.

Legalities

B ITTER LED ROCKFORD AROUND THE CORNER from the sheriff's office and two blocks further on to brother Luke's saddle shop and leather goods. He tied the reins to a metal hitchrail and pushed through the ornate door announcing "Bitter's Saddle Shop and Sundries" posted in gold letters on the upper half of the glass door.

The showroom was crowded with saddles, halters, reins, quirts, a rare leather raita, wide-brimmed leather hats, and a tall rack with various kinds of leather hides for sale. It was strictly masculine. Almost.

A young woman looked up from behind a counter where she was arranging a variety of expensive leather wallets, saddle bags, belts, and lady's purses. Her shiny blond hair was tied in a bun that belied her youth. She wore a snug, high collar blue dress which failed to hide a full, firm figure. Her deep blue eyes offset a clear, creamy complexion. She wore no rings, but she did wear a slightly mocking smile.

He couldn't say exactly why, but he was struck by a suspicion she was more than a salesclerk. *Lordy, Luke. I hope this isn't what it looks like.*

She smiled and said, "May I help you?"

"I'm Luke's brother. Is he in?"

"I thought there was a family resemblance." She held out her hand. "I'm Abigail Simmons, Mister Luke's sales assistant. So nice to finally meet the famous John Bitter."

"Infamous is more like it." Bitter shook hands and noticed she held his hand a bit longer than necessary. *Oops*, he thought. *Brother Luke, this one could be trouble. What is it about you and blond women?* Thoughts of Lydia, Luke's wife…and John's once upon a time fiancée…briefly crossed his mind and then were dismissed. Water under the bridge.

"Mister Luke is in back working on a saddle for a wealthy California rancher. A wedding gift for the rancher's daughter. A very ornate saddle, and very expensive." John Bitter heard a note of pride in her voice.

"Just go on back, Mister Bitter." She pointed to a Dutch door that was half open.

Bitter nodded and said thanks. He pushed through the door and was immediately wrapped in the warm, comforting odor of leather and saddle soap. A large ten-foot by ten-foot cutting table dominated the room, and benches lined the walls. Five men were seated at the benches, using awls, leather punches, needles, scissors, metal stamps, leather-headed hammers, and sharp knives––and all working to turn pieces of leather into polished goods. John's mind nibbled at the edge of understanding, of nearly getting a handle on the reason his brother loved working with leather…and maybe spearing a hint of why he was so profoundly good at it.

Luke looked up and smiled. He slid off his stool, put his tools carefully in their proper slots on the backboard, and untied his leather apron. "John! Nice to see you. What brings you to town?"

The brothers shook hands. John looked at the beautiful, ornate saddle Luke had been working on. "Is that one of those thousand dollar saddles you sell?"

Luke ran his hand over the silver saddle horn and grinned. "Yes. Yes, it is. Keeps the wolf from the door."

John nodded and then said, "I need to speak with my big brother."

Luke headed across the room to an office. John noticed Luke's limp, a gift from a nasty fall from a ladder a few years earlier. "And a blessing," Luke had said. "Gave me time to do what I like best…work with leather."

Luke ushered John into an office playing host to a large hardwood desk with a custom leather top. Bitter ran his hand over the surface and said, "Nice, Luke. Did you do this?"

Luke nodded. "Important people like to have important looking desks. They pay me important prices. Pride, John, pride."

John laughed and said, "That's the motto of my boss, Mark Anthony. He says pride keeps the Pinkertons in business."

Luke settled behind the desk in a beautiful rosewood captain's chair and pointed to a leather upholstered visitor's chair. "Have a seat."

Thirty minutes later, Luke's messenger boy was back with a message setting an appointment for John with Attorney at Law Bertrand Russell at one o'clock.

"Let's have some lunch," Luke said. "I'll see if Abby…I mean Miss Simmons would like to join us."

Catching Up

MISS SIMMONS DID INDEED WANT to join them for lunch, which, to John's surprise, was more business meeting than lunch. As soon as the meal was ordered and the coffee on the table, Abigail Simmons launched into a detail of the orders she had written during the course of the morning.

Prime among a list of ten orders came from a Mrs. Portia Harris to replace the leather seats and the leather top of the family carriage.

"She said the carriage was old, but her daddy had it shipped around the Horn from Boston and she just couldn't part with it. And how much would we charge for the work. I quoted her a price of twelve hundred dollars, and she never even blinked. Just wanted to know when we could get it done."

"If this keeps up we'll need to hire another man."

"Person," Abigail corrected.

"It takes strong hands to work leather."

"I'll find someone…a woman with strong hands."

Luke laughed and said, "Have at it."

Lunch over, Abigail excused herself with the explanation she had a customer coming in at 12:45.

John noted the way Luke stared at Abigail as she walked out the door. He finally said, "She's a pistol, that one."

"And she is helping me make a ton of money."

"What are you going to do with it."

"Lydia gets her share for the house and I invest."

"Invest?"

Luke gave John a wry smile. "Yep. Don't let it out, but I own the block the store is in, and I lease this space to George Zumwalt, the proprietor of this fine eating establishment."

John grinned and said, "Well, good. In that case, how about a loan?"

"You serious?"

"Just kidding. So how is Lydia and baby Eloise?"

Luke frowned and then shook his head. "Eloise is doing just fine. Love that little girl." He looked pained when he added, "But I'm afraid there won't be any brothers or sisters for her to share life with."

"Why not?"

"Well, Lydia is a jealous woman. She's jealous of her husband and of her husband's money. When I hired Miss Simmons, Lydia took one look and insisted I fire her. I refused and Lydia kicked me out of her bedroom. End of story."

"How long has this been going on?"

"About six months."

John shook his head. "Isn't that grounds for divorce?"

"I think about that, but I don't want to give up Eloise."

John nodded. "Understood…but I'll bet Miss Simmons wouldn't mind being Missus Luke Bitter. I saw the way you looked at her…and I would guess she feels the same."

Luke just shook his head. "Enough. Tell me about this Pinkerton business."

John brought his big brother up to date, including the hunt for Anna Franklin, about being shot out of the saddle and into the White River, and about the Dickson's.

"You've been busy, little brother. Or should I call you Marshal?"

Family

Lawyer Bertrand Russell, a solid-looking man with a neatly trimmed moustache, dressed in a black wool suit, wearing an air of superiority, was, in the words of John's brother, a man who can be trusted. John Bitter had yet to make up his mind.

At the end of an hour it had been decided to file a petition with the court for protective custody of Thomas McCarthy, a juvenile approximately twelve years old, to be followed by a request for adoption. John Bitter paid Russell twenty-five dollars.

"I'll send you a message when the court responds. That you are an established farmer, married, have a family, and that you are also a U.S. Marshal should be bone fides enough to convince the court the boy should be in your custody immediately. Adoption will take a bit more time."

"How much time?"

"As long as six months."

Bitter grumped and said, "In Missouri it takes about ten minutes."

"We escaped the war, Mister Bitter. We operate on a more civilized schedule."

Bitter shook his head. "When you have information for me, would you send a message to the Pinkerton office on Bridge Street?"

Lawyer Russell looked surprised. "May I ask why?"

"I'm an unwilling U.S. Marshal, but I'm also employed as a Pinkerton detective."

Lawyer Russell, studied the young man for a few seconds and then said, "You are a bit like your brother…into almost everything." And then he smiled, rose from his chair and extended a hand across the desk.

Bitter didn't get out of his chair. Instead he said, "I have a little more business I want you to tend to."

Lawyer Russell sat back down. "Okay. What is it?"

"I want to transfer the deed to the farm I bought from Luke. I want to give it to Ezra and Ruth Shipley."

"Easy enough. I have a record of the sale to you from you brother. I'll draw it up and you can sign it."

"My wife and I will both sign it. And I want another deed drawn up naming Morgan as co-owner of my other farm."

"You are pushing convention, Mister Bitter."

"I don't want her to lose the farm if something should happen to me."

"Are you a Democrat, Mister Bitter?"

"Nope. Just a simple soldier who fought three long years for the freedom of some other people. Right is right, Mister Russell."

"I'll do as you request."

Bitter frowned and said, "Well, to put the icing on the cake, Ezra Shipley is a black man who fought in the Civil War…a wounded veteran…and my close friend. I want to make sure he is also protected from seizure of his property."

Lawyer Russell rocked back in his captain's chair and then smiled. "That will be another twenty-five dollars."

Sanctuary

T HOMAS JERKED AWAKE BEFORE HE FELL off Horse as the big bay picked a path through the alder and cottonwood trees crowding Abiqua Creek. Owl reached back and caught him and then pulled Horse to a stop.

"Thomas, we'll trade places. You ride the saddle and I'll ride double…keep you from falling off."

Ethan reined Josey to a stop and waited. He watched the creek. A big rainbow trout rose to take a salmon fly. *Twenty inches, maybe*, Ethan thought. Aloud he said, "When you get fixed up, Thomas, we should come back here and catch some fish."

Thomas slid off Horse and winced when his feet hit the ground. "I'd like that. And I'd like to shoot a deer."

Ethan patted the butt of his Clemens .30 caliber rifle and nodded. "We'll do it for sure."

Secure in the saddle and in Owl's arms, Thomas slept most of the ten miles back to the Bitter farm. *Worn out*, Owl thought, and scowled at the thought of the beatings Thomas had suffered at the hands of the Dicksons.

Good thing we cleaned out that bunch. Otherwise I'd have to do it. Probably get in trouble. White men don't like it when Indians kill white men, even evil white men. His thoughts drifted back to the Oregon Trail and Butler. *Too bad. They cause trouble for all people.*

Take Chief Wild Horse. Caused his people a lot sorrow. Too many whites for them to win. A lot of dead Cheyenne is all he accomplished. Glad I'm not there to see it.

The trail they followed led to the county road. Owl looked at the fenced fields and shook his head. He turned and looked at Ethan and said, "Gonna be a lot of fences in the white world before it's over. I don't think even the white men are gonna like it."

Ethan frowned. Puzzled by Owls comment, he said, "We need to keep our stock in and keep critters out of the garden and the orchard."

Owl nodded and turned back to watching the roadside. "The fences won't be wood, Ethan. White men use rules to build another kind of fence."

Ethan gigged Josey in the ribs and rode up alongside Owl. "I don't know what you mean."

"You know the Golden Rules in the Christian Bible?"

Ethan said, "Well, some of them…like not killing people. And not stealing. And not lying. Those 'thou shalt not covet' rules don't make much sense to me."

"That's the beginning of rule-making. Probably pretty good rules, but human beings are not content to let people alone, and the bad ones won't follow the rules we already have, so you keep on making more rules. Pretty soon, there are fences on the trails of the mind, too."

"I don't understand."

Owl looked at him and nodded, "You will…in time."

MORGAN HAD A RULE OF her own…one about hitching horses to the corral rails and not near her front porch. "I don't want all those horse apples in my yard." But when she saw Thomas slumped in the saddle and Owl holding him in place, she hollered, "Bring him on over here."

Owl swung down and caught Thomas as he slid from the saddle. "He's sick," Owl said. "Gonna need a lot of rest."

From the front porch, Mikey said, "His heart is hurt."

Morgan nodded. Somehow those words touched her heart and brought tears to her eyes. "Mikey, how in the world do you know so much?"

"God tells me."

Morgan decided a pallet next to the fireplace would be the best place for Thomas to rest. Owl asked, "You gotta clean shirt he can wear?"

She nodded and went to the big trunk at the foot of her bed. Thomas was a bit taller than Ethan, but just as skinny. She dug out a gray cotton shirt and decided it would have to do.

Owl had Thomas's shirt stripped and was applying a black salve to the welts that still wept a little blood. When Morgan saw the welts and scars on Thomas's back, she was startled. "I didn't know anyone could be so mean."

Owl nodded, but he didn't answer. He said, "I'll need a clean cloth to cover his back. Keep the stains off the shirt. Keep his back clean."

Thomas said, "I'm sure thirsty."

Owl looked at Morgan and said, "He's got a little fever. I'll make a brew of willow powder and maybe you can give me some sugar and some of John Bitter's whiskey. Help Thomas sleep."

Ethan and Mikey watched Owl doctor Thomas and then Ethan, his face grim, said, "I think I'll go watch the road."

Morgan said, "If you see anyone who looks like the Dickson's, you come running. Don't try to shoot them. If they do come, I want you to take Sarah, Mikey and Thomas down to the creek and hide."

"What about you?"

She reached over the mantle and took down her Spencer rifle. "Owl will defend from the barn, and I'll defend from here." Her blue eyes snapped, and she seemed taller than her normal five-foot four inches. "No one is going to hurt any of my people. Understood?" She checked the load in the rifle and then leaned it against the frame guarding the front door.

"In the meantime, go take care of the horses. "If you get up in the barn loft you can watch the county road and see anyone coming."

Judge Deady

BITTER PAID LAWYER RUSSELL ANOTHER TWENTY-FIVE dollars and then asked for directions to Judge Deady's office.

"Chambers," Russell corrected. "But you will find his Chambers are in Portland."

Irritated, Bitter growled, "Portland, of all places. I don't have time for a trip to Portland."

Lawyer Russell said, "How about sending a letter. I'll help you compose it if you like."

When Bitter frowned, Lawyer Russell smiled and said, "At no charge, of course."

"Thanks, but I need to see the judge in person."

Lawyer Russell checked his pocket watch and said, "If you hurry you can catch the evening ferry to Oregon City."

Bitter tied the reins to the hitching post in front of the Pioneer Courthouse, an imposing but unfinished three-story edifice built with cut stone. Rockford tried to step on his boot and then tried to bite his arm. Bitter slapped him between the ears with his hat and said, "I know. There's not much to eat around here. You be patient and I'll fix that. First, I need to talk to the Judge, and then I'll find you some feed."

Bitter walked up a wide set of stairs to the second floor and found a polished mahogany door with a brass plaque stating "U.S. Judge Deady" on the door. He knocked and heard what he thought was, "Enter."

A short bustling young man in a black suit, white shirt and a black string tie, served as Deady's law clerk. He was a proud young man and he took his job…which he saw as protecting the Judge from pestering people…very seriously. When Bitter said he wanted to see Judge Deady, the young man, whose name it turned out was Marion Wilkes, asked if he had an appointment.

Bitter said, "No, but I need to see him nonetheless."

Marion said, "Who are you?"

"Let's try this again. I am U.S. Marshal John Bitter here to see my boss, Judge Deady on business. If he's in, I want to speak to him…now."

Marion caught the steely glint in Bitter's eyes and decided he really didn't want this pistol packer mad at him after all. It was quite a concession for Marion. He had faced down numerous angry citizens before, but none like this one.

"Just one minute." He hurried to an inner door and rapped twice with a knuckle. Bitter heard a gravelly voice say, "What is it, Mister Wilkes?"

Marion opened the door and stuck his head in. "There is a Marshal Bitter here to see you, your honor."

"Bitter? Who the hell is Bitter?"

"You appointed him, sir."

"Oh, I remember, now. That friend of Beecher's. Show him in, Mister Wilkes. I'd like to lay eyes on him. And bring us some coffee… with a little cream, please."

Wilkes pointed to the new-looking wide-brimmed hat on Bitter's head, indicating he should remove it, ushered him to the chamber door and closed it when Judge Deady rose and walked around his desk, hand outstretched. "The famous John Bitter. You are the first marshal I ever appointed without seeing him first. Nice to finally meet you."

Bitter pushed six feet, but Deady towered over him. Bitter shook hands and nodded. "Judge. Being a U.S. Marshal wasn't of my choosing, thanks to Beecher, but I have use for the badge. Let me explain."

Deady pointed to an overstuffed leather visitor's chair and said, "Sit. What happened to your scalp? That looks like a fresh wound."

Over coffee Bitter told the story of his search for Anna Franklin, about the outlaws shooting up his camp, and about being shot out of the saddle by an unknown person. "I think I heard one of the men say 'Alf'…like Alfred…Allen…something along that line. I'd like you to issue a warrant so I can legally go after him."

Judge Deady nodded, stroked his beard, then pushed an errant lock back on top of his curly dark hair. "Just a minute." He walked to the door and pulled it open. Bitter heard the judge ask Wilkes if any of the wanted posters carried a name like Alfred or Allen or any other names starting with "A."

Marion Wilkes may have been a bit prissy, but he had a steel trap for a mind. "Yes, we do." He opened a bottom drawer and set a stack of wanted posters on his desk. He rifled the stack and then pulled one out.

The picture on the poster was hand drawn and a bit crude, but the WANTED and $200 stamped on the bottom was clear enough. When Bitter looked at it, he nodded. "Alfred Swift. That's the man who shot up our camp."

"And you want to go after him."

"I do." Bitter smiled and added, "He owes me a new hat."

Judge Deady laughed, looked at the white streak in Bitter's scalp, and then said, "Well, you don't have the authority."

"I don't?"

"No. You haven't been duly sworn. Now, raise your right hand and repeat after me…"

Thirty minutes later, saddle bags loaded with Wanted posters of men who might be attracted to the Canyon City gold rush, Bitter rode Rockford to the Stark Street ferry to wait for a trip upriver to Willamette Falls. "We'll have to find a traveler's inn, Rockford. Push on home tomorrow. Dang, it, I didn't intend to get so deep in this Marshal business. I just want Alfred Swift."

Working It Out

ROCKFORD SPENT THE NIGHT IN AN Oregon City stable, a manger filled with hay and a bait of grain, sheltered from the drizzle that moved in overnight. He was half asleep when Bitter opened the door to the stall, bridle in hand.

"Come on, boy. The ferry leaves in an hour. I want to be on it."

Rockford was in a better mood than the night before, so he only kicked at Bitter once—more of a paw than a kick—and he only crow-hopped twice before giving up the struggle. It worried Bitter some. Maybe Rockford was starting to get old. Not a good thought. He was used to him. Knew he could count on the big horse…even if he was a mean cuss.

When he led a rain-soaked Rockford aboard the Corvallis, a side-wheel ferry owned by his friend Tom Beecher, Captain Kelly opened the window to the pilot house and hollered down, "Is that you, John? I thought I recognized that black horse."

Bitter waved and Kelly hollered again. "Get that horse stabled and come on up to the wheelhouse." When a deck hand reached for Rockford's bridle, Bitter shook his head. "No. I'd better do this. He's liable to bite your head off. Show me where to put him."

～

THE FERRY BELCHED SMOKE AS it bucked the current. Captain Kelly, Beecher's closest friend, turned the wheel to steady the Corvallis in the middle of the channel and pulled the whistle cord twice to acknowledge two young boys waving from the shore. He grinned at Bitter. "Those two seldom miss a chance to watch the ferry."

He waved at the boys and then held out his hand to Bitter. "Nice to see you again."

Bitter shook hands, and said, "You know, it was raining the last time I rode your boat."

Captain Kelly grinned again. "It does that now and again. Keeps the place green."

A steward brought Captain Kelly and Bitter steaming cups of coffee. Kelly set the cup on a wide dashboard in front of the wheel and said, "I hit a deadhead along about here coming down river last night. It's not so bad going down river, but it could stove a hole in this bucket of bolts if I hit it going upriver. You know…the butt sinks and the current keeps the floating end pointed downriver."

"Does the channel change much?" Bitter asked.

Kelly nodded. "Every time we get a flood, new shoals appear, and old channels are filled with rock. Finding the new channel makes for an interesting time every spring."

"You ever hit one…a deadhead?"

"Yep. Punched a big hole in the hull. Water everywhere, but I managed to run the Corvallis aground before we sank. Took a week to get the hole patched."

Bitter sipped the coffee, grateful for the warmth it gave, and thought about what he was going to do about Anna. He knew he had a chore ahead of him. He did not relish the idea of telling Peter Franklin he had found Anna, but she wasn't coming home. He took a deep breath and let it out slowly.

The problem with lying, he thought, *is you generally get found out. A reputation as a liar would reflect badly on the Pinkertons and on my personal reputation as well. Nope. Truth time for sure.*

"So. What brings you to this lowly form of travel?"

Bitter gave Captain Kelly a wry smile and said, "Necessity. I needed to meet Judge Deady…get a warrant for the capture of an outlaw."

"Deady?"

"Yes. Our mutual friend Tom Beecher had Judge Deady appoint me as a U.S. Marshal."

"And I suppose Tom failed to mention it to you. Right?"

"Right. But…as it turns out, I have a need for the badge."

Kelly eyeballed the swirling current, turned the wheel about forty-five degrees, and then said, "So tell me."

∿

BY THE TIME THE *CORVALLIS* reached the Ferry Street dock, Bitter had a pretty good idea of what was in store, and a pretty good idea of what he was going to do. Telling the story had firmed up what needed to be done.

When Captain Kelly said, "Some things are hard to duck. If you don't take care of this Swift fella, you'll lose lots of nights worrying." He stopped for a minute, intent on a big cottonwood drifting downstream.

"I'll let Beecher know what's up. He knows a lot of people, and some may have gone to Canyon City. Might give you some backing."

"You think that's necessary?"

Captain Kelly nodded. "The Alfred Swift types never run alone."

Nelson Goff

Nelson Goff was surprised to see John Bitter ride up to the hitching post and step down from the saddle. Goff hurried to the door and said, "Agent Bitter. How nice to see you…finally."

Bitter looked at him and said, "Don't go getting sarcastic with me, Nelson. I've been delayed."

"Sorry. Didn't mean to sound sarcastic. It's just been three weeks since you checked in."

"I know." Bitter removed his hat and pointed to the right side of his head. "Head wounds tend to slow a man down."

"I didn't know."

Bitter stopped and wondered why he and Goff always wound up in a pissing match. And then he smiled and stuck out his hand. "Nelson, how would you like to have my job?"

"Are you serious?"

"As serious as death."

"Why?"

Bitter took a deep breath and said, "I have things to do that don't include being a Pinkerton. Let me tell you what's been going on."

Goff was a good listener, and when Bitter finished with his tale, he said, "You aren't quitting because you were shot, are you." It was more statement than question. "You want to go after this Swift fellow."

Bitter nodded. "That's it. Now, pretend you really are my secretary and take a letter. "

Goff walked behind the desk, sat down and pulled a few pages of linen paper from a drawer, dipped his pen in the inkwell and waited.

"Let's see, now. Address this to Senior Agent Mark Anthony:

"My dear friend, I find myself sadly requesting release from my contract with the Pinkerton Agency. I have reluctantly accepted a commission as a U.S. Marshal and will be going to the Canyon City gold fields in pursuit of the outlaw who tried to kill me, even when he knew

I was a U.S. Marshal. It has been an honor and a pleasure to serve as a Pinkerton Agent. And it has been an honor to be your friend. I am suggesting you appoint Nelson Goff to be my replacement. He has a keen intelligence and the mind of a first-class sleuth. If he learns to temper ambition with patience, he will do well. Sincerely, your friend, John Bitter."

Bitter signed the letter and looked at Goff who was dumbstruck.

"Do you mean that…I mean the part about being your replacement and being a first-class sleuth?"

"I signed the letter, Nelson. That should tell you I meant it."

Nelson rose so suddenly from the chair behind the desk he stumbled and nearly knocked the inkwell over. He hurried around the desk and held out his hand, a hand that trembled just a bit.

"Thank you, Mister Bitter. I'll try to do you proud."

"I know you will, but first I want to tell you a story. During the war, we fought a tremendous battle against an impatient and ambitious Southern general, a general who will remain unnamed for this tale. His pride and his ambition overcame his military judgment. He wasted about ten thousand men in a frontal attack on entrenched Union forces. Didn't work out so well for him…or for his men. He never recovered his reputation. History will remember his blunder."

"Are you saying I lack patience?"

"I'm not sure, but I am sure about your ambition. Too much ambition can undo a man.

"But enough of that. You make our report to Agent Anthony. Tell him we found the girl, and tell him why you might have to give Peter Franklin his money back."

"Who is going to talk to Mister Franklin?"

"That's next on my list. I'll go see him today if I can find him home."

Peter Franklin

At Goff's suggestion, Bitter first looked for Franklin in his law office on State Street. Franklin's secretary, Jason Jackson, a serious young man whose beard was just beginning to fill in, looked up at the knock on the door. Bitter stuck his head in, and Jackson said, "May I help you?"

"Yes. I'm hoping for a word with Mister Franklin. I'm John Bitter."

Jackson said, "Just a minute," and walked down a short hallway to knock on an inner door.

Bitter looked at the leather upholstered visitor chairs, the horsehair love seat, and the wool floor rugs and thought, *Franklin doesn't scrimp, does he.*

A portrait of Anna stopped him cold. Puzzled, he decided it didn't square with the story she told about "Daddy" selling her to a "greasy old man." It spoke more of a man who loved his daughter.

Jackson walked back and said, "Representative Franklin will see you now."

A tad nervous, hat in hand, Bitter walked down the short hallway and into Franklin's office. Without preamble, Peter Franklin asked, "Did you find her? Is she alright?"

Bitter nodded. "I did find her. As for being alright, she broke her right leg when her horse fell."

"Where is she?"

Bitter took a deep breath and then gave Franklin a long hard look. "She told me she doesn't want to come home, and she asked me not to tell you where she is."

"Why in the world not? And for goodness sakes, don't just stand there, take a chair."

Bitter eased down in a leather upholstered chair and said, "Tell me, Mister Franklin, do you love your daughter?"

Franklin nodded and said, "Heart and soul. But, why do you ask?"

"Then why sell her…in her words…to a 'greasy old man'?"

Franklin looked shocked. "Why in the world would she say that?"

"Guessing…but she might have overheard you talking about a business deal with an older man."

"Good Lord! No…one of my business associates, Bill Hartman asked permission for his son…a boy about Anna's age…to come calling. I said yes, and we moved on to a business deal we were both interested in." He stopped, trying to recall the exact words exchanged with Hartman. "Hmm. You know, 1 suppose if you took a phrase or two out of context, you might think I was giving Hartman himself permission to pursue Anna."

And then he chuckled. " 'Greasy old man', huh? I sure hope Bill Hartman never finds out that's how she sees him."

Bitter breathed a sigh of relief, "In that case, I can tell you she is at Sherar's Bridge staying with Missus Jane Sherar who is looking after her." Along with a nice-looking young man. The thought of young Orin Sherar made it hard to stifle a grin, but he managed.

"I had hoped to hear from you before this, Agent Bitter."

Bitter nodded and then quickly related the story of finding Anna after Billy Bradford abandoned her, how she had shot Billy and how she wound up killing her horse. "The horse fell back on her leg when she accidentally killed it…while trying to get another shot at Billy Bradford. And, I should add, Billy 'sold' her as a whore to some teamsters. We took her to Sherar's bridge after we persuaded two teamsters they didn't own her after all."

Franklin shook his head. "Billy Bradford should be shot. I might do it myself." He shook his head again, and a slow grin worked its way onto his face. "She actually shot that sonofabitch?"

"She tried, and the teamsters who bought her said he had a bullet wound in one arm."

Franklin gave Bitter a wry smile and said, "Damn. I sure underestimated my daughter."

"When my friend Owl set her leg, she groaned a little, but that's all. I'd say she is one tough young woman."

Franklin nodded. "Okay. I want to go get her…explain what I was talking to Hartman about. But, I'm still miffed you didn't come to me sooner."

"Couldn't. I was laid up for almost ten days. An outlaw clipped my skull with a bullet."

"I wondered about the scar on your head. Glad he didn't come any closer. You going to go after him?"

"Day after tomorrow. I plan to ride a riverboat to The Dalles, and then follow the military road to Canyon City. That road crosses the Deschutes River at Sherar's Bridge."

Franklin looked at John Bitter in speculation, then asked, "Want some company? I'll pay the fare."

Bitter looked at Franklin for a good ten seconds and then nodded. "I'll be at the Ferry Street dock day after tomorrow. The ferry leaves for Oregon City about nine in the morning."

"I'll bring my buggy. It'll make for an easier ride for Anna…if she decides to come back."

Bitter rose, and said, "Pack for a few nights of camping." With a wave, he walked to the door and said, "See you day after tomorrow."

Late Night Plans

WHEN HE TURNED ROCKFORD DOWN THE farm lane to his log home, he could see Horse and Owl's pack horse tied to the corral rails by the barn and Owl sitting on the porch in one of Morgan's cane back chairs by her sipping table. Bitter pulled Rockford to a halt and grinned at Owl. "You headed home?"

Owl nodded, his long gray braids swinging alongside his face. He grinned back at Bitter. "Yes. Gotta go see if I'm still married to Woman. And maybe find a new place to live. Just waiting for you to get back."

Bitter swung down and walked the steps to the porch. "I'm grateful, old friend. And I hope you and Woman stay together."

Owl rose from the chair and shook hands. "If I hurry, I can get home in time for a nice drink of whiskey at O'Grady's tavern."

"Travel safely."

Morgan came out on the porch in time to hand Owl a beef sandwich wrapped in waxed paper. "For the road."

Owl nodded his thanks and started to walk down the steps, but Morgan stopped him. "No. No you don't. Not until I give you a hug."

Morgan, Bitter and the three boys stood on the porch and watched Owl ride down the lane. Thomas, lips quivering slightly from the sudden notion he might never see old Owl again, hollered, "You come visit. You hear?"

That evening, after the boys had yawned their way to the loft, and after Sarah had fallen asleep with a nursing bottle in one hand and her rag doll in the other, Morgan turned the bedroom lamp down and joined her husband at the sipping table. A chorus of crickets filled the yard with their raspy music, and a half dozen bats worked the insects flying in the warm evening light.

Morgan sat down, put her cider glass on the table, pushed a stray strand of red hair out of her eyes and said, "So, tell me, husband. Why did you quit the Pinkerton's?"

Bitter took a sip of lukewarm coffee and said, "I think it interferes with what I really want to do. And I'm tired of war. Three years was enough. After I arrest this Alfred Swift and bring him in, I'm also going to stop being a U.S. Marshal."

Morgan nodded. "And then what?"

"I'd love to show you Tygh Valley. No one has claimed it yet. We can homestead…each of us claim a section of land…and build a horse ranch. And there are quite a few wild horses we could round up."

Morgan frowned and then quietly said, "No."

"No? Why not?"

"Because the boys need to go to school. Ruth is a very good teacher, and I'm afraid we might not find another as good. Because I'm pregnant, and because Sarah will need a school and people around her as she grows up." She paused, a grin tugging at her lips before she added, "And because I just bought the Hill farm across the creek."

"What? You bought a farm?"

"Yes. I've been saving. The Hills wanted to move to Independence, to be closer to Missus Hill's family. So, I talked to Mister Hill and he gave me a price. I thought it was a good price, and you now have an extra one-hundred-sixty acres for hay and enough pasture for a larger horse herd. There's even a small barn and a three-room log house. And an apple orchard."

"Where did you get the money?"

"I know how to pinch pennies. And I've been putting away most of what the Pinkerton's pay you each month. I still have over six hundred dollars left."

"What did you pay Hill for their farm?"

"Four hundred dollars…in gold coins. He wanted five hundred until he saw the gold."

"I'll be damned."

"And, you and boys can still go chase wild horses for part of each summer, if you want." *And you'll be home enough to be a father*, she thought, but she withheld that comment.

Unconsciously he rubbed the scar on the side of his head, marked now by a stubble of white hair. *Ambushed*, he thought, *again. Just like when the judge in Missouri trapped me into marrying Morgan before I could adopt the boys. But she may be right. And we could grow the herd right here…closer to market.*

"And one more thing. We need a bigger house."

Bitter chuckled and said, "You are a pistol, Missus Morgan Bitter."

"I love you very much, John, and I want to grow old with you, not pine for you as a widow."

"Okay, a bigger house it is. We can start in when I get back. I still have this one last chore to take care of."

Morgan nodded. "I know. Alfred Swift. He has to be put away or we'll always wonder when he might take another shot at you. So, go get him, but do it safely. No nonsense about fair play. It's not a game, husband."

A small voice whispered, "Can I have my own room?"

Morgan's keen ears heard the sound and she turned in time to see the front door close. Quietly, she said, "Is that you Mikey?"

The door swung open again, and Mikey stood there in his night shirt. "Yep."

"Have you been listening in?" Bitter asked.

Mikey nodded.

"So, what do you think?"

"I'd like to chase wild horses. But our horse herd will grow right here anyway. The red mare is going to have a colt. Rockford did it."

Morgan laughed and held out her arms. "Come here, you rascal."

Woman

IT WAS EVENING BEFORE OWL RODE into the yard of his two-room cabin. Made from rough-cut lumber, wearing a cedar shingle roof turned gray by rain and sunshine, it was a snug house where he and Woman lived. He breathed a sigh of relief when he saw none of his personal belongings stacked by the front door. He might talk in fun about Woman divorcing him, but it wasn't something he looked forward to.

He guided the horses around to the back of the cabin and stepped down to open the gate to the corral attached to his small tack room and hay barn. "I'm getting too old for all this riding," he grumbled.

Woman's lilting voice said, "Then why do it, old man?"

He turned and looked at her, beautiful in the twilight, dressed in a pale blue dress that swept the ground, her braided black hair reflecting the last red ray of the setting sun. "I thought you would be married to O'Grady by now."

A quiet laugh was her answer. "No. I am married to you."

"I'm an old man," he grumped. "You need a younger husband."

"How old are you, old man?"

"Sixty summers, I think."

"And yet, look at you. Riding to the ocean, riding to see John Bitter. You still have a spring in your step, old man."

"I did maybe save John Bitter's life on this last trip. Help me put the horses up and I'll tell you what happened. And I did have to shoot two white men. I hope no one ever finds out about that." He would never know about the third man he had killed when he shot across the White River at a puff of gun smoke.

Woman undid the straps holding the pack in place, set the heavy bundle on the ground and then removed the packsaddle while Owl unsaddled Horse and turned him into the corral. Horse went down on his side and then rolled in the dust of the corral. It only took him two tries to finish the roll. He stood back up and shook his hide to shed the dust.

The packhorse shunned the practice of a refreshing roll in the dirt. Instead he just walked to the water trough to drink his fill.

A scoop of cracked corn for each horse in the feed trough and gear stowed in the tack room, Woman carried his personal pack to the house. He carried his rifle. When she held the door open, he could smell a nice beef stew steaming in the big pot on the wood cook stove. "Smells good," he said, "but you cooked too much."

She smiled and said, "I thought O'Grady might want some if you didn't make it back today."

"I think you make fun, Woman."

"Maybe. Now tell me what happened."

"That John Bitter is too nice for his own good." He poured a cup of coffee and sat at the small table in one of the two wood chairs that graced the cabin. "Now…let me see. What happened was…"

When he finished, Woman nodded, a serious look on her face. "A good man, John Bitter. But you are still an uncivilized savage."

When he started to protest he was a Christian Cherokee, she held up a hand to shush him. "Now, I have something to tell you. You listen. You are still a warrior and a big man. In six months. you will be a father…if you stop following John Bitter around. People are always shooting wherever he goes."

"No. Until we got back to his farm, I did all the shooting." He grinned and added, "I can still see pretty good." He studied her for a few seconds and then said, "I would like to be a father. Maybe I'll go drink from the ocean again."

She smiled and shook her head. "Eat and then go tell O'Grady his friend was shot."

Owl grinned and said, "I might need a whiskey to celebrate."

"Not more than two, then you come home to me."

He dug all but one of the gold coins out of his pocket and handed the rest to Woman. He figured for an Indian she was pretty smart about money.

She counted over two-hundred-twenty dollars in gold coins. She looked up in surprise. "Where did you get this?"

"John Bitter and I took five horses…and two pack animals away from some outlaws. We sold four saddles horses to the Army. And five saddles. This is my half."

"Good. We'll need a cradle and some clothes for a baby. The rest I'll hide in the fireplace chimney. Now, when are you going to open the school back up?"

"When the crops are done. Then I'll have to stay home."

She watched in silence until he had finished a plate of stew and three biscuits drowned in honey. She took his plate to the tub she used for washing dishes, and said, "Go on now. Go see O'Grady. And Beecher might be there."

〜

WHEN BEECHER HAD DECIDED TO back O'Grady and finance the building of a tavern, "Pub" O'Grady kept reminding him, he hadn't scrimped or squeezed the nickel. Whitewashed shiplap siding dressed the outer walls of a building forty feet wide by forty feet deep, with living quarters in back. Overhanging eaves sheltered a wide porch, and a long row of windows allowed a fair amount of light to escape the lamp lit room. The cedar-shake roof was home to a heavy wooden sign with shamrocks carved in each corner and with proud black and white letters declaring the establishment "O'Grady's Irish Pub." The shamrocks were green.

Inside, a craftsman had framed a long mirror to hang over the dark mahogany back bar. The mirror reflected light from four chandeliers… which so far had escaped damage from the Saturday night parties… and the mirror gave O'Grady a view of the room even when his back was turned to his customers.

When Owl walked in, Liam O'Grady was listening to a farmer who leaned on the polished bar with a boot hitched on a scuffed brass foot rail, a frothy mug of beer in front of him.

Three other customers sat at one of the five round tables lining the long room. They never looked up, busy eating beef hash and fresh baked bread. O'Grady raised his hand in greeting to Owl.

Dressed in blue wool britches, a white cotton shirt and a yellow deerskin jacket, Beecher was standing with his back to a cold fireplace in the end of the room, hands behind him. People just naturally back up to stoves and fireplaces, cold or not.

Silver hair trimmed and gleaming in the lamplight, his white beard a lot shorter than the last time Owl had seen him, Beecher was leaning forward and entertaining two dark-haired men sitting at a table near the fireplace, mugs of beer in hand. Owl heard just enough to know Beecher was yarning about his scouting days with the US Cavalry and his forays into the wilds of Idaho and Wyoming, chasing renegade Indians and outlaws.

He stopped in mid-story when he saw Owl. He looked at the two men. "This will have to wait for another time, gentlemen." The big man walked across the room, hand outstretched, and said, "You old renegade. Did you catch up with Bitter?"

Owl nodded.

"So, tell me. Where you been?"

Love Springs Eternal

Beecher led Owl to the far corner of the room. "Whiskey?" Owl nodded. He put a coin on the table, but Beecher shook his head. "No. You sit. I'll buy the drinks. I want to hear your story. When you didn't come back after the first week, I knew something was going on."

When Beecher walked to the bar to get Owl's drink, he overheard the farmer bending O'Grady's ear about the lousy roads in the valley. "Ever crick has to be bridged. And in the winter, the roads are too deep with mud for wagon travel. Why, just last year…"

Beecher cut in, "Abner, you were complaining last year about the roads. You built any bridges on your place?"

The farmer turned a shade red and shook his head. He took a drink of beer from his mug and muttered something about "too much to do."

Beecher shook his head. "I thought so. You're just going to wait until somebody else does it for you. I don't want to hear you complaining any more. Fish or cut bait, Abner."

The farmer took his beer and walked stiffly to an empty table. He jerked a chair back, slammed the mug down on the table and plopped his large butt in a chair. Beecher and O'Grady could tell hear him mumbling under his breath, but they couldn't make out the words.

O'Grady ginned at Beecher, glad to be shut of Abner's complaints. "Kinda sudden, aren't you?"

"Grumbling is just a damned excuse for not doing anything."

"I see Owl is back."

"Uh huh." Beecher studied the back bar for a full ten seconds before saying, "Liam, could Ellie fill in? I think Owl has something to tell us. Been gone too long for just a visit with John Bitter. I think you might want to sit in."

Ellie was one of two women O'Grady hired to help cook, tend bar, and clean up. After six months, she practically ran the place. At five-seven she could look O'Grady straight in the eye. A spinster at age twenty-one, a fact O'Grady found hard to understand. On O'Grady's scale of preferences, pretty and full of spunk ranked fairly high. And, he had to admit, Ellie was pretty and had plenty of spunk. "Maybe too much spunk," he told Beecher on one occasion.

What O'Grady hadn't noticed was the way she watched him as he worked the bar. She had her own scale of preferences, and Liam O'Grady scored pretty high…in spite of his Southern drawl…which was fading a bit. He was whipcord lean, moved with an ease and grace that was unconscious, and his blue eyes twinkled when he got into one of his story-telling phases. He was smart, and he made her laugh. Not many young men had managed that.

Liam nodded to Beecher and walked down the short hallway to the kitchen. She was busy washing beer mugs and dinner plates. "Ellie," he said, "would you spell me off? I got things to talk over with Beecher."

She turned to look at him, brushed a stray curl of dark brown hair from her forehead and nodded. "Be right there."

Something in her gesture, the movement of her hand, something he couldn't quite get a hold of squeezed a feeling he didn't understand, but suddenly Liam O'Grady, second generation cotton farmer and ex-Confederate soldier, knew he was in love with Ellie Ellis.

It stopped him in his tracks. She looked at him and said softly, "Is something wrong, Liam?"

He shook his head and managed to say "no."

"I'll just finish these dishes and be right out."

It didn't occur to him until later she had used his given name. Before this, she had always called him Mister O'Grady

When he joined Beecher and Owl at the table, Beecher said, "Okay, Owl, tell us what's been going on."

When Owl finished, Beecher said, "Do you know when he's going after this outlaw?"

"No. But John Bitter isn't one to wait. I think he will leave soon."

"Where to, I wonder?"

Liam said, "I'll bet this outlaw is headed for the Canyon City gold fields. Lots of bad men go there."

Beecher shrugged. "We're just guessing. I'll go visit the Bitters. I might just have to go along on this trip. I feel like I got him into this with that U.S. Marshal business."

O'Grady grinned and shook his head. "It's just too tame around here for you, Tom. Just too tame."

"You might be right. Shoot, I haven't seen any new country for almost a year now."

Owl sipped his whiskey and then looked across the table at Tom Beecher. "If you find him, you'll have to kill that outlaw. John Bitter won't do it. He thinks he has to bring him in because that's what the white man's law says. Might get him killed one of these days."

Beecher looked at O'Grady. "Want to come along? I'll bet Ellie can run this place for a week or two. You can double her pay if you want. I'll stand good for it."

"What about me?" Owl said.

"You look wore to a frazzle, old friend. I think you should rest up and get the schoolhouse ready for Fall. A couple of old scouts like me and Liam can handle this. Besides, I need someone here to keep an eye on things."

ᔕ

WHEN O'GRADY ASKED ELLIE TO run the place for a couple of weeks, he added, "I'll double your wages."

She was startled at the offer, but said, "Yes. I can run this place."

He just fidgeted with his sleeve garters and then said, "There's something I want to talk to you about when I get back."

"And what would that be, Liam?"

He swallowed hard, blinked a couple of times, and said, "Well, it's sort of…ah…sort of personal."

"Why, Liam O'Grady. Look at you. Red in the face and tongue tied. And you, the great storyteller of French Prairie." She laughed. "Why not speak to me of it now?"

Liam swallowed and plunged in. "I guess I should. Miss Ellie, I've fallen in love…with you. Don't know how that happened, but there it is. I think we should marry."

She smiled and then shook her head. "Not right away. You need to speak with Father first, and you need to come calling…at least twice… before we marry."

He took a step forward and she didn't retreat. "I'd like to kiss you."

She took his hand, leaned forward and gave him the gentlest, sweetest kiss of his life.

Warm Hearts

THE NOISY ROBINS IN THE BIG maple tree between Liam's log barn and the Willamette River were doing their level best to wake the world with their "cheery up, cherry up" song as he saddled his rose-colored Appaloosa. Some might figure a keg of whiskey, a blanket, his cavalry boots and a twenty-dollar gold piece was a high price to pay for a Nez Perce horse, but O'Grady never regretted it. He had thought about naming the big horse Georgia, after his home state, but the name was just too feminine. Even if the Appaloosa was beautiful to watch. He finally just settled on Appy.

O'Grady tied his bedroll behind the saddle, picked up the lead rope for the pack horse and mounted up. He knew Beecher would be at the Wheatland Ferry landing waiting for him. Beecher wasn't one to dally once a decision was reached.

The dirt road wound through a grove of young fir trees, down alongside a ten-acre walnut grove, and past the white-washed two-story Ellis farmhouse. He would never admit it, but he felt a touch of disappointment when he didn't see Ellie standing by the gate to her front yard. He pulled to a stop and looked the house over, hoping to see candlelight, a lamp…something.

And then he caught the flicker of a curtain and saw Ellie, backlit by a lamp, standing in an upstairs window. She waved and he waved his hat and grinned, the world suddenly looking a lot better. He pushed his hat back on his head, and gigged Appy in the ribs. The pack horse wasn't of a mind to trot, but the tug of the lead rope was too much to resist, so the pack animal, a small horse called Brownie settled into an awkward trot after the big rose-dappled horse.

Ellie smiled and blew an unseen kiss and hugged herself. "You come back safe, Liam O'Grady," she said softly, watching until he was out of sight. She let the curtain fall back in place, quietly slid the window closed, and then crawled back under the warm covers, a deeper warmth in her heart than she had ever known.

Beecher had a long-legged gray gelding ground-hitched and a sorrel horse packing his camping gear tied to a small oak tree. He waved when he saw O'Grady come riding up over the sandy berm that protected a deep slough from the Willamette River much of the year. Floods filled the slough with water on occasion, leaving behind a fresh supply of rainbow trout, and salmon smolt.

When O'Grady pulled Appy to a halt, Beecher pointed down river just as Captain Kelly pulled the wire on the steam whistle to warn the Wheatland Ferry operator the Corvallis was about to crowd the landing.

Beecher nodded a greeting and then said, "I thought you were going to miss the boat."

A little miffed, O'Grady frowned and said, "I didn't."

"Didn't what? Think you were late?"

"Uh huh. And I didn't miss the boat either."

Captain Kelly eased the Corvallis bumpers in against the dock and held her there with a slow churning of the big paddle wheel while the two men led their horses aboard. He backed away, let the current push the stern down river and then gently straightened the steamer in mid-stream. He added power and headed in the direction of Salem and the Ferry Street dock.

O'Grady remarked that Kelly sure knew his business.

"And a good thing," Beecher said, "because this old scow belongs to me."

"I think I knew that."

"Good."

∽

NOON SAW THE TWO FRIENDS riding side-by-side, leading their packhorses down the lane to Bitter's farm. A light breeze carried the smell of fresh apple pies.

O'Grady sniffed the air and said, "You suppose Morgan knew we were coming?"

Beecher nodded his gray head and said, "Maybe. Young Mikey knows things. He might have told her."

"You believe that?"

"I do. Mikey has the gift. It's sort of like a grown man who has a hunch about something without knowing why. Mikey hasn't learned to distrust his instincts about these things."

"It's a little scary is what I think."

"I thought you Irish believed in the little people…and a pot of gold."

O'Grady gave Beecher a half smile and said, "We do, but it's been hundreds of years since any of us found the Little People's gold."

"Maybe because you stopped believing in the Little People."

O'Grady just shook his head. "Not true. There just was never any gold to be found in all of Ireland after all."

Reunion

BITTER SAT AT MORGAN'S SIPPING TABLE on the front porch, a fresh cup of coffee in front of him, gently bouncing little Sarah on his knee. She giggled when he sang, "Ride a little pony, ride to town, you better watch out or you'll fall down."

At the sight of his friends, he shook his head, but he couldn't stop the smile that creased his face. "Morgan," he called through the open door, "Beecher and O'Grady just turned down our lane. Must have smelled your apple pies."

She walked out on the porch and stood by her husband, a warm hand on his shoulder. "I wonder what they are up to?"

He handed Sarah to Morgan and said, "I have a hunch Owl has been telling tales."

He stepped down from the porch and waited for his friends to finish the ride from the county road. The big black mule Lucifer brayed and charged across the pasture at the small cavalcade of horses, but stopped short of knocking the fence rails down.

Appy gave his rider a skittish dance, but the big gray Beecher rode just looked at the mule and ambled on down the road. The pack horses pulled back, but were bound by habit and ropes to go where the bigger horses went.

Bitter shook his head and said, "If Lucifer hadn't saved your hide back on our travels, Morgan, I'd be tempted to shoot him."

Defensively, Morgan said, "But he did save my life. Otherwise, I'd be in an unmarked grave in Missouri."

O'Grady was grinning when pulled Appy to a halt. He nodded and said, "Howdy, Missus Bitter. And you, too little Sarah." He stepped down from the saddle and walked over to Bitter, hand outstretched. "We were just passing by and smelled fresh pie. I couldn't keep Tom from stopping in to see if he could beg a piece."

Beecher smiled, and stepped down from the saddle. "Don't you believe a word of what this Irisher says. I never beg, but on the other hand, I'd never refuse a piece of fresh baked pie, either."

Bitter looked at the pack horses, skeptical about the coincidence, but he said, "Well, don't just sit there. Come on in."

Beecher pushed Bitter's hand aside and gave him a bear hug.

"Where are you two going?"

"Well," Beecher said, " it's been a mite dull lately, so we thought we'd go do some prospecting. Might look at that Canyon City country. We heard they found a passel of gold over there. And we thought you might like to go along."

Bitter asked sharply, "And why would I want to do that?"

O'Grady's smile slipped a bit, but he said, "Because we think you have some U.S. Marshal business over there. We thought we could travel together. Safer that way."

Morgan walked down the steps and handed Sarah to Bitter. She gave each of the men a hug and said, "You come on in. Let's talk about it over coffee and a piece of pie."

When it became clear he was not going to discourage Beecher and O'Grady from going along on his search for Alfred Swift, Bitter caved and actually felt better about his chances of surviving another trip into the deserts of Eastern Oregon. He unconsciously rubbed the white thatch of hair that was beginning to grow over the scar on the right side of his head. It wasn't like he had lost his nerve or his confidence, but that bullet sort of sobered him up about his own mortality—something several Civil War battles had failed to drive home. Without thinking about it, he had always assumed it would be other people who were wounded or killed, not him.

Morgan was relieved to hear her husband's acceptance of their company. Her confidence in the skills of Beecher and O'Grady was set in stone. She well remembered the two of them standing firm when Chief Pocatello led sixty yelling Shoshones in a wild charge right at the Bitter and Shipley wagons. She smiled at the memory of her husband telling her, after she had taken a wild shot with her carbine, "Take your time and aim."

She still had an occasional nightmare even though Captain Bradford's troopers had arrived in time to chastise the Indians. It was always the same dream—a wall of yelling, painted Indians shooting rifles and their horses thundering straight at her and the boys.

News

O'GRADY INTERRUPTED HER MEMORIES WHEN HE said, "We stopped by the Silverton post office. Y'all got some mail. Looks like both are from Missouri."

Morgan smiled and said, "Did you read them?'

O'Grady laughed. "Tempted, Missus Morgan, tempted."

"And there is one letter for Mister and Missus Shipley of Abiqua Creek," Beecher added.

Morgan said, "John, use your pen knife to open ours, please."

She sat down at her sipping table to read. The men stood in the yard, watching her intently, looking for any sign that would help them guess the contents without appearing to be too nosey. After all, letters were rare, and any news from "back east," as it was termed, regardless if it was from the East Coast or Texas, was welcome to a news-starved population. The men waited patiently while she read the letters. When she finished, she looked at each of them and said, "This one is from Sarah McBeth, one of our close-by neighbors in Missouri. She and Harley have married, and they are coming West…this year.

"She says the Union doesn't know whether to treat Missouri as a rebel state or a loyal state, and the carpetbaggers have moved in and just about taken over. So, they traded the home places, both hers and Harley's, for a wagon and a team of mules and enough supplies and money to make the trip."

She blinked back a tear at the thought of seeing Harley again, regained her composure and added, "The other letter is from our friends Wanda and Jack Bellamy. They should be here in late August or early September. Wanda wrote that the Pacific is supposed to be pretty calm in August, so they are coming from New Orleans by ship to the Isthmus of Panama, on over to the Pacific, and up the coast by ship."

Bitter said. "I'll be glad to see Wanda and Jack. When was Sarah's letter dated?"

"March 14."

He nodded. "Four months ago. They could be here by late September… if they don't have trouble on the trail."

Beecher said, "Does she give any details about the carpetbaggers?"

Morgan just shook her head. "No. Just that they were moving in."

He nodded. "Give greedy men an excuse and they will steal from the church."

Mikey sneaked in behind the group gathered around Morgan's table and tugged on O'Grady's shirt sleeve. "Hi, Mister O'Grady." He paused and looked up at Beecher. "Hello, Mister Beecher. You going with Pa to catch the outlaw?"

O'Grady nodded. "Uh huh."

"Good. There's too many outlaws."

"Amen," Morgan said. "Well, come on in. The pies have cooled enough for eating."

Bitter said, "Where are the other boys."

"Swimming."

"Go tell Ethan and Thomas I have a riding job for them."

"Riding job?"

"Yes."

"I can ride."

Bitter studied Mikey, and then nodded. "Okay. Go fetch the little red mare. I want you to take this letter to Ruth. And ride bareback. If you fall off, you won't get a foot caught in the stirrup."

Morgan heard John and came out the front door in time to say, "Tell Ruth we are going to have a party this evening along about seven."

Mikey nodded and said, "I will, Mama."

Bitter watched Mikey bounce off the porch and run to the barn. Not fifteen seconds later he emerged from the man door with a hackamore and a small bucket of oats. When he banged on the bucket and whistled, the horses in the upper pasture headed for the barn.

Beecher wiped crumbs of pie crust from his bead and stepped outside in time to watch. "He does have the gift."

"I don't know how it works," admitted Bitter, "but it does. He really seems know what animals are thinking."

Mikey open the corral gate wide enough for the red horse and then shut the others out. Rockford stamped a foot when he discovered he wasn't getting any oats.

Mikey pored a dab of oats in the feed trough for the mare, and bridled her while she snuffed the grain. Then he led her to the corral fence and climbed the rails until he was high enough to slide onto the horse.

Mikey waved, the letter in one hand and the hackamore rope in the other, and gigged the horse into a lope up the lane to the county road.

Celebration

Evening saw a bonfire popping and crackling in the yard surrounded by a circle of wood blocks for sitting. O'Grady offered an amber liquid in a clear glass bottle, complete with cork stopper, that brought tears to his eyes if taken in large doses. "I call it Irish Delight."

Beecher took a swig from the bottle, choked and coughed. "More like Irish Revenge, I'd say."

That brought the expected chuckles.

Ruth and Morgan, little Sarah on her lap, listened contentedly from the sipping table to the murmur of the men, and the boys. Thomas, Mikey, Ethan and little Davey, Ruth and Ezra's son, pushed quietly into the circle to listen to some tall tales and some serious man talk as well.

Ruth said quietly, "If you want boys to become men, they need to spend time with men. There sit four of the strongest men I ever met."

"They do get things done, don't they."

"And they don't shirk their duty."

Morgan smiled and said, "Amen." Having settled that, they each took a sip of cool cider.

Morgan said, "Is your next one a boy or a girl?"

Ruth, her pregnancy showing, patted her stomach and said, "I'd bet on a little girl This one is carrying higher than Davey."

"It would be nice if Sarah had a friend close by."

They overheard Ezra say, "The letter we got is from my Uncle Rufus. He wants us to move to Corvallis. Says there is a sight more black people living there than here, and he thinks there is safety in numbers. He also offered me a share cropping job."

Beecher said, "What does he do?"

"He runs a general store, but he wants me to work his farm."

"You aren't going to, are you?" Bitter asked worriedly. "I mean, you already have a farm right here, and a trade. People are saying you are one of the best blacksmiths in the valley."

"Well, I don't want to, but there is the question of family."

"If he really is worried about safety, you could offer him a share cropping job right here," Bitter said.

Ezra laughed. "Now there's an idea."

Beecher passed the jug to Bitter who held it to the firelight with suspicion.

O'Grady frowned and said, "And what are you looking at?"

"I was just making sure you hadn't added any snake heads to the brew."

Even O'Grady had to laugh at that one. He turned to look at the ladies on the porch and said, "I haven't heard any zither music since we left the Oregon Trail. You wouldn't want to treat us to a song or two, now, would you?"

Ruth looked at Morgan who nodded. She handed Sarah to Ruth and went into the house. In less than two minutes she returned, a shiny rose-colored zither in hand.

Bitter brought the ladies' cane-backed chairs to the circle by the fire and took Sarah from Ruth. "So, you can play," he said.

Ruth took the zither and seated herself in a chair. She looked at Morgan and said, "Aura Lee?"

Morgan nodded and Ruth strummed the strings. When Morgan's sweet voice reached the chorus, "Aura Lee, Aura Lee, maid with golden hair…" even Beecher had a lump in his throat. The men and boys all clapped, Sarah mimicking them, and Beecher cleared his throat and said, "Sweetest thing I've heard in a long, long time."

Morgan said, "Thank you, but you should hear Ruth sing." She turned to Ruth and said, "How about Cheer Up My Brothers?"

Ruth nodded, and said quietly, "You come in where you feel like it. A little harmony is always welcome."

The talking stopped and Ruth strummed the zither with a pick made from the quill of a hawk, and sang, "Cheer up my brothers, live in the sunshine, we'll understand it all by and by…"

Bitter shook his head. *Damn, but I wish they wouldn't sing that. Brings back memories of Mother at the kitchen sink, washing dishes and singing that song. Enough to break a man's heart.* He gave little Sarah a gentle hug and said, "I wish you could have known your Grandma."

Morgan harmonized with Ruth on the last chorus, and the men clapped when they had finished. O'Grady smiled and said. "Beautiful, ladies. Just beautiful."

Mikey said, "Sing the crawdad song."

It was nearly ten before the songs were sung. A little Irish Delight made one last circle, and the fire was doused. O'Grady and Beecher headed for the hay mow, and Ezra and Ruth put Davey in their wagon…sound asleep. "I think the boys had a good time, " Ruth said.

Morgan nodded. "I haven't done much singing lately."

"Trouble can make us forget the good things in this life. Thank you for a lovely time, Morgan."

Best Laid Plans

AN HOUR OR SO BEFORE DAYLIGHT, O'Grady lit a lantern so he could see to saddle Appy and strap the pack saddle on Brownie, a horse not given to fuss. Brownie just stood still, looking his usual calm self while O'Grady tied his trail gear to the pack saddle.

Beecher, beard wet from a quick wash in the horse trough, nodded. "You're pretty good at that…for a tavern owner."

"Pub," O'Grady automatically corrected him for about the thousandth time.

As Beecher bridled the big mouse colored horse, and smoothed a saddle blanket over its back, he said, "I've been meaning to ask you, Liam. Are you having any fun with this Pub business? I mean, it looks like a lot more work than I ever thought it would be. And you have to put up with people like Abner."

"I am having fun, Tom. And I'm grateful. Work is part of life, and it's a lot easier in some ways than the cotton farming I did in Georgia. Ever pick cotton?"

"No, and I don't intend to start in either."

"Backbreaking work, Tom. Brutal, hot, dirty backbreaking work."

Beecher finish saddling his horse and started to pick up the pack saddle when his back just popped so loud O'Grady could hear it."

"You all right, Tom?"

"No, Liam. I don't think I am. I can't straighten up." He grunted with pain. "Damn, but that hurts. Don't know what I did."

"Well, I guess you won't be going with me and Bitter then. Can you walk to the house? Just put your hands on your knees for support and take short steps."

Through clinched teeth, Beecher said, "What the hell do you know about backs?"

O'Grady shook his head. "You are not the first man I've known to throw his back out."

They could see lamp light through the curtains on the kitchen window, and the shadow of someone moving about. A hand on Beecher's shoulder to keep him from falling, O'Grady eased him on over to the porch. Beecher looked at the steps, dim in the moonlight, and shook his head. He backed up and perched his butt on the second step. "This is as far I go…for now."

"I'll get some help."

The door opened, and Bitter said, "Don't just sit there. Come on in. The coffee's hot and Morgan has hotcakes in the skillet."

"Can't," Beecher said while trying to look back over his shoulder at Bitter.

"Why not?"

"My back gave out."

"Oh, damn."

"You said it. Guess you and Liam will have to go without me."

"Has this happened before?"

Beecher groaned and then laughed. "Not out of bed."

"Well," Bitter said, "Let's get you in the house." He nodded at O'Grady and set one of Morgan's sipping chairs off the porch. "You think you can make it to the chair?"

Beecher nodded and pushed himself into a stooped position, turned, and plopped his butt in the chair.

"Hang on," Bitter said and then he and O'Grady muscled the chair up on the porch.

Thirty minutes later Beecher was sitting on a stool, back turned to Morgan's wood cook stove, hoping the heat would ease the pain in his back. When Bitter and O'Grady said goodbye, Beecher just shook his head. "Get on out of here. And watch your backs. People die almost daily where you are going."

Morgan kissed her husband's cheek and hugged O'Grady. "Thanks for going with him, Liam."

Mikey's little voice carried from the loft. "Bye, Pa. Be careful."

River Travel

A STEAM WHISTLE TOLD TEAMSTERS IN CHARGE of the twenty wagons lined up along Ferry street that the Corvallis was coming, ready to load cargo and passengers before heading downriver to the loading ramps above the Willamette Falls.

Peter Franklin fussed and worried Bitter would miss the boat until he saw him riding down Ferry Street on a big black horse, leading a pack mule. A second rider on a beautiful rose- colored Appaloosa rode beside him. Franklin could tell the two men were talking about something. He didn't know they had decided to hide their friendship. Just pretend to be two travelers headed for the same destination. Bitter figured it might give them an edge when they got to Canyon City.

Bitter stopped beside Franklin's leather-topped buggy and stepped down, but the second man stayed in the saddle.

"Mister Franklin," Bitter said and pointed to O'Grady, "this gent is going to keep us company. If that's all right with you. He's headed for the gold fields in Canyon City."

O'Grady nodded. "Liam O'Grady at your service."

Franklin nodded in return, but didn't say anything. He did, however, ask Bitter how long he thought the loading would take.

"I don't know. I've only been on the Corvallis a couple of times—upriver when we finished crossing the Oregon Trail, and recently to see Judge Deady. Why don't I go see? I know Captain Kelly."

When Bitter stepped around the stevedores and teamsters loading cargo, a deck hand stopped him. "You can't come aboard just yet." Bitter started to say something when Captain Kelly called down from the wheelhouse. "Mister Bitter, come on up." The deck hand gave Bitter an appraising look and stepped aside. "I guess you can."

Bitter grinned and said, "It depends on who you know."

In the wheelhouse, Kelly offered him a cup of hot coffee. "If you have steam," Kelly said, "you always have heat in the galley. Cookie keeps a pot of coffee going all the time. Where are you headed?"

◡

THE TRIP FROM PORTLAND THROUGH the Columbia Gorge was as impressive as Bitter remembered. But slower than he remembered from the trip downriver when the Bitter-Shipley party was headed home to Abiqua Creek. The sidewheeler *Oneonta* was bucking a strong boiling current this time instead of being helped along by the strong flow of the Columbia River.

He found Peter Franklin busy at the job of listening to O'Grady tell Irish tales, both men idling, leaning on the rail forward of the wheelhouse, gawking at the tall cliffs that lined the gorge, at the waterfalls on both sides of river that seemed to just appear out of the sky, some looking to be five hundred feet high. An osprey slammed the water and rose with a fish that looked too big for the bird to handle. Wingtips beating, catching a little water, the bird turned into the downriver wind until it caught enough air to rise and head for a nest along the south side of the river.

Franklin said, "Look at that. Quite a sight." And then he added, almost as if embarrassed, "I've got to get Clarissa and come back and see this all again. Been too damned busy to go see much outside of the Valley." *And too busy being a politician to be a husband and a father,* he thought, with a touch of regret.

O'Grady said, "Well, now. You should bring your wife to French Prairie. There is a nice Irish pub there down on the river that serves a fine stew. It's called O'Grady's."

Franklin smiled, the smile reaching his eyes. It was perhaps his first smile in a long time. "And I suppose you know this O'Grady?"

Liam cocked his head sideways and smiled. "Been walking around in his hide since I was born."

Franklin nodded. "I thought so. I tell you what, when this business is done, I'll bring Clarissa out for a dinner."

"First dinner is on me," O'Grady said.

Bitter pointed to a massive monolith on the north side of the river. "Beecher told me that one is called Beacon Rock. Said it was the biggest lone rock he ever saw. Biggest rock I've ever seen, for sure."

❧

NOON FOUND THE *ONEONTA* TIED in against the docks below the boiling water of the Cascade Rapids. A few boats ran the rapids when the water was high from the spring floods, but not always with success. Failure generally meant a good dunking and a better chance of drowning. Ventures downriver during spring flood were generally more successful.

A dozen stevedores and deck hands placed bridging planks from the deck to the loading ramp and began hauling cargo to the rail cars hitched to a small steam locomotive named the Oregon Pony. A hundred passengers, mostly men seeking fortune in the gold fields, and a half dozen women sprinkled in the mix, were ushered by a young deckhand to waiting passenger cars.

To Bitter it seemed like a lot of work and time for a fifteen-mile train ride—and kind of expensive. He thought about just heading upriver along the railroad right of way, but he remembered Rockford—stumbling—twice—during the search for Anna Franklin. *No*, he thought, *it'll save him a few miles*.

He said, "Let's go get our gear and unload the animals."

Fifteen miles above the rapids, the process was reversed and cargo, passengers and animals were loaded onto a sternwheeler named the Whittaker, once named the Drake until it rammed a rock and sank. The owners were happy to sell it where it sank. And the new owners were happy to raise it, repair the hull and refit it to the business of portage. It was simply a steam-powered open deck—no staterooms, no galley. A few benches were bolted to the deck down the center of the ship for use by passengers, a concession to the balance and stability of the hull. The captain presided over the operation in a small wheelhouse mounted forward on posts and reached by a steep, narrow set of stairs.

"Hmm, Franklin said. "No frills. I'm sure glad it isn't raining."

Bitter laughed. "And there is always wind when the boat moves."

"But it moves faster than horses and it's easier on horseflesh," O'Grady said.

"Well," Franklin said, "I think I'll go sit in my buggy…maybe take a nap."

O'Grady smiled and said, "In that case, we'll watch the sights for you."

Beecher Goes Home

MORGAN MADE UP A PALLET IN front of the fireplace, hoping the warmth would ease the pain in the old man's back. She also heated water and mixed up some of Owl's willow tea, complete with sugar and whiskey.

She smiled when she handed a cup to Beecher who propped himself up on one elbow with a grunt, trying to get high enough to drink the tea. Morgan said, "I don't know if the willow tea or the whiskey is the magic in this brew, but it seems to work."

After a nap, Beecher said he was feeling better. "You know, I lived with the Nez Perce one winter. That was the first time my back gave out. Their medicine man's daughter was about your size. He told her to walk on my back. That time something snapped, and by gollies I was well again. Would you walk on my back?"

"Lord Almighty. I'm afraid I'd hurt you."

"No. No you wouldn't. Wish I'd thought of this before the boys left."

"The men, you mean."

Beecher laughed. "Missy, at my age you are all boys and girls. Now, I take you seriously, because you are building this country…and doing a da…darned good job of it. I certainly mean no disrespect."

"I should hope not."

"Well," he said, "you going to walk on my back or not."

A small voice from the loft said, "Don't do it, Mama. Mister Beecher is hurt worse than he thinks."

Beecher said, "Is that you, Mikey?"

"Yep."

When Mikey climbed down the ladder to the main floor, in a kindly tone the old man said, "What do you know about backs, Mikey?"

"Your bones are getting brittle. You should not let Mama walk on you. You should go see Owl. He can make you well."

"And how would I get there?"

Morgan said, "We'll fix up a bed in the wagon and take you there."

Beecher nodded. "I hate to be such a bother, but you might have to."

✒

Owl sat dozing on a block of wood he used for a stool, leaned back against the big maple growing alongside the road. He often sat there to see who was coming and going, and because he really wasn't much for working his little farm. The distant jingle of harness bells brought him fully awake and interested in seeing who was on his road.

When the Bitters' wagon rounded a bend in the road, he recognized the mules. Morgan was at the reins, little Sarah sitting beside her. Ethan on Lucifer, Thomas on Josey, and Mikey riding bareback on the red mare, led the parade. When Owl saw Beecher's horse tied on behind, he stood up and walked to the edge of the road.

"Hello," he said. "You are a long way from home. I see Tom Beecher's horse."

Beecher yelled, "I'm in the wagon, Owl. I need your help."

Morgan pulled to a stop and said, "He hurt his back. Can't ride or walk worth a darn."

Owl said, "Take him on up to his house. It's a half mile straight ahead. I'll take a look at him there."

At the sound of Morgan's voice, Woman came to the door and waved shyly.

"Woman!" Morgan exclaimed. "It's so nice to see you."

Woman nodded and said, "You come back after you take Tom Beecher home and I'll feed you."

"Thank you. We'll take you up on that," Morgan said.

An hour later, Woman had Sarah on her lap and watched contentedly as the boys and Morgan dug into a thick beef stew and fresh bread.

"The bread is very good," Morgan said.

Woman smiled. "O'Grady taught me." She paused and said, "You stay here tonight, please."

Morgan said, "I'd love to. It's too far to get home at this hour."

Woman said, "The boys can sleep in the hay. I'll make a bed for you and Sarah by the fire."

"Lonesome?" Morgan asked.

Woman shook her head. "Not really. Tom Beecher's wife, Martha, and I are friends, and some of the other women here have been very nice to me. Owl is very kind, and he is right…the old ways will soon be gone. We want our child to have a safer life."

"Child?"

"In early winter, I think."

"Wonderful. Congratulations!"

"Thank you. And you?"

"We will have another child this fall."

"Good. And O'Grady will marry soon. To a woman called Ellie Ellis. You will come to the wedding?"

"We certainly will. Wouldn't miss it for the world."

The Dalles

THE BUSTLE OF UNLOADING THE STEAMER at The Dalles roused Peter Franklin from a dream-plagued sleep. He sat up, stretched and rubbed the sleep from his eyes. Mercury and Midnight were still in harness, but they weren't too fussed by the noise of hand carts rumbling across the gangplank that connected the Whittaker to the loading ramp. In high water, the top of the ramp was nearly up against the back door of the Umatilla, a prominent waterfront hotel.

O'Grady walked to the buggy and said, "I think we'll need to find a room someplace. Bitter is determined to work the saloons here for information about Alfred Swift."

Franklin pointed to an imposing three-story building just across the street from the loading ramp. "That's the Umatilla Hotel. Colonel Sinnott is the owner. He's a friend of mine. I'm sure he'll have rooms for us."

O'Grady looked at the crowd off-loading their freight, horses, and personal gear. "You sure? There looks to be more people than town."

Franklin smiled and said, "Daniel will have rooms for us. Guaranteed. I'll get us checked in and then let's have dinner in the hotel." Without waiting for agreement, he slapped the reins, and Midnight and Mercury pulled the buggy across the bumpy, rutted landing.

Bitter and O'Grady found a livery stable two blocks from the Hotel. For a dollar each, the hostler, a stooped old man, his stubble of whiskers gray with age, watered the horses, fed each a scoop of oats, and agreed to stash the camping gear in his tack room. "How long do you plan to stay?"

Bitter pulled his jacket open to expose the silver star stamped U.S. Marshal. "It depends. We're looking for a man named Alfred Swift."

The old man shook his head. "Nope. Don't recall anyone by that name. What's he done?"

Bitter pulled his wide brimmed hat off and pointed to the white patch of hair covering the scar on his scalp. "For starters, he shot me off my horse. And he robs travelers."

The old man cocked his head sideways and asked, "Is there a reward for this outlaw?"

Bitter set his saddle bags down on a feed sack and unbuckled the flap. He pulled out a stack of wanted posters. Alfred Swift's was the top sheet.

The old man nodded. "Yep. He was in here last week. Put his horse up for the night. Riding a big bay with a black mane. Mean looking guy. Made me nervous."

"But he's gone now?"

"He is. Two other men rode out with him the next day. I heard one of them ask this wanted feller how far it was to Canyon City."

"You mind going through this stack of posters? You might help me identify the other two."

The old man grinned and held out his hand. "Ben Colin at your service. I work best with some Irish sipping whiskey."

Bitter smiled and shook the man's hand. The twinkle in the old man's eye reminded him of Owl. "I'm John Bitter. I think we can find a little whiskey."

O'Grady shook hands and said, "Liam O'Grady at your service. You know of a nice pub?"

The old man smiled. "Gibbon's Saloon and Eatery is just across the street and down a block. Give me a minute. I need to let Samuel know I'll be gone a while. And bring those posters with you, Marshal."

They took a table in the back corner of the tobacco smoke-filled saloon, the hubbub of voices just shy of a roar. Ben caught the eye of one of the two busy bartenders and held up three fingers.

The barrel-chested bartender hurried to set a bottle and three glasses on the table. "Evenin', Ben."

Ben pointed at Bitter and said, "Andy, this gentleman, is a bona fide U.S. Marshal. He's hunting a man named Alfred Swift. I think I recognized him." The old man looked at Bitter and said, "Show him the poster, Mister Marshal."

Within five minutes, Andy had every poster in Bitter's stack making the rounds in the saloon. One man held up a flyer and shouted, "I saw this guy in Canyon City about a week ago!"

Bitter walked over to the man's table and asked, "Which one?"

"This Swift guy."

The other two men Ben Colin mentioned went unidentified. "Well," Bitter said, "at least we know where he was…and where he might still be."

Ben said, "That calls for another drink." He poured two fingers of amber liquid in each glass. "Liam O'Grady, I detect a hint of an Irish accent beneath your southern drawl. I think you're not long from the old sod."

"Second generation cotton farmer from Georgia."

"Aha…that explains the mix of accents."

"Your accent is not so pure either."

"I'll drink to that."

Bitter stacked the flyers, Swift's on top, and slid them back into his saddle bag. "Mister Colin, thanks for the help. I'd like to buy you supper at the Umatilla Hotel in about an hour."

The old man rubbed his stubble and then shook his head. "Thank you, no. Marshal Bitter. I'd have to shave, and the Umatilla, now… that's a bit out of my class"

Bitter rose from his chair, shook hands with Ben, and said, "If you change your mind, come on over."

The Curse of the Press

AT THE FRONT DESK OF THE Umatilla, Bitter and O'Grady were told
Representative Franklin expected them for dinner at 6:00. They
each signed the register, but when they tried to pay for the rooms, they
were informed by a very proper desk clerk that Representative Franklin
had taken care of the bill.

Then they were shown to separate rooms on the second floor by a
bellboy. Bitter found a quarter for a tip. "Can you bring me some hot
water?" he asked the boy.

The boy said, "Hot baths and a barber can be found one floor
down…on the river side of the hotel."

Freshly shaved, his hair trimmed for the first time in two months,
dressed in clean gray wool britches and a long-sleeved blue cotton shirt,
his boots as shined as much as a boot black could make them, Bitter
decided he was as dressed as he could get for his dinner with Franklin
and O'Grady. He debated about wearing his pistol, and finally settled
for slipping the two-shot .44 derringer in his jacket pocket. The badge
he left in his saddle bags. His new black hat graced the polished top
of an armoire.

He took a peek at the wharf where men were still busy loading
freight wagons for the gold fields. *And the Umatilla Hotel right in the
middle of all this fuss*, he thought.

A waiter in a black jacket ushered Bitter to a large table near the
back of the restaurant where Franklin was holding court. A tall, upright
man with a salt and pepper beard laughed as Bitter heard Franklin
say, "That's when my darling daughter shot Bill Bradford. Who would
have thought?"

The smaller man just smiled, his glasses reflecting light from the
chandelier overhead.

Franklin looked up and said, "Gentlemen, let me introduce Marshal John Bitter. He rescued Anna, for which I owe him a debt I'll never be able to repay. He's a remarkable young man."

Geared more for trouble than for praise Bitter nearly blushed, but managed to say, "Remarkable is a word that should be reserved for Miss Franklin."

Franklin grinned at his companions, and said, "Perhaps we should add 'gallant' to his list of accolades. As for my daughter, she does have courage, but you are the hero of the day." He pointed to a chair and said, "Please sit."

The gentleman with the beard turned out to be Colonel Sinnott, owner of the Umatilla, and the smaller man who looked bookish behind his glasses was Mister Cowne, owner and publisher of the Mountaineer, a small daily paper that fed news—and advertising—to the community of The Dalles.

Cowne said, "My sources tell me you are looking for a man named Swift."

Bitter nodded, and then added, "And several other men wanted by the law."

"But the primary character you are chasing is Alfred Swift. Right?"

"How do you know that?"

"Ben Colin is a friend of mine."

Bitter shook his head. "It's a small world, isn't it."

Cowne just smiled.

O'Grady, who evidently had seen the same barber as Bitter was ushered to the table in time to break the silence that was settling on Franklin's companions. He pulled a chair out and sat down without invitation. "Howdy, y'all. I hope I'm not late. I'm as hungry as horse. Something about travel gives me a good appetite."

Franklin smiled and said, "Let me introduce you to my friends."

Drinks before dinner, wine with dinner, and some kind of sweet after-dinner liquor that O'Grady privately thought he would never touch again, loosened up the conversation, and Cowne, who was on all occasions a journalist, asked, "Why are you here, Mister O'Grady? Are you a prospector?"

"Not really." He looked across the table at John Bitter who just shrugged as if to say, "Go ahead."

"You see, I owe John Bitter my life. So, I'm here to back him up if Alfred Swift gets too obstinate. I wouldn't want to go back to Abiqua Creek and tell John's wife I didn't protect him."

"Your life?"

"Well, yes. You see a big battle was brewing, and my orders were to scout the Union lines. We swung wide, trying to find the right flank of those old boys, when all of a sudden we find Captain Bitter and a bunch of blue bellies. Blue bellies in front. Blue bellies in back. Blue bellies on each side.

"Captain Bitter says, 'Welcome to the end of your war.' Then he offers me a drink because he says there won't be any whiskey where I'm going.

"Now the way I figure it, Captain Bitter saved my life. If I had fought in that battle, given the number of Confederate dead, I'd probably been one of them. So…you see…my friend John Bitter saved my life. I owe him. Especially for that last sweet drink."

The men chuckled at O'Grady's story, so he said, "Now, one other time…"

Later in the evening Cowne asked to see the poster on Alfred Swift. When Bitter returned from his room with the poster, Cowne unfolded a thin piece of parchment and traced the image. "Just in case I see him," he said.

A Little Politics

Just before daylight, the rap of a knuckle on his door brought Bitter awake. He heard O'Grady say, "Y'all awake?"

John padded across the floor and opened the door a crack. "I am now."

O'Grady thrust a single sheet of newsprint through the narrow opening and said, "I'll see you downstairs for breakfast."

The headline of the Mountaineer read "War Hero Seeks Whereabouts Of Outlaw." The story was clear, concise, and brief.

Former U.S. Army Captain John Bitter, decorated war hero and now a U.S. Marshal seeks to locate and apprehend the outlaw Alfred Swift. A reward of $200 is offered for Swift's capture. Leave messages at the Umatilla House.

It was followed by the hand drawn image of Alfred Swift, a pretty good drawing.

Bitter thought for a minute and then folded the one-page Mountaineer and stuffed it in his saddle bag. He dressed hurriedly, doing his best to quell his irritation at Cowne. He shook his head and muttered, "The cat was out of the bag as soon as Ben Colin showed the wanted poster to all those men in Gibbon's Saloon. No need to get mad at Cowne. I'll bet this puts a scare in Swift. He'll have every pistol packer in Canyon City looking for him. I wonder if I can get there before this newspaper does?"

O'Grady was sitting at a back table with Peter Franklin and Colonel Sinnott, amazed at how much the Colonel knew of Oregon politics. "I live much closer to Salem and Portland. I hear a lot of tavern talk in my pub, but I don't know half of what you know."

The Colonel smiled. "The Umatilla is the hub for travel to the interior and to the east, as well as an informal post office. Take this morning's story in the Mountaineer. Mister Cowne says to leave information at the Umatilla. That gives us the inside track on information, and information is the key to success."

Bitter walked to the table, pulled a chair back and sat down. "I heard that, Colonel. My Pinkerton secretary—make that former secretary, since I have resigned from the Pinkertons—keeps his finger on the pulse of Oregon politics. When the Oregon House is in session, he makes sure he is there to watch and observe. I'll bet he can name every state representative who has ever been elected."

Conversation ceased while a waiter poured coffee for Bitter and refilled the other cups, and then Franklin asked, "What has he told you?"

Bitter laughed and said, "Nothing lately. He doesn't really like me."

The men chuckled, and then the Colonel asked Franklin, "Do you think Governor Gibbs will be successful in his bid to be our U.S. Senator?"

Franklin shook his head. "No. He made too many enemies trying to get the Fourteenth Amendment passed. Too many Southern sympathizers in the House. No. They'll pick someone else. The hell of it is, the Amendment will pass in the next session. Gibbs is just a sacrificial lamb."

The Colonel nodded. "Yes, he is. It's too bad for Gibbs, but President Grant will keep him busy. He's too good a man to be put out to pasture. I wish I was half the orator he is."

O'Grady said, "Fourteenth Amendment?"

Franklin said, "It grants citizenship and voting rights to Indians, Negroes and former slaves. The blanket definition is 'persons born or naturalized in the United States.'"

"I thought President Lincoln took care of that," Bitter said.

"No," Franklin said. "That just freed the slaves, and there is some thought that Lincoln didn't really have the power to do even that. Hence, the Fourteenth Amendment. Puts the question to rest—if it ever is put to rest."

The Colonel looked quizzically at Franklin. "What do you mean by that?"

"I mean, the South is being pillaged and plundered by rapacious Northerners. I'm not sure the South will ever forgive or forget."

O'Grady shrugged. "I think y'all fixed that when Sherman burned Atlanta. That was mean."

Franklin nodded. "That certainly didn't help." He looked squarely at John Bitter and nodded. "I think you would do well in politics, my young friend."

"God forbid! Meaning no disrespect, sir. I guess someone has to, but not me."

Franklin smiled and said, "We'll see. Now about getting to Sherar's bridge. The Colonel tells me I can be there by this evening if I take the stage. They have fresh horses at Fifteen Mile Creek, at the foot of Tygh Ridge, and at Sherar's bridge. I think Anna might be more comfortable in the stage."

The Colonel looked at his pocket watch and said, "Which leaves in about an hour. I'll look after the buggy and that nice matched team of yours."

Two waiters brought steak and eggs, fried potatoes, biscuits with wild blueberry jam, and fresh coffee. In the manner of Western men, conversation ceased while they ate.

Bitter cleaned his plate, took another sip of coffee and said, "I'd best go make my manners to the local magistrate…and to the commanding officer at the Fort."

The Colonel nodded. "Good idea. Do you know a Captain Bidwell?"

Bitter nodded. "He's a close friend of mine."

"He and his men had a run-in with some Indians in Tygh Valley a couple days back. One trooper was wounded, but the Indians got away. You boys be careful going through there."

"We will," Bitter said.

Sherar's Bridge, Again

PAYING HIS MANNERS TO THE COMMANDING officer took a bit longer than Bitter liked, and it was after eight o'clock before O'Grady and Bitter put their horses to the hard task of climbing the first set of big, rolling grass covered hills south of The Dalles. They were over the top of the first grade and grateful for a few miles of fairly flat road when the stage rattled on by, the wheels pulling ropes of dust from the road.

Franklin leaned out the window and hollered, "See you at Sherar's Bridge."

"Long before we get there, I'll bet," O'Grady grumped.

"Yep. We'll be there by dark, but the stage will be long gone. There's a stage stop on Fifteen Mile Creek. They'll get fresh horses and just keep pushing."

"We could have taken the stage."

"Uh huh, but there's no guarantee we won't need horses when we get to Canyon City."

"Might. You know, I keep wondering what will become of this part of world when the gold is all gone?"

"Somebody will want to ranch or farm it."

"Think so?"

"Wait until you see Tygh Valley. Pretty as a picture. The rye grass is stirrup high to a tall horse. I'd love to have a horse ranch there... someday."

Bitter turned and looked at O'Grady. "Did I tell you Morgan bought one-hundred-sixty acres across the creek from our place. Didn't tell me about it until it was a done deal."

"What you gonna do with it? You ain't home enough to farm the one you got."

"Now don't you start in on me, too." He frowned and then said, "Did I tell you I quit the Pinkertons?"

"You did?"

"Gone too much from the home place. And," he pulled his jacket back to expose the silver star, "I'm gonna get rid of this badge when we get back."

"I think that's a good idea. Look what happened last time."

"Don't rub it in, Liam. Old Owl blamed me for not shooting Swift in the first place. You know, for a civilized Christian Cherokee, Owl is plumb blood thirsty. Told me you never just wound an enemy."

"It's a hard way to look at the world, but he could be right."

"Sad to think so."

"Might be good advice. He told me I am to kill Swift if we find him because you won't do it." O'Grady flicked Appy with the end of the reins and said, "Come on, John Bitter. I fancy a drink and a steak at Sherar's Bridge tonight."

They watered their horses in an oak grove where Tygh Creek wandered into the Tygh Valley. O'Grady said, "It's as pretty as you said. If I get tired of the pub, I might just stake out a homestead here."

"Alone?"

O'Grady nearly blushed. "Well, I guess now's a good a time as any. I'm gonna get married as soon as I ask her daddy for her hand…and come calling, she said…twice."

Bitter grinned and held out his hand. "And who is this fair maid?"

O'Grady, charmer, cavalry scout, war veteran, story teller, stammered and turned red before he got it out. "Ellie. Ellie Ellis. She works in the pub…cooking, cleaning up."

"Congratulations, Liam. When's the wedding?"

"Don't know yet, but I'd like you to be my best man."

Bitter wrapped an arm across Liam's shoulder and said, "Honored, my friend."

❧

ANNA WAS SITTING IN A wicker chair on the front porch of Sherar's trading post, her broken leg propped on a wooden stool. Orin brought her a glass of cider and plopped into a chair next to her. "Sun feels good, don't…ah, doesn't it?" he said. "How's the leg?"

"That's two questions in one, Orin. Which one do you want me to answer first?"

"Well, let me see. Maybe I didn't ask if the sun felt good or not. Maybe I just sort of said the obvious. So that takes care of one question…which might not have a been a question at all. So just move on the second question."

"I think I'm a lot better. The pain didn't keep me awake last night. And I managed to walk out here without my walking stick."

"Good." He stopped for a minute and then looked sideways at her and said, "What are you going to do, Anna, if you can't go home?"

A smile flirted with her lips and she said, "Why, Orin, what if I just stayed here?"

Orin blushed and stammered, "Oh, I guess that would be just fine. Mama could sure use some help with the kitchen and the store."

She smacked him on the arm. "Is that all you've got to say?" She started to get out her chair when the sound of hoof beats told her the stage was coming.

Orrin said, "I'd best see to getting the fresh horses hitched up. Old man Wheeler doesn't like to wait too long before he pulls out."

She plopped back down, fussed for sure, but not too sure why. She had known Orin for barely four weeks, so why would he "say" anything anyway?

The stage pulled to a stop in a cloud of dust, and before she could get away from it and back in the store she heard her father say, "Anna?"

Since she couldn't run…and that meant she couldn't run away… she just sat back in the chair, put her hands over her face and started to weep. She wasn't sure why she wept. Later she would wonder if it was from relief or despair. Or if there wasn't a certain amount of joy that her father had found her.

Franklin did not try to hug his daughter. He did that much right. What he did instead was tell her what John Bitter had told him…about her conviction she was being sold to a "greasy old man."

"I explained to Bitter I was talking to Mister Hartman about his son, a boy about your age. The Hartman boy wanted permission to come calling. Good Lord, girl, I wouldn't marry you to a man older than me. I want you to have a life."

She raised her head, trying to decide if he was telling the truth. A hint of tears in his eyes convinced her. "Oh, Daddy," she said and raised her arms to hug him and be hugged back. They both held tears at bay.

⌇

By the time O'Grady and Bitter rode into the yard of the trading post, it was clear to Franklin his daughter had forgiven him. *But I'll have to try and forgive myself*, he thought, *for neglecting this beautiful child.*

"Anna," he said, "I've been a terrible father. It wasn't until I thought I had lost you that I realized how much I truly love you."

Anna smiled and said, "In that case, I would like it if Orin Sherar came calling."

"Where is he?"

She pointed to tall, square shouldered young man hitching fresh horses to the stage. "That's Orin. He's really very nice. And smart."

"It's a long way to Salem from here."

"You can pay his fare on the riverboats."

Peter Franklin was prepared to do anything his daughter asked if it meant taking her home.

The Sherar's, O'Grady and Bitter, and father and daughter celebrated the return of Anna Franklin to her family. O'Grady sipped whiskey and told Irish folk tales while Orin and Anna held hands under the drape of the tablecloth.

Anna looked at John Bitter and said, "I owe it all to you, Mister Bitter. If you hadn't come along…"

He smiled but didn't share his thoughts. *And you wouldn't be in love with Orin, and he in love with you.*

Dayville to Canyon City

A shout urged Bitter and O'Grady to clear the road for the fast-moving Wheeler stagecoach. They watched six strong horses pull the stage through the low water ford on the South Fork of the John Day River.

Bitter opened his jacket to expose his badge and keep the driver and his partner, who rode shotgun, from getting spooked. He kneed Rockford alongside the stage. "Howdy. I'm Marshal Bitter. We're just wondering how far it is to Canyon City."

The driver nodded down the road and said, "About thirty miles or better. You here for the trial?"

"What trial is that?"

"We heard about it on our last trip, some hombre gunned down the local sheriff, but one of the deputies got the drop on the shooter. Trial starts tomorrow."

"Got a name?"

"For the shooter?"

"Yes."

"A bad man named Swift. Judge Joaquin Miller is holding trial tomorrow."

"Joaquin Miller? I know of a writer by that name."

"One and same."

"I'll be darned. Imagine that. Well, Swift is the name of the man I'm chasing."

"So was every hungry prospector in Canyon City. That story in the Mountaineer put him in every man's gun sights. From what we heard, the sheriff got a tip that Swift was hiding in a whore house. When the sheriff went to arrest him, Swift gunned him down. Swift will hang for sure."

"Witnesses?"

"Three whores and two deputies saw the whole thing. Swift never gave the sheriff a chance. Just up and shot him." The driver paused and then said, "We best be going, Marshal. Got a schedule to keep."

Bitter nodded and said, "Thanks for the information."

O'Grady and Bitter watched the stage without speaking until it rounded the toe of a little hill. When the dust settled, O'Grady said, "We turning back?"

"Should, shouldn't we."

"Maybe it would be useful if you were there for the trial. You could testify."

"To what?"

"Well, he did shoot you."

"I didn't actually see him shoot at me. I only heard someone shout, 'You got him Alf, you got him.' That's a little too iffy to be evidence in a trial."

"Not for me," O'Grady said.

"Might be enough for me, too, but let's go see this Swift person. Just to be sure."

For the most part the road was just a set of wagon ruts that followed the John Day River east through a long valley squeezed at times by the foothills of the granite-bound Strawberry Mountains to the south and an edge of the pine tree covered Blues on the north.

The river was flanked by alder, willows, meadows of wild grass and cottonwood trees with a mix of cedar here and there. In the next six hours they forded the river four times, the water muddy brown from upstream dredging.

"You know," Bitter said, "this valley sort of reminds me of Star Valley…the way the open foothills rise to meet the slopes of the mountains.

I see some mountain mahogany and pine timber, and a few junipers up there. Beautiful. I can see people wanting to ranch and farm this country."

"Not me," O'Grady said. "Too damned far from everything."

"Like Ellie Ellis?"

"Like Ellie Ellis for sure."

After about one hundred-eighty miles in six days, O'Grady's pack horse was tired enough to just lay down in the road, and Appy and Rockford weren't looking a whole lot better. The men walked their horses down a street lined with the first buildings of what was recently named John Day City, marking it as an area distinct from the mining town of Canyon City. A small Chinese boy waited until they crossed Canyon Creek, then asked, "You want stalls for your horses, mister?"

Bitter nodded. "We surely do, son."

The boy sort of half bowed and then said, "Follow me."

For three dollars the horses were watered, fed, and led to stalls where hay was tossed into the mangers. The boy accepted a two-bit piece as a tip from Bitter and said, "You want to meet my sister?"

Bitter shook his head. "No, that's not what we came for. What we want is a meal and a room for the night."

"My sister has a room she rents."

"Ah, I thought you meant something else."

"You want?"

"Let's take a look."

The boy's sister, coal black hair shining in the lamp light from the door of a well-built two-story cabin, led them to a set of outside stairs climbing to a loft. Three beds were arranged u-shaped along the walls and across the end. It was as neat and clean as the rooms they had at the Umatilla—and a whole lot cheaper at a dollar each. Bitter paid six dollars for three nights and then asked, "Where can we wash up and get something to eat?"

The girl pointed through the one lone window at a café across the street. "Charlie's. There is a bathhouse next door. If you have clothes to wash, I take."

They put their gear on two of the beds and hid their rifles under the cotton blankets. "Not bad," O'Grady said. "Beats camping in the field with fifteen or twenty thousand other men. Talk about a smelly business."

"I know what you mean. There were times during the war I thought I'd never sleep in a bed again. Or ever get more than a cold-water bath in a muddy creek."

They changed into clean clothes, wadded dirty clothing in a ball and took them down the stairs to the young Chinese girl. "Ready tonight," she said. O'Grady shook his head. "Tomorrow night will be soon enough."

Charles McShannon

THEY PUSHED THROUGH THE DOOR INTO Charlie's to be greeted by the smell of frying meat. It was crowded with men dressed in rough workmen's clothing and scuffed boots. Food was served at two long communal tables. The smell of unwashed clothing competed with the scent of warm yeast bread.

They took seats at the end of one of the tables with their backs to the wall in response to an inborn need to see who might come through the door. A hand-painted sign read: Coffee 25 cents, Pie 50 cents, Steak and Spuds $1.00. O'Grady thought about the prices at his pub and said quietly to Bitter, "Pretty steep."

Bitter smiled and said, "I'm just glad to find hot food. I'm so hungry I'd eat the bark off a tree."

A rough-looking man whose face said he had survived small pox brought them each a heavy mug and poured coffee from a big granite pot without saying a word. Ten minutes later he brought two plates, each piled high with fried spuds, a decent looking fried steak, and two thick slices of warm bread. The fat on the steak still bubbled a bit. Again, the waiter didn't say anything, just set the plates in front of them and turned back to the kitchen.

For a place filled with men, it was pretty quiet, the intermittent conversation spiced with "pass the butter," or "salt and pepper, please."

It suited Bitter and O'Grady who dug into the spuds and cut steak into edible sizes. When they finished, the waiter gathered their plates and dumped them into a big tub of soapy water. It almost startled them when he said, "Pie?"

"Blueberry?" Bitter asked.

He nodded.

O'Grady said, "I'd sure like a piece."

Bitter nodded and said, "Make that two."

A husky, well-dressed man sitting across from them grinned and said, "That's the most I've heard Wilcox say in the past two weeks. Normally, he doesn't say anything at all. Just sets the pie down and leaves. Must like you two."

"You from here?" O'Grady said.

"Well, as much as any newcomer. Wasn't but seven people living up Canyon Creek when the gold was discovered. I got here early, staked a claim and hired a couple of swampers to help. Found enough gold to keep me in comforts for the rest of my life." He laughed and added, "Just can't find a woman to go with it. I might have to visit Portland or San Francisco to find one."

The man reached across the table and held out his hand. "Charles McShannon at your service."

O'Grady turned his head slightly and leaned back, studying the man. "And this place is Charlie's. You wouldn't be owner, now?"

"Ah, I hear a bit of the Irish hiding under that southern drawl."

"Liam O'Grady of French Prairie. And this gent is Marshal Bitter."

Bitter shook hands but didn't say anything.

"Here for the trial?"

"In a way." Bitter paused and then added, "We've been tracking a man named Alfred Swift, a wanted outlaw."

"Well, you'll be disappointed then. This man is Roger Swift, and I'm his attorney."

Bitter frowned and said, "Could we get a look at this gent?"

"I think that could be arranged." Then he grinned and said, "The pie is on me."

∿

THE JAIL WAS A HALF-MILE walk up Canyon Creek from Charlie's. The sound of the creek, the cool evening breeze coming down the narrow canyon, and the call of a nighthawk eased Bitter's soul until they approached a cut stone building serving as sheriff's office and jail. A tall, clean-shaven man with a silver star pinned to his shirt sat in a ladder back chair, a shotgun on his lap.

"Evening, Deputy Richards," McShannon said. "We've come to see Swift."

"Go on in."

Bitter studied the man lying on a cot and said, "Stand up."

"Why? They gonna hang me for sure. And I didn't do anything."

"I want to make sure you aren't Alfred Swift."

"Good old Alf. I've been blamed for Alf's dirty tricks all my life. And now this."

Bitter's temper flared and he said, "If you don't stand up, I'll shoot you right now and save the city the trouble of hanging you. Now, stand up!"

Slowly, Roger Swift swung his dusty boots off the cot and then stood up.

O'Grady looked at Bitter and said, "Well?"

Bitter shook his head. "He sure enough looks like Alfred, but he's not as tall, and he's twenty pounds lighter. Nope, this isn't the gent that shot up my camp and then tried to kill me. But I can see why people might mistake him for Alfred."

"Alfred's my brother."

Bitter said, "How did you come to be at the whore house?"

"I'd gone to warn Alfred the sheriff was coming to arrest him."

McShannon said, "If he's been such a pain in the ass, why would you do that?"

"He's the only family I got."

O'Grady said, "God forbid."

Bitter said, "Do you know where Alfred might be?"

Roger Swift shook his head. "All I can say for sure is he likes whore houses."

Deputy Richards said, "You seen enough?"

"I guess," Bitter said and walked back through the office and out to the porch.

McShannon said, "What do you plan to do, Marshal Bitter?"

"Me? Why I'll just keep working the saloons and whore houses until I find out where to look for Alfred Swift. I still have a warrant for his arrest."

McShannon said, "What did you think about Roger's story?"

Bitter shrugged and said, "Might be the truth. Maybe you can get this trial delayed until I find Roger's errant brother. Might get him to confess to save Roger."

"Maybe."

"Come on, O'Grady. Let's work the saloons and whorehouses this evening. See if we can turn up anything."

A Break

I F A VISITOR DIDN'T KNOW CANYON City kissed the southern limits of John Day City, he might think it was all one town. To John Bitter it wouldn't have made any difference anyway. He and O'Grady took the wanted poster to every saloon in both towns, knocked on the door of three whore houses and came up empty.

Frustrated, Bitter said, "He might have left the country."

"Maybe, but where would he go? We know he was here three days ago."

"If we don't turn up something pretty damned soon, I'm afraid I'll have to give up the hunt."

"Well, you can guarantee that almost everyone in these two towns knows you are hunting him. And the two-hundred-dollar reward has not been claimed. Might stir up some business for us."

"Well…I know what I'm going to do about it for now. I'm going to head back to our room and get some sleep."

"I'd say amen to that."

❧

S OMETHING WOKE BITTER FROM A dreamless sleep. He didn't stir, just laid there and listened, trying to figure out what had disturbed him. A step creaked on the outside stairway and he held his breath, waiting. He reached up and slipped his pistol from the holster hanging on a peg over his cot. Thumb on the hammer of his gun, he slipped out of bed, walked barefoot across the room, and stood to one side of the door.

Finally, a timid knock and a whisper confirmed his caution. "Marshal? Marshal Bitter. I have news of Alfred Swift."

Bitter heard O'Grady slip out of bed, cock the hammer of his pistol, and slide into place on the other side of the door.

"Who are you?" Bitter asked through the door.

He heard a man say, "Is that two hundred dollars still good?"

Bitter took a deep breath. "I'm going to let you in. Keep you hands in the air when I open the door. If you don't, I'm liable to shoot you."

"I'm unarmed," the man said.

Bitter said, "Wait a minute." He struck a match and walked to the lamp hanging from the ceiling. When it was lit, he nodded to O'Grady, slipped the latch and opened the door.

A small blond man, maybe five foot four, wearing britches with the knees out and run-down shoes, inched through the door. Arms raised, hat in hand, the quaver in his voice a loud signal to his fear, he said, "I come in peace."

Bitter's pocket watch told him it was two-thirty. "At this time of night?"

The man shrugged and said, "It took me that long to walk from Prairie City. I could not get a ride to save my soul."

"Why not wait until morning?"

"Cuz Swift will be gone in the morning. And I need the money. I'm near broke." Once started, the man was set on telling his story. "I was working on the Dixie dredge, but I fell and buggered up my knee. I couldn't work, so they laid me off. I been working the dredge tailings, but it's awful slim pickings. Some days I make five to ten dollars… and some days I don't make anything. And everything costs so darned much. The other day, why I paid fifty cents for a small hen's egg. I'm nearly starving. That's why I need the money. If I get it, I'll ride the stage out of here."

Bitter took advantage of the man when he took a breath and interrupted. "Okay. Where is Swift?"

"Oh." The man laughed. "Guess I didn't get around to that part. He's holed up in a whore house run by Goldie…over there in Prairie City. She's a pretty good old gal, but she has the ugliest whores I ever seen. Why this one…

"Enough. Tell me how you know this?"

"Oh. Okay. I saw that story in the Mountaineer bout him…the one with the drawing, so I know what he looks like. I was having a beer in the Pastime over in Prairie City this evening and Swift was in there. Drunk as a skunk. Got to bragging about he shot the sheriff and how he aimed to kill himself a U.S. Marshal in the near future. It was all brag, but I think he was feeling guilty about letting his brother hang for it. But he's a skunk, so maybe he wasn't feeling guilty. I don't know, maybe people like him don't feel guilt."

"But?" Bitter said.

"Well, anyway, the bartender finally told him to go back to Goldie's and sleep it off."

"What makes you think he won't be there tomorrow?" O'Grady asked.

"Oh, that. Cause he said he was riding the stage to The Dalles in the morning. Going hunting is what he said. Gonna kill that marshal. I think he means you."

Bitter said, "What's your name?"

"I'm Olaf Olson."

"Well, Olaf. You sit right there on that cot. I'm going to get us some horses and we, that means you, me and my friend with the pistol over there, are going to pay a visit to Goldie's. And you are going to show us where it is. If he is there, and if I capture him, I'll pay you two-hundred dollars."

"I…I don't want go back there. If he finds out I told you, he's liable to kill me."

"No, he won't. He'll be in irons or he'll be dead. And another thing, you will have to testify to what you heard him say about killing the sheriff. So, here's the deal. You get two-hundred when we capture Swift, and another fifty when you testify to Judge Miller about what you heard."

"That wasn't the deal."

"It is now. Look, a man's life is at stake. He's liable to be hanged for something you know he didn't do. You've got to do this. It's your duty, Olaf."

Olaf looked miserable, but finally he straightened his shoulders, took a deep breath and said, "You are right. I'm just not a very brave man. And I don't own a gun."

O'Grady laughed. "Can you use one?"

"I fought in the Civil War. I was with the First Wisconsin Infantry. I know how to use a rifle."

Bitter looked at him, eyebrows raised. "They saw some heavy fighting. Did you stick?"

Olaf looked insulted. "Of course."

"Then why turn mouse on me?"

He shrugged and looked miserable. "I guess poverty does that sometimes. Fear just creeps in and keeps you company until you lose your courage."

"Well, you won't be broke much longer."

When three mounted men rode up to the jail and banged on the door, Deputy Richards rose from his bunk in the corner of the jail, shotgun ready. He shouted through the door, "What do you want?"

"Richards, this is Marshal Bitter. I need you to tell Judge Miller I have evidence to prove Roger Swift did not kill the sheriff. Alfred Swift did. He's holed up in Prairie City and we are going to fetch him back here in the morning."

"You sure about this? There were witnesses."

"I can prove it. I'm going slide a note under the door. Take that to McShannon for me."

"I surely will."

"See you along about noon or sooner."

Goldie's

THE SUN WAS JUST PAINTING A few morning clouds with desert pastels when Bitter, O'Grady and Olson rode into the yard of a single-story log house that looked to be about forty feet long.

Bitter whispered, "Is there a back door?"

Olaf nodded. "Leads to the outhouse."

O'Grady nodded to Bitter and stepped down. He handed Appy's reins to Olaf, and slipped around the corner of the house. Bitter dismounted and handed Rockford's reins to Olaf as well. "You lead these animals back to the main road. When you hear me call, bring 'em back. If you stuck when the First Wisconsin was in the fight, you can stick now."

To make Olaf feel better, Bitter handed him his .44 derringer. "Just in case."

Without looking to see if Olaf was doing as told, Bitter walked to the front door and tried the latch. "Locked," he said in disgust, so he settled for pounding on the door with his left hand, right hand full of cocked pistol. It took a good three minutes for a heavy-set blond to open the door a crack and say, "We're closed. Come back tonight."

Bitter just pushed her out of her way, showed her his badge and said, "I'm after Alfred Swift. Where is he?"

Goldie sighed and said, "Thank God. He's the meanest customer we ever had. Loves to hurt the girls. He's in the last room on the right and good riddance."

"Alone?"

"He is now."

Bitter slipped quietly down the narrow hallway, senses alert, keyed up and ready, and then he saw the open back door. Suddenly and loudly O'Grady said, "Bitter! Come here! I got him."

Bitter stepped through the door and nearly laughed at the sight of Alfred Swift, pants down around his ankles, hands raised in the air."

"Swift," he said. "Why is it every time I see you your bare ass is showing." And then he laughed in relief. "I am arresting you for murder, for attempted murder, for assaulting a police officer, and for robbery. As I think of additional charges, I'll let you know. Now then, where's your horse? We are going to need it to take you back to Canyon City."

Goldie was standing in the moonlight, arms crossed. "We had nothing to do with this, Alf, but I'll be damned if I'll be sorry to see your rotten ass hanging from the scaffold."

"I'll get you, Goldie. I'll make you pay every day of your life."

Goldie walked closer and said, "Not in this life, Alf." She unfolded her arms and before O'Grady or Bitter could react, she shot Alf between the eyes with a .44 derringer. Alf fell backwards and landed in the outhouse.

Goldie said, "Are you going to arrest me, Marshal? He killed one of my girls a few days ago."

"Why didn't you report it?"

"Think about that. Who cares if an old whore is killed? Who's going to avenge her? Not a soul gives a damn. And I'm afraid of him. But you had him covered, so I shot him while I could. I'll take whatever comes."

Bitter looked at O'Grady who just shrugged. "What if we didn't find him, John?"

Bitter chuckled and said, "No. That's not what happened. He was about to shoot us when Goldie came to our defense and shot him. Yes. I think that's what happened. She saved our lives."

He bowed and said, "Thank you ma'am."

Goldie took a deep breath and said, "Can I make you gentlemen some coffee? How about some breakfast? How does ham and eggs sound?"

Both men nodded and followed her back into the house. Three frowzy-looking women peeked at them from behind half open doors. One asked, "What happened, Goldie?"

"Let's just say, Alf won't beat on any of my girls again."

Bitter said loudly, "Thanks for saving us, Goldie. It was careless to let him get the drop on us."

That taken care of, Bitter walked through the house and out into the front yard. "Olaf, you can come on in now."

Parade

O'GRADY PULLED ALFRED'S PANTS BACK UP before they loaded him on a horse he had undoubtedly stolen from some place. Bitter tied his denim jacket behind his saddle to make sure the badge pinned to his shirt pocket was easily seen. He mounted and kneed Rockford over beside Olaf's horse. "I'll take that derringer, Olaf. I don't think you need to worry about getting shot by Swift.

Olaf looked a lot happier than he had when Bitter insisted he guide them to Goldie's, but he still had hoped Bitter would forget about the pistol. Reluctantly, he fished the gun from his pocket and carefully handed over. Bitter grinned and said, "You can afford to buy your own gun now."

Olaf nodded. "I will. It's no good feeling defenseless."

O'Grady said, "Amen."

IT WAS AFTER TEN O'CLOCK when they forded the John Day River and rode the dusty road up a long grade and into John Day City. Curious citizens came out of doorways and stores to stare at the little cavalcade.

Bitter and O'Grady kept their eyes moving, looking for threats, but saw none.

They turned at the junction of the Canyon City road and rode to the jailhouse. Deputy Richard's stepped out on the porch of the sheriff's office and watched them ride up. "Got 'em, I see."

Bitter nodded. "Did you get my note to McShannon?"

"Did."

"What did he say?"

"He was by a few minutes ago. Said you were to go on up to the courthouse when you got here."

"That's all?"

"That's all he said."

"Okay, then. That's what we'll do."

"Hold on a minute. I'm to walk Roger Swift up there. You can kind of help keep an eye on him, if that's all right with you."

Bitter nodded. "Bring him on out."

∽

A DOZEN PEOPLE HEADED FOR THE courthouse following the small parade of horses—one carrying a dead man—and Roger Swift in handcuffs walking up the street guarded by well-known Deputy Richards. They all smelled a chance for one of the West's best entertainments: a trial. And while a killing now and again wasn't unknown, it wasn't often they chanced to see a dead man across his saddle.

The hubbub drew Judge Miller to his office window. He did not recognize the three riders, but he was familiar with Roger Swift and Deputy Richards. *The rider wearing a badge must be that U.S. Marshal McShannon talked about*, he thought. *This could get interesting. I wonder who the dead man is? And how did he get killed?*

The riders stopped at the hitching rail in front of the courthouse, a small two-story stone building only recently constructed on the site.

It looked new, the scars on the ground from the construction still unwashed by winter snow or summer rain.

"Mister Updike," Miller called through the open door. "Bring your pad to the court room. I think you'll have an interesting tale to record. And then I want you to find Mister Campbell, our fine prosecutor, and get him back here."

Stephen Updike served as Judge Miller's clerk. An energetic young man barely old enough to shave, Updike was a recent graduate of Willamette College. In his spare time, he was reading for the law. He said, "Yessir."

McShannon was standing on the walk to the courthouse, impatiently waiting for the cavalcade. He looked at his watch, stuffed it back in his vest pocket and took a few steps closer to the street. "Howdy, Marshal. What have you brought me?"

"Alfred Swift."

"What happened?"

Bitter looked at O'Grady who was the better liar and nodded. O'Grady was up to the task. He shook his head and said, "We bring sorrowful news." He pointed at the corpse hanging over the horse. "We were mighty careless in our effort to capture this outlaw, and danged if he didn't get the drop on us. I think we'd be dead if it wasn't for Goldie. She up and shot him before he could shoot us. I call it a miracle. The Good Lord sent us an angel just in time."

"Who is Goldie?"

"She runs a leisure house for gentlemen in Prairie City."

McShannon laughed. "You mean she's a madam. That seems an unlikely angel."

O'Grady swept off his hat and said, "The Lord works in mysterious ways."

McShannon spotted Updike leading lawyer Campbell up the street to the courthouse.

Judge Miller stepped out the door and said, "Mister McShannon, Mister Campbell, I'll see these people in the courtroom…now."

The three riders dismounted and followed Deputy Richards, McShannon, and Roger Swift into the courthouse. Alfred was left hanging over the saddle. A dozen citizens followed them in and sat down on benches set up in the back of the room for that purpose. Judge Miller enjoyed an audience, and he was good at playing to it.

He pointed to a row of chairs behind a couple of tables in front of "the bar" which separated the onlookers from the serious business of the court.

"Hats," he commanded, and Olaf, O'Grady, and Bitter hastily removed theirs. "Now then, this is just a preliminary hearing to determine if any new evidence has been uncovered that might be cause to dismiss the murder charges against Roger Swift."

He pointed at Updike and said, "Swear these people in. I don't want to do it more than once."

Bitter, O'Grady, and Olson raised their right hands and swore to tell the truth. Judge Miller said, "That includes you too, Mister Swift. Get your right hand in the air." Roger Swift did his best. He held his handcuffed wrists up and slightly to the right. "Mister Updike?"

Once Swift was sworn in, the judge said, "I'm told you are Marshal Bitter. Do you have proof of who you are?"

Bitter stood up and pulled a folded letter from the shirt pocket guarded by the badge. He handed it to Updike. Miller read the letter, looked up and stared at John Bitter. "Okay, I accept this letter as the genuine article. I know Judge Deady, and that is definitely his signature. Now, why were you hunting Alfred Swift?"

Bitter told the tale of Swift attacking his camp, of being shot out of the saddle and hearing someone say, "You got him Alf, you got him!"

Lawyer Campbell interrupted. "Judge, may I ask a question?"

Miller nodded and said, "Go ahead.

"And that was enough for a warrant?"

Bitter said, "There is a wanted poster in my saddle bags. Judge Deady issued a warrant for his arrest. So…whether he was the one who shot me or not, he was still a wanted outlaw."

"And who are the men with you?"

"Liam O'Grady, and Olaf Olson. Olaf is claiming the reward. He brought us the information as to where Swift was hiding."

"Mister Olson," Judge Miller said, "tell us what you know."

When Olaf got to the part of his story where he heard Alfred Swift bragging about shooting the sheriff, Judge Miller said, "You're sure about that?"

"Yessir. That's what he said. He also said he was going hunting. Gonna kill him a U.S. Marshal. I reckon he meant Marshal Bitter, sir."

"Possible. Well, as to the matter of Roger Swift, I'm starting to think he is wrongfully accused. There is a strong possibility he was mistaken for his brother. Tell me, Deputy Richards, how dark was it at the whore house when the sheriff was shot?"

"Well, sir, there was a wall lamp at the end of the hall, but it was pretty dim."

"Could the witnesses have been mistaken?"

Richards shrugged. "I guess so, but I caught him going out the back door."

McShannon rose to his feet. "Your Honor, Roger Swift swears he was in the whore house to warn his brother the sheriff was coming. When the sheriff came down the hall, Roger tried to leave the premises. Your Honor, I suggest we go look at the body of Alfred Swift. I think you'll agree there is a strong family likeness."

Judge Miller rose and said, "All right. Let's do that."

They all trooped back out of the courthouse and surrounded Alfred Swift's horse. McShannon lifted Alfred's head and said, "Alfred and Roger could be twins."

Judge Miller looked at Roger and then back at Alfred. "Except for the bullet hole in this one's forehead. Okay, back inside."

Bitter watched Roger Swift's face and would have sworn he smirked at the sight of his dead brother. *I wonder what that's about.*

Everyone found a bench and the judge sat down behind his podium. The crowd was busy talking in loud voices about what they had just witnessed. The harder it was to hear what was being said, the louder the voices became. Judge Miller rapped his gavel twice before the crowd noise fell a low murmur.

"In view of Mister Olson's testimony, I am open to a motion from the defense…or from the people for that matter."

McShannon shot to his feet and said, "I move to dismiss."

The judge looked at Campbell. "Well, Mister Campbell?"

Campbell rose slowly to his feet. "I'm not entirely convinced by this story, but I think there is enough doubt about the guilt of Roger Swift. And since we have a witness who claims Alfred Swift bragged about the killing, I won't object."

Judge Miller rapped his gavel and said, "Case dismissed."

Deputy Richards unlocked the handcuffs from Roger Swift and said, "I reckon you are free to go."

Doctor Kam Wah Chung

WHEN ROGER SWIFT HELD OUT HIS hand to Bitter and said, "Thank you," Bitter refused to shake. He touched the thatch of white hair growing over the scar of Alfred Swift's bullet and said, "I got you off…or rather Olson did…but I have no reason to like the Swift's. Let's call a truce, but from now on, you Swifts stay out of my way. Now, the horse out there with your brother's body on it is yours… although it was probably stolen. So, take the horse and your brother and get out of my sight."

O'Grady watched until Roger Swift had led the horse away before saying, "That was kind of sudden."

"Was it? What if they were both involved? That question was never asked, and it didn't occur to me until the judge had dismissed the case. I'm not sure I'd trust Roger Swift any further than I would Alfred."

"But you didn't say anything."

"Too damned slow in the head. Speaking of heads, mine is killing me. I swear it's just going to explode."

McShannon overheard Bitter and said, "We have a very good doctor here. A Chinese fellow. Kam Wah Chung. He has a store in John Day City just north of the wagon road. Let me get my horse. I'll show you."

Bitter nodded thanks and mounted up. O'Grady was left to lead the packhorse. Bitter was too distracted by his headache to even notice.

⌒

KAM WAH CHUNG'S STORE WAS a bouquet of odors, spices, dried plants, and tea. The small man took one look at Bitter and pointed to a ladder back chair. He wasn't a doctor in the traditional sense, but he was the only healer within about a hundred and fifty miles. And people swore by him.

"Sit," he said. "Now…why have you come?"

Bitter pulled his hat off and gently rubbed the thatch of white hair growing along the groove on the left side of his scalp. "Ever since I was shot, I've been having headaches. And the scar is sore to the touch. Sometimes it hurts just to put my hat on."

Mister Chung used gentle hands to feel the scar, and when Bitter winced, he said, "You have something in there. Keeps the wound from healing. I think I should cut it out."

"Really?"

Chung smiled and said, "Unless you don't want it to get better."

"No. I guess we should find out what's in there. Go ahead. Work your magic."

Chung nodded and filled a basin with some of the warm water from the stove. Chung kept the water hot, ready for his tea. He took a bar of soap and a clean rag and gently washed Bitter's hair, especially along the bullet scar.

He handed Bitter a clean towel and said, "Dry, please." And then he walked behind the counter where a wall of shelves displayed medicines kept in what seemed like hundreds of small bottles. Chung selected one and set it on the counter, and then added a jar full of cottony looking material. He nodded and said, "Okay."

Chung's scalpel was a thin slice of nearly translucent obsidian. With deft hands he made a half-inch incision and, with a small pair of tweezers, extracted a tiny piece of wood maybe a half inch long and thin as a needle. He held it up for Bitter to see. "Now your wound will heal. Your doctor didn't get the wound clean." He handed Bitter a cloth. "Hold that on the cut until the bleeding stops."

Chung opened a jar filled with some type of oily looking paste and dabbed it on the incision. "For healing," he said. And finally, he opened the second jar and patted a spider web dressing over the wound. "No washing for five days." He added water to his tea pot and waited for it to heat again.

When John started to get up, Chung said, "Wait. I will give you some powder to take with you…for your headaches, but you drink some now. I'll give you an envelope with the medicine. Put a spoon of it in your coffee each morning. Add sugar, because it is sour to taste."

A knock on the door, followed by a grimy miner with his hand wrapped in a bandana interrupted Chung's instructions. O'Grady watched Chung gently pulled the miner's dislocated finger back in place and then wrap it back up with the bandana. "Do not use for three days," he scolded.

The man said thanks, turned and left without offering to pay.

Chung said, "He won't listen. He is too hungry to miss work."

Bitter felt a great sense of relief. At least I know what's been keeping my scalp sore. And maybe Mister Chung's medicine will take care of the headaches.

O'Grady said, "Mister Chung sure knows his business. Who would have thought that black obsidian was so sharp."

Chung said, "I learned it from the Indians."

When the sour tea was drunk, and a packet of the headache powder stuffed in his jacket pocket, Bitter fished a silver dollar from his pants pocket. Kam Wah Chung waved it away. "No need. Rest until tomorrow." Bitter put the coin on the counter anyway, and held out his hand. "Thank you. I'm feeling better already."

A man walked in holding his stomach and grimacing. "Mister Chung," he said, "I think I've been poisoned."

Bitter and O'Grady watched Chung sit the man down on the ladder back chair and ask, "Now. What did you eat last?"

✑

Bitter slept the afternoon away, and O'Grady took the time to find a bath. Dressed in his freshly laundered clothes, hair slicked up, boots polished, he left a note written on a scrap of brown paper bag. He placed it on Bitter's bundle of clean clothes. "Gone to Gibbon's. Back for dinner. I paid the girl for doing our clothes."

Bitter woke to the faint smell of Bay Rum aftershave, a scent associated with barber shops and a fresh shave. He rubbed the bristle on his cheeks. When he found the note and the clean clothes, he decided O'Grady had the right idea. He dressed in his dirty clothes and carried the bundle of clean clothes to the bath house across the street. Thirty minutes later, the dust and sweat of travel soaked off, Bitter put on his clean travel clothes, bundled his dirty clothes, strapped his gun belt on, and headed for the barber shop for warm lather and a sharp razor.

He followed a boardwalk past a building that was on its way to becoming a dry goods and mining supply store, stepped down to the dust of the street, and Roger Swift walked out between two buildings, his pistol cocked and ready. In a mild voice, he said, "I can't have you walking around thinking suspicious thoughts. And I can't have you killing any more Swifts."

Without thinking, Bitter took a step to his left and drew, all in one fluid motion. Swift's bullet cut the air where Bitter had been standing, and then Bitter shot him…about midway between his belt buckle and his chin. Swift had a look of disbelief that faded as he dropped his pistol, and then he fell face down in the dirt.

A man from across the street, a broom still in his hand said, "You all right, mister? I saw the whole thing." The man leaned his broom against the wall of his bakery and walked across the street. "He laid for you with his gun drawn and cocked. Why you ain't dead is a mystery I'll take to my grave."

"Would you mind sending someone to get Deputy Richards?"

"He's not our deputy. In fact, we don't have anyone doing police work in John Day City…not yet at any rate."

"Well, humor me. He is a deputy county sheriff and the actual sheriff until a new one is elected. That covers this town as well. And find an undertaker while you are at it."

"Who are you, mister?"

Bitter pulled the flap of his jacket back to reveal the star. The man said, "I know about you. You're that U.S. Marshal been hunting Alfred Swift. Saw it in the paper."

"Yes, and this is his brother."

"Why did he lay for you?"

"I think he was afraid I'd figure it out…that he was in on the shooting of the sheriff."

"You think so?"

"Can't prove it, but I'm pretty sure."

"I'll be back."

Deputy Richards rode up on a big black and white pinto and stepped down. "Okay, tell me what happened."

Bitter started to explain when the store owner interrupted. He pointed at Swift's body and said, "This guy, the dead man, laid for Marshal Bitter. Had his gun out and cocked. Marshal Bitter stepped aside and Swift missed. Marshal Bitter did not…although by rights we should be looking the marshal's corpse now instead of this one. Plumb unbelievable is what it is."

Deputy Richards said, "Sounds like self-defense to me." He looked at Bitter and said, "Not going to arrest you or charge you. But, wherever you go, you seem to wind up in some kind of shooting. I'll be glad to see you out of our town."

Bitter looked at him as he thumbed a shell into the empty chamber of his pistol. "And I'll be glad to be gone."

By sundown, patrons in every bar in town were hearing the story of how John Bitter, with blinding speed and a cool head, had faced a man who had his gun drawn and cocked. One man said, "I heard about him back in Missouri. He's sudden and he's fast."

"And accurate," another man said so quietly hardly anyone noticed.

The Wilcox Telegraph

SUPPER AT CHARLIE'S WAS TOPPED by another piece of blueberry pie, delivered without comment by Wilcox. He did refill their coffee cups without being asked.

McShannon smiled. "No doubt about it. Somehow or another you rank high in the Wilcox system of approval."

"What makes you say that?" O'Grady asked.

"Wilcox does not believe in giving away free coffee."

O'Grady looked disgusted. "If he doesn't talk, how in the world would you know that?"

McShannon grinned. "He's my ears. At the end of each day, he tells me what he hears, who to watch out for, who's claim jumping, who plans to rob my bank. That kind of thing. Because he doesn't say anything, people forget he's there, so they talk out of school. Saves me a lot of trouble."

"Huh," Bitter said. "I never heard such a thing, but I guess it would work at that. Crooks just aren't very smart. Otherwise, we'd never catch them."

Wilcox smiled as he walked up. "I heard that."

McShannon said, "Dagnabit, Wilcox, you're gonna spoil the game."

"Just thought the marshal and his friend should be very careful going home. Word is the marshal is carrying quite a bit of cash. Some folks would like to have that. And they think you'll go home soon."

With that Wilcox stalked off, his pockmarked face once again impassive.

"See what I mean?" McShannon said.

O'Grady and Bitter took time to clean their rifles and pistols and reload with fresh ammunition purchased at the local dry goods store. When Bitter pulled the .44 derringer from his jacket pocket, O'Grady just raised his eyebrows.

Bitter looked at him and said, "Took it from the kid that was fixing to ambush Owl and me. Somehow, I just feel better if people don't know I carry it. Call it my 'just-in-case' gun."

O'Grady nodded. "You always were one step ahead of everyone else."

"Sure. That's why I only got shot, not killed."

O'Grady ignored that bit of sarcasm and asked, "How's your headache?"

"Gone. Just gone. Forgot all about it."

"That doctor fella sure seems to know his business."

"Amen."

"Well, Marshal, what say we go buy what we need for the trail. I don't think the mercantile is open very late."

The Scouts

AT FIRST LIGHT, O'GRADY AND BITTER mounted up and led their pack horse, Brownie, quietly through the little town. They forded Canyon Creek and headed west, planning to reach the Dayville stage stop before dark. Neither had noticed the man hiding between two buildings a half block down the street. When Bitter and O'Grady rode by, he slipped back to where his horse was tied. He mounted and put his long-legged bay into a ground- eating canter.

The road was wide enough to allow the two friends to ride side-by-side. Bitter was quiet. Not brooding quiet. Relaxed quiet. And it was driving O'Grady nuts. He liked conversation. Even nonsense was better than silence. Finally, he said, "How's the head?"

"Slept like a baby. Didn't even wake up to pee."

"Doctor Chung's headache powder must work." He paused and grinned, "I wonder if it would work on a hangover?"

Bitter chuckled and said, "You are not getting any of this to try."

"Just a thought. You know, if you could come up with an easy cure for a hangover, you could get rich."

"And sell a lot more beer and whiskey at O'Grady's Pub."

"That, too."

Five miles of easy riding brought them in sight of the first river crossing west of John Day City. They rode warily, rifles across their knees. Trees crowded the river, and they both felt a nervous tension as the horses splashed across and up out of the river. But nothing happened.

When they were out in the open meadows again, Bitter slid his rifle back in the scabbard and stated the obvious. "I guess this wasn't the place where they plan to ambush us…if they are planning to. How much stock do you put in Wilcox's story?"

O'Grady said, "I think he's a damned good spy. He and McShannon are right. People who don't talk just fade into the background." He nodded, more to himself than Bitter, and added. "They'll try something between here and Dayville."

Bitter had a good memory and could picture each of the crossings they would have to make. "You remember the first crossing this side of Dayville? Lots of trees?"

O'Grady nodded. "I do."

"What if we don't cross there? Leave the road and skip that spot?"

"Or sneak in on the crossing from the north. I recall a low ridge that runs down close to the river there."

"I don't want to look for a fight, Liam. Just avoid one."

O'Grady grinned and said, "Not much fun in that."

They lapsed into silence for half an hour. Finally, O'Grady said, "You know, that old whore surprised the hell out of me when she shot Swift. But from what she told us, he had it coming."

Bitter looked at O'Grady and shook his head. "As if any of us deserves to die."

"Some folks don't leave you any choice, Marshal Bitter."

Bitter shook his head. "I just pray there isn't a third Swift brother someplace."

Indians, Maybe

As they neared the last John Day River crossing between Canyon City and Dayville, they swung northwest and rode up on a little ridge running south towards the river. They dismounted behind a thicket of juniper and tied the horses with enough rope to give them room to graze a bit.

Bitter slipped his rifle from the scabbard and fished his field glasses from a saddle bag. "Let's go take a look."

They settled on a grassy spot in the shade of a big juniper and took turns glassing the trees close to the crossing. A movement caught O'Grady's eye. Quietly he said, "I saw something move down there. See that big pine? Look just to the right of it."

Bitter adjusted the field glasses and brought the pine tree into focus. Then he said, "There's a horse there. I think you must have seen its ears moving. That's about all that's visible. Here, you take a look."

O'Grady adjusted the focus and studied the grove of trees. "I see another horse. Rusty colored."

"See any people?"

"No. But horses move around unless they're tied up. Those aren't moving. I bet they're tied." He scanned the area again and then stopped. "Ah. There they are, behind that big downed cottonwood. I see three of them."

"Do you suppose they are waiting for us?"

"Don't know that. They could be waiting for anybody as far as I can tell."

"Let's go pay them a visit."

Using the cover of the junipers, they slipped into the alder grove behind the men watching the road. When they were within about thirty yards, Bitter and O'Grady stopped and waited. The two former Army scouts, one from the Confederate Army and one from the Union Army, watched intently until they spotted a fourth man next to the big pine, watching the horses.

O'Grady pointed at himself and made a walking gesture with his fingers. Bitter nodded and watched O'Grady slip quietly down the hill in the direction of the horses. Ten minutes later, he stepped around the backside of the big pine and waved at Bitter.

Their flanking approach went undetected until Bitter stepped on a pine cone buried in about six inches of pine needles. The dry crunch had the three men who were watching the road turning and reaching for pistols. O'Grady's voice stopped them cold. "No. No, you don't. Draw and die. Now take your guns out carefully and drop them on the ground. And then back away."

One of the men, a skinny runt with a dark face that looked like he hadn't shaved in quite a while, a white-tipped eagle feather tied to a greasy braid falling alongside his face, said, "There's three of us and one of you." A thin weasel-faced man wearing a brown cowhide vest backed up a step and nodded. "That's right, Ollie."

Bitter startled them. "Not quite. Liam, I get the mouthy one. Which one do you want first?"

"Aw, hell, Marshal, that's the one I was fixing to shoot. Pick a different one."

Reluctantly, the men dropped their pistols and backed up. While Bitter covered them with his pistol, O'Grady searched them one-by-one. Except for a knife in a belt sheath, they had no weapons other than their revolvers and one carbine—probably stolen from the U.S. Army.

"Whew," O'Grady said, "You search the next bunch. These old boys are pretty ripe." He wrinkled his nose. "You boys ever hear of bathing?"

Bitter said, "Sit on the ground. On your hands."

The skinny one who might pass for an Indian–if he shaved–asked, "What you want with us?"

Bitter said, "I can't figure this out. Are you Indians trying to look like white men, or white men trying to look like Indians? I'm thinking you were going to rob the stage and let them blame the Indians for the robbery. Right?"

The third man whose brogue exposed him as Irish, spat and said, "Not me. I'm for finding honest work."

O'Grady said, "I'll get our other prisoner, and then we can get down to business."

At the end of fifteen minutes, the men hadn't budged. They would not admit to anything but resting their horses. When O'Grady asked them why they were hiding behind the log, the Irishman said, "Because the Indians are raiding the road."

Bitter looked at him and then laughed. "I knew the Irish would have an answer. O'Grady I can't think of a single reason to arrest these guys. I don't believe them, but let me go get our horses. I want another look at the posters. See if any of them match."

Plotting

MORGAN AND THE CHILDREN STAYED AN extra day in French Prairie. The boys made friends with a twelve-years old named Alex whose family lived neighbors with Owl and Woman. He seemed to know everything a twelve-year old boy should know. He showed Thomas, Ethan, and Mikey where an old beaver was working the willows to build a beaver house on a slough blocked from the main river by a low sand bank. The boys waited patiently for over an hour to be rewarded with the sight of the beaver paddling down the slough.

And Alex knew where the nesting bald eagles lived, and where the osprey built their nests, and he showed them his hideout in a big old oak tree, a tree house built from old scraps of lumber, tied together with wire and odd rusty nails. They had to climb a knotted rope to get up to the narrow door and into a slightly slanted room which was topped by an old piece of canvas with just the right number of holes.

The boys were impressed, and Mikey, after struggling up the rope climbed in and said, "Good. When it floods you can be safe up here."

"Nobody knows where this is," Alex said proudly. Ethan nodded and said, "We have a hideout near Abiqua Falls. We even used it once when Thomas ran away from the Dicksons. We'll show you when you come over."

Thomas nodded, and then Mikey piped up, because Ethan and Thomas has never taken him along, "Yeah, and old Owl found it without any problem."

Huffy, Ethan said, "That's because we didn't have a place to hide Josey."

Alex led them to a warm water pond where they skinny-dipped until sunset—diving and splashing, capturing turtles, and building a raft from drift wood, returning for supper about the time the bats appeared, dark against the evening sky, darting about, sweeping mosquitoes from the air over the river.

Alex said, "Gotta go before Ma gets mad."

"Bye," Mikey said, and Alex said, "See you later."

"Thanks," Ethan said, and Thomas waved goodbye to the barefoot boy running down the sandy path along the river.

Morgan looked at the wet heads and smiled. "Did you have fun?"

"Yep," Ethan said.

Sarah was learning to walk by holding on to Woman's hand. She pointed with a free hand and said , "Mikey, or something like that. For certain there was an "E" in there someplace.

Mikey jumped up and down and shouted, "She talked! She talked! She knows my name."

Ethan was less than happy about that, wanting to hear "Ethan" instead.

He walked over and knelt down and said, "Sarah, can you say Ethan?"

Sarah smiled and said, "Thin."

Thomas said, "Okay, Sarah, can you say Thomas?"

She pointed at him and said something that sounded more like "Mom" than "Tom," but Thomas was not disappointed. He was certain she knew him.

All in all, it was a grand time, and Morgan realized they needed to broaden their horizons.

They were outside, the boys on a swing Ethan and Thomas made from a rope tossed over a limb of the big Maple, when Owl walked down the lane.

He held his knobby, polished walking stick in his left hand and shook hands very formally with each of them, and said, "Boys," and then walked over to the cabin. Morgan and Woman sat just outside the door drinking apple cider, watching Sarah crawl after Woman's new kitten.

Morgan said, "How is Mister Beecher?"

"Gonna live, but he is a very poor patient. Won't do what I tell him to."

"Which is?"

"Rest, take a hot bath every day, and rest some more. His spine is okay. Not bent, but his back muscles are a very tied up…and very hard. He has cramped his back."

"Well," Morgan said, "I'm glad he'll be all right."

"Good thing you brought him home."

❧

BY EIGHT O'CLOCK THEN NEXT morning, the wagon was packed, two hours after Woman's rooster crowed and an hour after a breakfast of ham and eggs. Morgan gave Woman a hug and said very formally to Owl, "Thank you."

"You come and stay anytime, Morgan Bitter. Woman likes company."

❧

ALONG ABOUT FOUR IN THE afternoon, the mules pulled the wagon down the Bitter's farm lane.

"Ma," Mikey said, "there's a strange horse in front of the house."

Morgan touched the revolver hiding under a wool shawl on the wagon seat. "I wonder who it is?"

She recognized Mark Anthony as he walked back from the outhouse, and then Mikey was loping the red mare down the lane shouting, "Uncle Mark!"

Hugs all round and Sarah perched on Mark's lap at the sipping table, Morgan said, "All right, Mark Anthony, what's going on? You do know my husband resigned from the Pinkerton's."

Anthony smiled and nodded. "Yes. Our loss."

"You aren't trying to get him to go back, are you?"

"No. No, I'm not. I respect his wishes, but given the death of Representative Brown, a Republican, the imbalance between Democrats and Republicans in the state legislature has worsened. The Republicans very much need a solid citizen to join the ranks.

"The vacancy left by Brown means a special election. We…I mean the powers in Salem, including Tom Beecher, have put John's name in the pot. Any idea what he'll say to that?"

"He'll say no for certain. He's not political at all, except in cases of injustice. Then he can be very determined."

"I thought you would say that, but what if you urged him to run… for the good of the District…and for the good of the state?"

She mulled it over, wanting very much to have her husband home more. And she was tired of feeling vulnerable at night when John wasn't home, and she wanted him in a safer occupation. One war was enough.

She nodded slightly and then said, "You are a devious man, Mark Anthony."

He smiled and said, "It's one of my better qualities. So, you'll do it?"

"I don't know. All John wants to do is breed horses and stock a horse ranch." She paused and added, "We now own one hundred sixty acres just across Abiqua Creek from our place. That's enough to get him started."

"But you will tell him we plan to run him for office, won't you?"

"Yes, but I won't try to persuade him. It'll have to be his decision."

Anthony rose and handed Sarah to Morgan. "Thank you. I hate to run, but I need to get back to the Salem office. Thank you, Morgan."

She watched as he rode the lane to the county road out of sight. She sighed and struggled with the business of trying to think of what was good for John, what was good for the family, and what was in her heart.

Itinerants

BITTER FOLLOWED THE RIDGE BACK TO the horses and led them back down the hill. He stopped to untie the man O'Grady had walloped into a troubled sleep. Bitter held his hand on the butt of his pistol and motioned in the direction of the road. "You'll find your friends by that cottonwood log. You go first."

At first the four men were surly and uncooperative, but when Bitter held up wanted posters and looked at each man, the dark faced one, the one with the eagle feather said, "Hold on. Let me see that last one." He held it arm's length, a certain sign he needed glasses. "Walter Winston, wanted dead or alive, one-hundred dollars."

All four men studied the drawing, read the caption and nodded. The dark one said, "I know that guy. He's living on a claim near the top of Canyon Creek." He squinted at Bitter and said, "How do we collect the bounty?"

Bitter said, "Take him to the sheriff's office. They'll pay you."

"Even if he's dead?"

Bitter nodded. "But it's a lot nicer to transport a live prisoner than a dead one. The dead get to smelling pretty ripe."

O'Grady laughed. "The way these old boys smell, it wouldn't bother 'em none."

The Irisher said, "Will you knock that off. We haven't been where it's easy to bathe. Hell, we ain't had a meal since yesterday. Too broke to buy food."

O'Grady looked at him and nodded. "Where you from?"

"New York."

"I mean before that."

"Oh. County Cork."

"What brings you here?"

"You've seen the signs. "No Irish need apply." We was working on the railroad and heard of the gold strikes in this Oregon country. But we got here a bit too late. The gold is starting to peter out, and the claim we bought was dry. Worked for over three weeks and never found enough gold for a drink of whiskey."

"So. You thought robbing people was the thing to do?"

"No such thing. We were just resting and decided it was best to fort up."

Bitter shook his head. "Hard to believe."

He looked over at O'Grady and said, "What do you think?"

O'Grady grinned. "Let's feed them, and then I think I'll take this Irish lad to fist city. Just because."

The men gathered dry limbs for a fire, and dusted off cups from their saddle bags, waiting for the coffee pot to boil. Bitter dug into the packs on Brownie and handed cold biscuits to the men. They each said thanks and bolted the food. *Well*, he thought, *the part about being hungry is true.*

Seated on the log, the men shared two cans of beans without heating them, and then stared hungrily at the bacon in the skillet. The Irishman said, "Reminds me of the war. Old Grant pushed the rebels hard, but he pushed us hard as well. This is more than we had for days at a time. Supply just couldn't keep up."

O'Grady said, "What's your name, lad?"

"Darrin McGill."

"I'm Liam O'Grady, and this fine gentleman is Marshal Bitter."

The dark man would not give his name, but the husky one said, "Delbert Huff."

Bitter pointed at the third man. "And you?"

"Winston Merriweather, formerly of Boston."

Bitter nodded. "Long way from home."

"Sometimes I wish I was back there, but this country grows on a man. What I need is a job and a fresh start."

"Jumping U.S. Marshals is not the way."

"No. You got it wrong, but I don't suppose we could change your mind."

The men grew silent as they ate bacon and sopped the grease from the plates with more dry biscuits. Finally, Bitter softened. "Wait right here," and then walked behind the big pine where he undid his money belt and took out two twenty-dollar gold pieces."

He walked back and said, "Who minds the money in this crowd?"

Delbert said, "Winston. He comes from a rich family. Knows about money."

"Okay, then." Much to everyone's surprise, including O'Grady's, he handed Winston the two gold pieces. "If you can manage to make it to Sherar's Bridge, you'll find they are going to build a hotel. I think they will put you to work. And Mrs. Sherar makes a mighty fine pie.

"And listen closely. You will behave or you will find me hunting you. And I won't be so nice next time. We'll be leaving now. I'll leave your guns about a hundred yards down the road. You wait until we are out of sight before you make a move."

O'Grady hid a smile. He had seen Bitter in action and nice wasn't a word used to describe it, but this scene was simply unbelievable. *What does John see in these men that I don't?*

When the four felt it was safe, they found a small bar of lye soap in the grass next to their weapons. Winston held up the soap and smiled and said, "Well, there's a nice pool upriver. We could take turns."

✄

O'GRADY DIDN'T SAY A WORD until they were around the first bend. "What was that all about, Marshal Bitter?"

"Don't get cynical on me, Liam. Truth is I'm not sure, but three of those men seemed like solid citizens about to take the wrong step. Desperate men do the wrong thing sometimes. Maybe this will keep them from going bad."

"Think they'll actually go to Sherar's Bridge and ask for work?"

Bitter shrugged. "Maybe, or maybe they'll turn bounty hunter."

✄

THREE DAYS LATER BITTER AND O'Grady stopped to see the Sherars and stare at the foundation of the new hotel being built on the east side of the Deschutes.

Over a cup of coffee and piece of fresh baked apple pie, O'Grady said, "Impressive, Missus Sherar. Impressive. Might have to bring my wife back for a visit when it's done."

"If it's ever done. The problem," Jane Sherar said, "is we can't find enough workers to get the hotel built very quickly. Everyone is bent on heading for the gold fields, certain they'll find a bonanza and get rich."

Bitter smiled and said, "I believe there are three or four fellows about a day behind us that might need some work. I'm pretty sure I'd hire two of them, even if one is Irish."

O'Grady frowned and started to growl at Bitter until he saw the impish grin on Bitter's face.

Bitter said, "Where's your son, Orin?"

Jane shook he head and smiled. "He's gone courting. That Anna girl has him twisted around her finger, but we've grown to love her, too."

"That's a match that will probably work. Both come from good stock," Bitter said.

"Thank you, Marshal Bitter."

Resignation

Bitter and O'Grady stopped in Portland on their way home. Bitter said, "I need to talk with Judge Deady and turn in my badge."

O'Grady just said, "That shouldn't take long. I'll hold the horses and discourage the thieves who have taken up residence along Front Street."

"Now, who's being cynical?" Bitter said.

"It's not cynical to be realistic. I hear talk in the tavern." He grinned and added, "Some of which is true."

Judge Deady listened carefully while his clerk Marion Wilkes wrote Bitter's story down. When Bitter finished, Judge Deady said, "A very good report," and fished a wanted poster from a stack of papers on his desk. "Now, we will want you to find this man as well."

Bitter shook his head. "No, sir. I'll not do that. I said the last time we talked I would do this one job and that would be it. When Goldie shot Alfred Swift, my job was done."

Judge Deady shook his head and said, "Dammit, boy, we need men like you if we are going to civilize this state."

Bitter shook his head. "I think I've done my part...for now. My family needs me, and I have a new piece of land that needs tending. I'll be raising horses now. It's what I do best."

Judge Deady shook his head. "It's what you do second best. You are a natural law man."

"I had all the killing I need during the war. The rest of the trouble was brought to me. I didn't go looking for it."

"Didn't you? What about the search for Anna Franklin? I know her father, of course."

"That was a matter of just stumbling into a dangerous bunch of men. Old Owl told me Swift was a hater, but I was slow to believe it."

Deady looked at Wilkes who was faithfully scratching away, recording the conversation between Deady and Bitter. "Dammit, Wilkes, you don't need to take down this side conversation."

Bitter placed the letter signed by Deady and the silver badge on the edge of the desk. "Judge, I do appreciate the confidence you placed in me, but I'm resigning."

He stood up and Judge Deady rose and offered his hand across the desk. "Well, good luck young man. If you ever need a job, come calling. And, by the way, you have another one hundred dollars coming."

"Why?"

"That's the bonus I pay my marshals for dangerous, successful jobs." He turned to Wilkes and said, "Pay this man, and then get busy finding me another marshal."

Deady sat back down and picked up a file and started reading. Bitter half smiled and shook his head before walking out the office door.

Wilkes said, "The judge is miffed, but he'll get over it." He handed Bitter five twenty-dollar gold pieces. "Good luck," he said and held out his hand.

⁓

O'GRADY WAS SLAPPING ROCKFORD WITH his hat when Bitter emerged from the courthouse. He looked over at Bitter and said, "Blasted horse. He stepped on my foot and then tried to bite me."

Bitter laughed, partly because he was finally free of the burdens that went with being a Pinkerton and with being a U.S. Marshal, and partly because he was happy to see Rockford being his old self. "It's a sure sign of love, Liam. That horse loves me the same way. I was beginning to worry. He hasn't tried to buck me off for at least a month. I thought he was losing his spunk."

"Well, you get down here and take charge of this loving beast. We got to get out of here. Three people have tried to buy Appy and Rockford. I didn't like the looks of them. They might try to steal our horses."

"All right. Let's go catch the Corvallis and go home, Liam. And at the risk of sounding mushy, I'm glad you decided to ride with me. It made Morgan easier in her mind, and me as well. Now, the judge gave me a hundred dollars. A reward, he said, for a job well done. I'm going to split it with you."

"No need."

"I know that. I'm doing it all the same. Buy Ellie Ellis a nice wedding ring."

"You've never met her."

"Yeah, but I will. Count on it."

✍

THE CORVALLIS PUSHED IN AGAINST the loading ramp at the Wheatland Ferry landing, the wheel turning slowly while O'Grady led Brownie and Appy across the ramp. O'Grady turned and waved, and the Corvallis reversed and backed into the current before heading upriver to Salem. When the ship was at midstream, Captain Kelly pulled the whistle wire and listened to the pure sound echoing up and down the river.

He centered his ship in the channel and looked at Bitter who was sharing the pilot house with Kelly. "I hear O'Grady is getting married."

Bitter nodded and said, "That's what he says. Some nice woman named Ellie Ellis."

"Don't know her."

"Well, you'll have to come to the wedding. Then you can meet her."

Kelly made a correction with the wheel and nodded. "Tom Beecher loves weddings. Says it means the country is growing and getting civilized."

"Well…maybe he's right. Families are the glue that holds civilization together."

"That sounds mighty profound, John Bitter."

Bitter shook his head. "Just common sense, Captain Kelly. Just common sense. In the end, family and a few friends are all you have. The rest just doesn't matter much."

Horse Farm

Lucifer's braying alerted Morgan before she saw Bitter riding down the lane. She ran down the steps and into the yard when Bitter pulled Rockford to a halt at the barn. He was stripping the saddle from the big horse when she grabbed him from behind and squeezed so hard he thought his ribs would break. She said, "Are you still a U.S. Marshal?"

"Not on your life. I resigned early this morning."

She hugged him tighter and said, "Thank the Lord. I can stop worrying now."

He grinned and said, "Easy now, Morgan. I got to breathe."

She released him, spun him around and gave him a kiss that convinced him he made the right decision in quitting the U.S. Marshal Service.

Breath a bit short, she stepped back and said, "Hand me your saddle bags and your bedroll, and get Rockford tended to. I'll go fix something to eat…if you're hungry."

"All I've had today is some jerky and a cup of coffee on the Corvallis. Good coffee, but a little too thin to keep my appetite at bay."

He opened the corral gate and shooed Rockford inside. "You get a big bait of oats, you old flea bag." He studied the horse and decided he was going to need another horse to ride. "And you get turned out to stud, old timer. You've earned it. Some wild and wicked rides we've seen. It's kind of amazing that we're both still alive and in one piece."

Bitter set the saddle over a sawhorse set in the tack room for just that reason, hung the bridle on a peg alongside several other bridles, and hung the saddle blanket on a line so it would dry. When he banged the bucket scooping up a bait of oats, Rockford snuffled and stamped a foot. "Hold on, Rockford. I'll be right there."

When he walked into the corral to dump oats in the feed trough, Rockford nudged him with his nose.

"You get pretty friendly when it comes to food."

While Rockford lipped dry oats and ground them with his big teeth, Bitter rubbed him down with a piece of burlap sacking. The big horse actually leaned into Bitter, something he seldom did unless he was fixing to step on Bitter's toes.

Surprised, Bitter said, "I'd almost think you liked me some. And after all the times you tried to buck me off." And then he laughed.

A cup of hot coffee was sitting on Morgan's sipping table when he closed the man door to the barn and walked to the house.

Morgan peeked out and said, "Be quiet, now. Sarah is napping. There's hot water in the basin by the back door."

He splashed warm water on his face, ran his fingers through his hair, scrubbed his hands with soapy water and dried with a piece of cotton towel cut from a flour sack. It was a bit thin, but Bitter didn't mind. He was home.

He walked back and sat down at the sipping table. Morgan brought him a cold beef sandwich and a sliced apple, and then sat down opposite him. "Okay, then. Tell me what you've been up to."

He grinned and said, "Well, I stopped at the mill in Silverton."

"Why?"

"I wanted to see what a new house is going to cost us."

"Seriously?"

"You said you wanted one."

"I've thought about that. I think what I want is a bunkhouse for the boys, an extra room for Sarah and one for the new baby. I've also been thinking we can drill a well, and pipe water to the kitchen. That can all be done as we get the money."

"No new house?"

"Not yet, but in time. After our horse ranch makes us some money."

"Well…sounds good to me. Where are the boys?"

She pointed across the creek. "I have them fixing the fences on the Hill place. I haven't gone over to see how they are doing, but I hear some chopping and a hammer going, so I think they are still busy."

He grinned and said, "You know, when were kids, Luke and I knew how to make it sound like we were pretty darned busy when all we were doing was making noise."

Morgan laughed. "I'll bet you two were pure hellions."

"No. Just boys. How do they get over there?"

"They have to ride back to the county road, take the bridge on the Scott's Mill road and then ride back up the other side of the creek."

"Hmm. We'll have to fix that, build us a wagon bridge. I'll scout that out. Right now, I want to eat."

She waited while he ate the sandwich and crunched the apple slices. When he rocked back in the chair a bit, she said, "I have a surprise for you."

"You do?"

"Yes."

"Okay. What is it?"

"Walk out behind the barn and look in the upper pasture. You'll see it."

Mystified, he did as she told him. When he spotted a medium-sized roan, he stopped dead in his tracks. He shook his head in wonder. "What have you done, my love? That's one of the most beautiful mares I ever laid eyes on."

He walked back to the house and sat down just shaking his head. "Where did you get that beautiful mare?"

"I had nothing to do with it. A man brought her over from Salem two days ago." She handed him a folded note.

My dear friend, John,

Thank you for saving my daughter. It means more than I can ever say. The mare is a gift from my family to yours.

In friendship,
Peter Franklin

p.s. I'll send the pedigree papers by post, soon. Breed wisely, keep records of the studs you use and the mares, where they came from, who owned them, their names, the birth date of each foal, everything you can find out. The records will become extremely valuable over time.

Bitter looked at his wife and nodded. "This is the true beginning of our horse farm, Morgan."

She reached across the table to take his hand. "You deserve it, John Bitter, and I'll help anyway I can. Now tell me about your trip. Did you find Swift?"

As succinctly as he could he related the details of the trip, about Goldie shooting Swift, about Kam Wah Chung and the splinter in his scalp and the spider web dressing and the headache powder, about the four men he and O'Grady fed on the way home, about Judge Deady trying to persuade him to stay on, about O'Grady and Ellie Ellis, and about his decision to put Rockford out to pasture. The only part he left out was Roger Swift trying to kill him. He felt a momentary pang of guilt because he and Morgan had always been totally honest with each other.

And then he changed his mind. "One other thing I didn't want to mention. I didn't shoot Alfred Swift, but I did shoot his brother. He laid for me, but while he was busy talking, I was busy shooting. Got lucky again."

A little voice from inside the house saying, "Mama, Mama," interrupted the tale. Morgan got up and said, "We can continue this tonight. Since Sarah is awake, I think I'll call the boys home."

The Big Cat

THE BOYS SPENT THE MORNING REPLACING broken rails in the split rail fence on the Hill farm or stacking the ones back up that had fallen from where they were intended. They were proud of the job. "That'll keep the horses in," Mikey had said while he tried to pull a small sliver from the heel of his hand.

"Won't keep Lucifer in," Ethan said. "He can jump that…easy."

"Yeah, but the horses don't know they can jump a fence," Mikey said.

Thomas said, "See that big old maple down by the creek. I bet we could build us a tree fort down there. Maybe bigger than the one Alex built. Let's go see."

The faint clang of the iron triangle hung on the front porch of the house echoed across Abiqua Creek and out to the meadow where the boys were eyeballing the maple tree, mentally trying to match the old boards they found behind the barn with the span of two big limbs about eight feet off the ground.

Rusty, curled in the grass, soaking up the sun, raised his head and sampled the air, trying to catch a scent to let him know what was happening.

Ethan said, "Sounds like Mama wants us home. I wonder what's going on. Pretty early for supper."

Mikey said, "I think Pa is home."

Thomas shook his head, "How do you know these things, Mikey?"

The boys rounded up their horses—Thomas on old Misery, Mikey on the red mare, and Ethan on Josey—and forded the creek in a shallow they had found. Rusty stared at the water, dipped a paw and then finally just leaped in and paddled across. His distaste for moving water was pretty strong since his experience on the White River.

The boys laughed when he shook himself off, filling the air with a stinky dog mist. Mikey said, "You need a bath, Rusty."

When they trotted their horses down the lane past the orchard, Lucifer played his usual game of charging the fence. Josey laid her ears back and bared her teeth at him.

Mikey laughed. "Josey doesn't like Lucifer charging the fence. And Lucifer doesn't care whether she does or not."

Ethan said, "I think that's Pa sitting on the porch."

Mikey yelled, "Yippee," and dug his heels into the red mare who broke into a gallop straight for the house. Thomas and Ethan just shook their heads and watched. Mikey was prone to falling off, and they waited to see if he would make it to the house this time without bouncing off the ground.

Mikey pulled the red mare to a stop—without falling off—and dropped to the ground. "Pa," he said, and ran up the steps and into Bitter's waiting arms.

Ethan and Thomas were more formal. After unsaddling and turning their horses into the upper pasture to keep company with Rockford and the new mare, they walked over to the porch, each offering a calloused hand to shake with Bitter. "Glad you're home, Pa," Ethan said.

"Me, too," Thomas added.

"I'm glad to be here, by gollies. I want you to know the lazy days are behind us. I quit the Pinkerton's and the U.S. Marshal Service. Now we're going to build a horse ranch." He paused and then said, "How's the fence building coming?"

Proudly, Ethan said, "We got all of the fence around the big pasture done. Had to cut and drag some poles to patch a spot or two, but the place is in pretty good shape."

"Good. After supper let's ride over there and you can show me this farm your mother bought us."

Rusty caught Rockford's scent and followed it to the upper pasture. Horse and dog sniffed, and then Rockford went back to cropping grass while Rusty curled up in the meadow and soaked the sun, content to be with Rockford again.

The new mare grazed her way warily toward Rockford. Rockford suddenly raised his head, ears forward, looking beyond the mare. Alerted, Rusty gave a low growl. He couldn't see what Rockford was staring at, but an errant breeze brought him the scent of a cougar. It was an unfamiliar scent, but he knew it instinctively for an enemy.

Rockford watched the tawny animal slip down the fence line, stop and stare at the horses. Rusty inched forward in the grass, and then both Rockford and Rusty walked across the pasture toward the fence.

When he was within about thirty yards of the fence, lips pulled back, teeth exposed, Rockford whinnied a challenge and charged straight at the big cat, Rusty barking, running with him.

The cat turned and bounced back into the band of trees flanking Abiqua Creek just as Rockford and Rusty cleared the fence and gave chase.

If the cat had been older, he might have gotten away, but he was spooked and climbed the closest tree he could find, an old oak with a big limb about twenty feet off the ground and that's where the cat stayed, hissing and growling at his tormentors below.

Rusty barked and then bayed three times, circling the tree, anxious to tangle with the cat. Rockford backed away and stood still, ears forward, eyes locked on the cat.

The barking of the big hound, coupled with the sound of hoof beats brought Bitter from the house, rifle in hand, Ethan with his rifle right behind him.

"What's going on, Pa?"

"Something's wrong. Let's go see." Bitter sprinted to the upper pasture gate, saw the new mare, head alert staring upstream. "Rockford's gone! You don't suppose Rockford jumped the fence?"

"He can, Pa. I've seen him."

They climbed over the upper fence and followed the sound of Rusty's baying. Short of breath, Ethan panted, "I never heard Rusty do that."

"I think he treed something. He's not moving off."

About two hundred yards upstream, they found Rockford and Rusty. "Easy boys, easy now. What have you got?"

Ethan pointed at the big limb on the oak tree and said, "It's a cougar, Pa. They've treed a cougar."

"Call that dog over here and hold him. And back Rockford away. I'm going to shoot the cat, and I hope he's dead when he hits the ground. If not…there could be hell to pay."

Thomas, his voice sounding a little winded from his run through the pasture, said, "I've got Rockford," and looped a short piece of cord around the horse's neck and tugged him a few steps back. Ethan wrapped an arm around Rusty's neck and hung on.

Unblinking, the cat watched Bitter line up the sights and squeeze the trigger.

Ethan and Thomas flinched when the cat's body thumped into the grass below the tree limb, but there was no doubt it was dead.

Rusty growled and sniffed at the cat, and Thomas prodded the yellow corpse with the toe of his boot. He said, "You gonna skin it, Pa?"

Bitter shook his head. "No. We'll just leave it. Might help scare off any other cougars in the neighborhood."

"Can I have the hide?"

"What for?"

Thomas looked at Ethan and said, "It'll look good in our tree fort."

"Do you know how?"

"Sure. I watched the Cheyenne women skin animals a lot of times. You start on the inside of the legs and go from there. Me and Ethan can do it."

"Okay. Go ahead. I'll take some rails down so we can get Rockford back in the pasture. And then I'll go tell your mama what the fuss was about." He squinted slightly at Rockford, a thoughtful look painted on his face. "Rockford, who in the world ever heard of a horse treeing a cougar…or chasing one for that matter."

Skinning

T HE SILENCE FOLLOWING THE SHOT WAS slowly replaced by the normal sounds of the land along Abiqua Creek. A dove cooed in a big cottonwood down along the creek, house sparrows chirped again, and a calf bawled over on Ezra and Ruth's place. Bitter could hear the murmur of talk from Thomas and Ethan as they worked to skin the animal. Two quail called from the hedgerow along the county road.

His boots pushing tall meadow grass aside, he slipped through the pasture gate. Morgan sat on the porch, Sarah on her lap, and a pistol played hide and seek under a dish towel on the sipping table. Mikey jumped off the porch and ran over to Bitter.

"What was it, Pa?"

"By gollies, Rusty and Rockford chased a young cougar and treed it."

"Did you shoot it?"

"I did."

"Can I go see it?"

"Sure."

Morgan said, "We'll all go."

⌇

AN HOUR LATER, BITTER HELPED Ethan and Thomas nail the hide to the back of the barn to let it dry. Thomas said, "I think I can cure it like the Cheyennes did."

Bitter hid a smile and nodded. "Okay. Give it a try."

Ethan said, "Pa, do you suppose there's any more cougars hanging round?"

Bitter shrugged. "I don't know. Maybe. Ezra tells me he knows a hound man. We might just invite the hound man to hunt around here and see if he can scare another one up. In the meantime, carry your rifle. And Thomas should carry Morgan's carbine."

He looked at Thomas and said, "I need to get you a proper rifle. I'll tend to it the next time I stop in Silverton. In the meantime, both of you get a bar of soap and go wash up in the creek. You look like you've been in a knife fight. Blood all over your hands."

Mikey huffed and crossed his arms. "What about me?"

"Well, let's see, in about three years when you turn ten, I'll get you a rifle. In the meantime, we'll teach you to shoot Ethan's light Clemens rifle. Okay?"

"Boy, I'll be glad to grow up."

Truth Time

AT THE SUPPER TABLE, ETHAN SAID, "Pa, we saw some folks looking the Hill Farm over. Me and Thomas think maybe we should start sleeping over there. Keep a lamp on at night, build a fire. Make it look like somebody lives there. Might be good to put Josey and Misery in the pasture."

Before Morgan or Bitter could object, he added, "We'd take Rusty with us. And we found a shallow place to cross the creek if we need to."

Morgan looked at Bitter with raised eyebrows. He nodded and said, "You know, boys, that's a fine idea. Keep any squatters out until Uncle Harley gets here. I'm thinking we'll move him and Sarah in on the Hill place when they get here."

"You'll needs blankets," Morgan said. "Did the Hills leave a lamp?"

Ethan shook his head. "No, they didn't."

"We'll hitch a couple of mules to the wagon and get you set up proper," Bitter said.

Mikey didn't say anything until it was clear he was being left out "I'd like to go too."

Bitter shook his head. "I need you here, Mikey. I just can't spare you. Somebody has to watch Sarah and help me work the horses." He paused. "We'll bring one of the yearling foals back from Ezra's so you can train it. Deal?"

Mikey nodded. "I guess so."

❧

Two hours later the boy's bedding was unloaded, a water bucket and a dipper sat inside the kitchen door, and a cupboard held bread, cheese and jerky. Bitter grinned and said, "Well, boys, come to breakfast. We'll see you in the morning."

Ethan said, "We'll keep the squatters out, Pa."

Bitter hid a smile and said, "I'm counting on you."

Mikey said, "Bye," with a sad note in his voice.

Ethan gave him a hug and said, "See you in the morning, Mikey."

Sarah waved her fingers in imitation of a goodbye and managed to make a noise that had the cadence and intonation of some kind of English. Somewhere in there they all heard "Thin" and "Moss."

Mikey laughed and said, "She's talking now."

They climbed in the wagon and Morgan looked over the yard of the Hill's farm and decided it sure enough looked occupied. The yellow light of a coal oil lamp lit the kitchen windows and a thin column of smoke wrapped around the chimney and drifted out across the meadow. When Rusty started to follow the wagon, Bitter said, "Stay, Rusty."

Confused, the dog retreated to the stoop of the Hill House and watched the wagon until it was out of sight.

Worriedly, Morgan said, "Do you think they'll be all right?"

"Safer than on the Oregon Trail, I'd say."

"I sure hope so."

∾

THAT EVENING, AFTER MIKEY HAD gone to his bed in the loft and Sarah was asleep in her crib, Morgan and Bitter sat at the sipping table with a cup of coffee.

"John, I've something to tell you. Actually, two somethings. First, you should know Mark Anthony rode over from Salem. Someone named Jones died and left a vacancy in the Legislature. That means a special election.

"Some of the leading politicians…and that includes Representative Franklin and Tom Beecher…are going to run you as the replacement for Jones."

Bitter looked startled. "Hell, I won't do it."

"I told them that would be your answer, but Mark insisted they would run you for office anyway. He tried to talk me into persuading you, but I said I would not. You would have to make up your own mind."

"Well, you can tell them I have made up my mind. I'm going to be a horse breeder and a stay-at-home husband and father."

"There is this other news you should hear before you make up your mind. While you were gone, Doc Hardy sent Ezra to Salem to pick up some kind of machine. A boring machine, I think. Something to do with making rifle barrels.

"Anyway, three white men got to cussing Ezra and picked a fight. They kept saying things like 'Nigger, go back to the South' and other things. When one of them tried to punch Ezra, he simply caught the man's fist in his big hand and squeezed. I'm told he broke every bone in the man's hand. One of the others pulled a knife and Ezra cut himself taking the knife away. And then he knocked the other men out."

Bitter shook his head. "Only three of them?"

"Only three."

"That might not be enough."

"Well, it wasn't, but Ezra was arrested and jailed overnight. Doc Hardy got him out the next morning, and a witness talked to the sheriff. Said the three who tackled Ezra started the whole thing."

"Well, I'm glad he's okay. The cut must not have been too bad."

"It wasn't, and he's back at work at Doc Hardy's blacksmith shop, but there is a sentiment going around that doesn't make much sense. As a State, we are anti-slavery, but the State Assembly tried to pass an exclusion act, banning all blacks from living here."

"What?"

"As Mark explained it, during the war, the Republicans held a majority, but with the end of the war the Democrats have gained popularity and now hold the majority. Jones sided with the Republicans, so naturally the Republican leaders want to replace him with another Republican."

"I'm not Republican."

"No, but you are not a Democrat either. If those folks have their way, they will forcibly remove any black people living here. That must not happen."

"Well, damn. I just want to farm and raise horses."

"Something else to consider, the legislative sessions are held for sixty days every two years. They start in October. That's not much to give up." She paused, "And it's a lot less time than you have been spending as a Pinkerton…and a U.S. Marshal."

Bitter sipped his coffee and stared at the gathering twilight. He took a deep breath, and then said, "Why me?"

Morgan gave him a slow shake of her head. "John Bitter. You don't really know the impact you have on other people, do you?"

"I guess I don't."

"You are the one person everyone looks to when something needs done. You act. Others wait for you to lead." She teased, "Who else mounts up and charges a band of Indians all by himself out in the middle of nowhere."

"I had to. O'Grady and Hackett's horses were about done."

"Exactly. They needed you, and you did what you had to."

Bitter was silent for a few minutes, and then he said, "I'll go see Ezra in the morning. I need to bring those horses he's holding for me back down to the Hill 's place. We'll pasture half of the fields and cut the other half for hay."

"How many horses do we have now, John?"

"Oh, let me see. There's the eight Luke left me…and two yearling foals. That's ten. Ezra has them on one of his pastures. And then there's Josey, Misery, Rockford, the red mare Franklin gave us, and the red mare I took from the outlaws. That makes fifteen, plus, the six wagon mules and Lucifer."

"Looks like a good start."

"It is, but I might have to take the boys and go chase some wild horses in that Tygh Valley country next summer."

She smiled. "You'll probably need to do that."

Persuasion

Ezra was headed for the back door with a galvanized pail of fresh, warm cow's milk when Bitter rode into the yard. He set the pail down on the back stoop and waited until Bitter swung down and ground hitched Rockford.

Quietly Ezra said, "You're up kind of early, John."

"I am, Ezra. Wanted to catch you before you headed to work."

"You managed that. Just got Queeny milked." He stopped and said, "Ruth heard a rifle shot yesterday afternoon. You know anything about that?"

"You won't believe this, but Rocky and Rusty treed a cougar. I heard Rusty baying and went to take a look. I shot it."

"And good riddance. Think it was alone?"

"Hard to tell. You don't suppose you could get your friend with the hounds to come and hunt the area, do you?"

Ezra laughed. "It would cost you a fifth of good whiskey."

"I'll give him two fifths if he'll do it."

"Okay. Next time he stops at the smithy, I'll talk to him." Ezra paused and said, "Is that why you came so early in the day? Or do you have something else on your mind?"

"I do. Beecher has been messing with my life again. First the U.S. Marshal business and now this."

Ezra studied his friend and then smiled. "Must be pretty awful, whatever it is. Let me see the wounds."

"Don't make fun, Ezra. This is serious."

Ezra poured an inch of the warm milk from the bucket into an old wash basin for the barn cats who were busy circling his boots. He pushed one aside with the toe of his boot and then pulled the screen door open.

Ezra set the milk on a table on the back porch by Ruth's newest gadget, a marvel of technology that separated the cream from the milk. When she cranked the handle, the milk spun inside a bright copper pipe with a coil of copper tubing that drained the milk off. Ruth had a few local customers for her milk, cream, and butter. She was open to trade, but she liked coins best.

Ezra pushed the kitchen door open and said, "Ruth, look who's come calling."

The smell of fried potatoes, eggs, ham and white bread toasted on top of Ruth's wood cook stove made Bitter's stomach rumble. "Sure smells good in here."

Ruth turned from the stove and said, "Why John Bitter. Come here and give me a hug. We haven't seen you for a month of Sundays. Come to think of it, we haven't seen you in church much either."

Ruth's head just about made it to the top of John's shoulder—if she stood on a low stool. He gave her a hug and ignored her comment about his churchgoing. "How's the new reverend working out?"

"Reverend Jackson. He's God fearing and preaches a good fire and brimstone sermon. You should come see for yourself. We're having a baptism next Sunday."

Bitter stepped back and looked at the small black woman. "Morgan told me you are expecting."

"Does it show?"

"In a beautiful way, Ruth. In a beautiful way."

"All right you two," Ezra said. "That's enough billing and cooing. John's got something to talk over."

Without asking if he was hungry, Ruth set two plates of eggs, potatoes, ham, and stove toasted bread on the table. "Sit."

"I know Ezra has to get to work, so I'll try to make this short. It seems that Tom Beecher has put me up as a candidate for the State Legislature. I was fixing to turn it down when Morgan told me what happened to Ezra in Salem."

Ezra frowned and said, "Why would that make a difference?"

"When I heard about the exclusion law, it got my attention. We can't have that."

Ruth looked at Ezra, concern painted on her face. "Tell him, Ezra."

Ezra sipped his coffee and then set the cup down. "There aren't a lot of black folks in Oregon...maybe fifty or so...all freedmen. The folks in Corvallis are pretty much okay with us living there. And the folks in Silverton…with a couple of exceptions…are friendly. In fact, a couple of white families make the drive out to our church on Sunday. They say they like our brand of religion.

"But the word I get from Uncle Reuben is we best stay out of Southern Oregon. And Portland isn't a whole lot better."

"I didn't know that."

"Well, Ruth and I don't talk about it much, so I'm not surprised." He paused and then said, "You think you can win the election?"

"Beats me. Beecher and Mark Anthony seem to think so."

Ruth said, "I know I'd feel a whole let better if you were there."

Bitter speared a bite of ham with his fork and then set the fork down. "I don't know if I'd have any influence if I did get elected."

Ezra laughed. "With Tom Beecher and his friends behind you? Of course you would. It isn't what you know as much as who you know when it comes to politics."

"How do you know this, Ezra?"

"Well, my great grandfather was a house servant. He kept his ears open and his mouth shut. After a while, the owners just forgot he was there. And when they talked about politics, he listened. That's how I know it's who you know that counts."

He watched the frown on his friend's face, saw it relax, and knew Bitter had his mind made up. "Well?"

Bitter gave Ruth and Ezra a rueful smile and said, "You know when I found Ethan fishing for bass on a Missouri slough with stinging worms, I sensed a change in my plans, and when he brought Mikey to my campfire, I knew I'd have to rethink my trip over the Oregon Trail. This feels like another one of those changes. I just got used to the idea of being a horse breeder, and then this comes up."

Ruth poured Bitter a fresh cup of coffee and patted his hand. " 'The Lord works in mysterious ways, his wonders to perform.' "

"Wonders. That's an interesting word. The Lord has sure got me to wondering." Bitter laughed and picked his fork back up, the food suddenly tasting better. "By the way, Liam is getting married. I'm to be his best man, but he hasn't told me when I'm to do that."

Ruth frowned and then said, "Well, good for him. Maybe a good wife will make him stop drinking."

"How does that go, Ruth? 'Judge not...'?"

"I just worry for him, is all."

Davey, looking taller than his seven years, eased into the kitchen and slid onto a kitchen chair.

"Morning, Davey."

"Morning, Mister Bitter."

"You get taller every time I see you. Mikey is going to be jealous if you get to be taller than he is."

Davey smiled and said, "I already am."

⌇

ON THE RIDE BACK HOME, Bitter decided he had best go see Tom Beecher—find out what he had in mind. He unsaddled Rockford, turned him back into the pasture and watched the big horse arch his neck and sniff the air. "Looking for another cougar, Rockford?"

The two red mares looked up and watched Rockford as he began grazing, taking a slow step at a time in their direction.

"I've got to find another horse to ride. Some horse breeder, I am," he snorted, "Don't have but one saddle horse of my own. Need to fix that."

The smell of fresh coffee greeted him when he pushed through the door into the log house the Bitters called home. Morgan set a cup on the table and filled it from her blue granite coffee pot.

"Breakfast?"

"Thanks, but Ruth fed me."

Morgan sat across from Bitter and waited.

"You know," he said, "if people would just mind their own business and leave other people alone, we wouldn't need a legislature. Well, maybe for taking on projects too big for a single person…roads and bridges…that type of thing. And for defense, I guess."

Morgan nodded. "We still need some rules for the sticky things, though."

"Sticky things? Like what?"

"Inheritance, land ownership, divorce…those kinds of sticky things."

"I guess." He paused, and then said, "I need to go see Beecher, find out how this thing works. Maybe we should all go."

Morgan shook her head. "No. We need to do what we are doing. It's past time to cut the suckers away from my fruit trees. I'm going to put the boys on that this morning."

"Why don't you wait. We'll tackle that first thing when I get back."

"Make it a quick trip, then."

A Short Race

ROCKFORD WAS MORE INTERESTED IN MARES than in making another trip away from the farm, and he showed his displeasure when Bitter threw a saddle on him and mounted up. Rockford sidestepped and then went to bucking. This was a game both rider and horse understood.

Bitter swatted Rockford between the ears with his hat, and said, "Go ahead, you old flea bag. Do your best."

Rockford twisted, humped up, came down stiff legged and pitched forward with his head as close to the ground as he could get. Bitter just grinned and pulled hard on the reins, taking control, just like the first time he rode Rockford. No one had ever ridden the beast until Bitter chose him from a small herd of cavalry mounts. He and Rockford rode unharmed through the last year of the war, and when he mustered out, he bought Rockford with his mustering-out pay. The horse wrangler had said, "Good riddance."

Bitter heard Mikey shout, "Ride him, Pa! Ride him!"

Bitter sensed Rockford didn't have his heart in the fuss, and when Rockford just stopped and waited, Bitter patted his neck and said, "Okay, old timer. Let's get to moving."

Rockford was long legged and had a ground eating pace he could keep up all day without seeming to tire, but Bitter felt the ride in his bones when pulled the big horse to a stop in front of O'Grady's pub. He sat and looked at the shamrock sign and the polished windows. "Nice," he said to no one in particular.

O'Grady came to the door, a bar rag in his hand and said, "A bit early for the wedding, John."

Bitter swung down and shook hands. "Came to see Beecher."

"About running for office?"

"Yes. You heard, I guess."

"Might keep you from getting shot."

"Might at that, Liam. You know if Beecher is home?"

"He's not. He is inside sipping on his morning tea."

"Tea?"

"Yes. Owl has him drinking some kind of brew he calls tea. Says it's good for Beecher's back. Personally, I think a hot toddy would work better."

"It might. If he was Irish."

"Well," O'Grady said, pointing at the pub, "What do you think?"

"It's nice, Liam. I'm proud of you."

"Come on in."

Beecher sat at a back table near the cold fireplace, grimacing as he took another drink of Owl's tea. Bitter walked over, hand outstretched, and smiled. "You'd think Owl could brew something that tasted better. Wait until you've tried his willow bark tea."

Beecher folded Bitter's hand in his big paw and pushed a chair out with his boot. "So far, he's managed to take the fun out of my life." He held the glass out and gave the brew a scowl. "He has this notion that whiskey will make my back worse, but I'm about to try that instead of this foul stuff." And then he laughed." I suppose you've come to thank me for running you for office?"

"That wasn't exactly my intent. In fact, I said no the first time I heard about this ridiculous scheme." A note of exasperation in his voice, he said, "That was before I heard about this exclusion law business. That's got to be stopped."

O'Grady set a beer down in front of Bitter and sat down. "I'd shoot any sonofabitch that tried to run Ezra and Ruth out of the state."

Beecher nodded. "It does need to be stopped. To do that we need more Republicans in the Legislature. That's why we picked you, John Bitter."

"I'm not a Republican. For that matter I'm not a Democrat either. I'm a horse breeder."

"And a principled man. The kind we need leading the fine people of Oregon regardless of which party you belong to."

"Okay. I'm in, but I have no idea what that even means."

"The Democrats have picked someone they think is a shoo-in, so he'll not be doing much campaigning. Just rest on his laurels. That's where you come in. My older son, Ira, is in the newspaper business. He's going to write a series of articles about you, your rise from private to Captain during the Civil War, your service as a U.S. Marshal… create a picture of a responsible farmer and family man. All of it true, by the way. And it doesn't hurt to be Luke Bitter's brother. Luke isn't going to run for office, but he has a lot of powerful clients who will vote for you simply because you are his brother.

"Franklin and several of his political friends will endorse you, as well. And I have the Governor and Judge Deady lined up. That should get you the votes you need."

"I don't need to tour the district. Give stump speeches?"

"This is going to be a quick election. The voting takes place next week. Next time, you'll need to campaign."

Bitter looked grim and said, "There isn't going to be a next time."

Beecher smiled and said, "We'll see."

"Okay. I guess I'll find out how it all works. Right now, what I need is a good saddle horse until I get some of my younger ones broke to ride. Old Rockford needs a rest. I'm just going to put him out to stud and let him get fat and lazy."

Beecher looked at O'Grady. "Didn't Oliver Johnson talk about having a horse for sale? A big buckskin gelding?"

O'Grady nodded. "He said he wanted a hundred dollars for it."

Interested in what a hundred-dollar horse looked like, Bitter said, "Where is this horse?"

Beecher rose and said, "I'll walk to the house and send one of the grandkids to the Johnson place. Have Oliver bring the horse up so you can look it over."

"Obliged."

O'Grady said, "Now, since this business meeting is over, I'd like you to meet my intended."

"She's here?"

O'Grady sounded a bit defensive when he said, "Yes. She works here. She keeps the books and fills in when necessary."

Bitter grinned and said, "Aha, I see what happened."

"Nothing of the sort. We just became friends and then…ah… well…" O'Grady stammered, "she just sort of grew on me. I can't think of not having her nearby."

"I think that's called love."

"Might be."

Ellie looked up from the ledger she was working on when O'Grady opened the office door. She pushed a lock of luxuriant dark brown hair back in place, and then closed the ledger. "Ellie, I want you to meet my friend, John Bitter."

She stood up, smiled, and reached across the desk to take Bitter's hand. "The famous U.S. Marshal Bitter. I've been curious about you. Liam insists you saved his life."

"I wish Liam would let that tale rest."

Ellie nodded and changed the subject. "I have some good Irish stew on the stove. Let's have lunch."

"First, I need to take care of Rockford."

She nodded. "There's a corral around back. Help yourself to the hay."

A Hundred-Dollar Horse

Bitter was scraping the bottom of his second bowl of stew and eating another slice of warm yeast bread when a tall, lanky man pushed through the front door of O'Grady's pub.

He wore a leather vest over a blue denim shirt, black cotton britches, dusty boots, and a flat brimmed black hat. O'Grady looked up and said, "Oliver, my lad. Come meet my friend, John Bitter."

Bitter rose and shook hands. "Pleasure."

"Oliver Johnson, at your service. I'm told you are looking for a good saddle horse."

"I might be."

"Well, I've got one tied outside if you'd care to come and look."

"I would."

Bitter stood on the porch and looked the big horse over. *Maybe sixteen hands*, he thought. *Looks sound. Maybe six or seven years old. I wonder why Johnson wants to sell him.*

Johnson looked sideways at Bitter and said, "You may be asking why I want to sell this fine animal, and I'll tell you. He has a mean streak and is prone to bite you, step on your foot and buck you off if he can. But…if you want a stayer that can run like the wind and keep going all day, that's Alamo for you."

"Alamo?"

"Yep. He's a Texas horse and the name just stuck."

"Are you a horse trader?"

Johnson grinned, "After a fashion."

"Good. I'm breeding horses out on Abiqua Creek. I plan to have some ready for sale next year."

"Come see me."

"I might at that. Now, about this horse, I'd like to ride him before I make an offer."

"You mean before you buy him for one hundred dollars."

Bitter shook his head, "No. I mean before I even think about making an offer."

They led the horse around to the corral in back of the pub where Bitter's saddle straddled the top rail. Johnson clamped a fist around Alamo's ear while Bitter slipped the bridle over his head and pushed the bit in the big horse's mouth. Alamo just stood there when Bitter threw the saddle blanket on his back, but he humped up a bit when Bitter set the saddle in place and pulled the cinch tight. Bitter kneed him in the ribs and the big horse let out a breath, and Bitter pulled the cinch two inches tighter.

He grinned at Johnson. "Uncooperative brute, isn't he?"

Johnson just nodded and then said, "I'd get away from the corral before you mount up. He likes to smack your legs against the corral if he can. And watch any low hanging limbs. He'll cut right under one to scrape you out of the saddle."

Bitter frowned, "And you still want a hundred dollars?"

"Yep. He's what you might call an outlaw horse. Not that's he's killed or hurt anybody very much. He's just the kind of horse an outlaw would want if he was trying to outrun the law. He's game."

Bitter just said, "Let's see." Johnson held Alamo's head down while Bitter stepped aboard, and when Bitter was ready, Johnson turned loose and stepped back. Ellie, Liam, and Beecher got there just as the fun began. Alamo bucked, swapped ends, and slammed against the corral. Thanks to Johnson's warning, Bitter got his leg out of the stirrup and up out of the way. He swatted the big horse between the ears, pulled Alamo's head up and kicked him into a gallop down the road and out of sight.

Old Alamo was dripping wet when Bitter loped him back up the road. Bitter stepped down, took the saddle off and went to rubbing that horse down with a burlap bag. The horse leaned into him. Johnson was surprised, because it looked as if the horse liked the attention Bitter gave him.

Bitter never said a word to Johnson, just dug out a hundred dollars and handed it to him. Then he said, "I'll keep this one."

Later, O'Grady asked Bitter why he wanted a horse that rough, and he said he needed him to chase the wild horses in that Bake Oven and Tygh Valley country. But O'Grady suspected Bitter just liked that big brute.

⌁

IT WAS DUSK BEFORE BITTER turned Rockford and Alamo into the upper pasture. Morgan sat at the sipping table with a cool glass of cider and watched Sarah pet a new gray kitten. When her husband sat down in the second chair, she said, "I see you brought a new horse home."

Bitter grinned, poured cider in a cup and said, "I had to. He's the only horse I've ever ridden that has the heart and stamina of Rockford. And, he's a gelding, so he and Rockford will get along." He paused,

"But he's nearly as mean as Rockford. I don't think any of our boys should try him."

Mikey stepped into the doorway and said, "Can go I go see him?"

"Sure. His name is Alamo."

They watched him cross the yard to the barn, climb the gate to the upper pasture and head for the horses grazing near the south fence.

⌇

M ORGAN NODDED. "BY THE WAY, now that you are home for a while, I'm going to start riding Lucifer again. He's gotten fat and lazy."

"Okay, but what difference does that make if he is?"

"There is going to be a horse race at the county fair. I'm going to enter him. He needs to be ready."

"But you're pregnant."

"I won't ride him in the race. Ethan will do that. He's lighter, and he takes after you. He can stick."

"I'm not his actual father."

"Yes, but he looks up to you like you were. And you are his father in all the ways that matter."

"Seen Thomas and Ethan lately?"

Morgan smiled. "Only at mealtimes. They brought down the horses from Ezra's place, and I think they are starting to work with the colts. I suspect they want to surprise you."

"We're lucky, my love. They are fine boys."

Mikey came trotting back, climbed the gate and said excitedly, "The red mare, the one you brought home from Eastern Oregon, is having a colt right now."

"Any trouble?" Bitter asked.

"No. She's fine." Mikey paused and then said, "That Alamo horse. I'll ride him when I'm thirteen."

"Think you can?"

"Yes. He likes me. Can I have some cider?"

August

A WARM AUGUST MORNING THAT PROMISED TO turn downright hot brought Lucifer's braying up and down Abiqua Creek. It was his habit to announce the presence of unwanted people, horses, dogs or strange mules.

Bitter carried his coffee cup out on the porch to see what was fussing the big brute just as a buggy pulled by a matched pair of bay horses turned down the lane. He could make out two people sitting in the buggy. One appeared to be a woman.

When Lucifer charged the fence, the geldings thought about bolting, but a strong hand on the reins checked their impulse. Bitter just shook his head. "I think I'll move him to the Hill Farm and keep him away from our lane."

Morgan slipped an arm around his waist and said, "That's a good idea…just as soon as you get a bridge built between the Hill Farm and this place. I don't want to walk two miles just to ride him."

"How about a foot bridge?"

"No. We need a wagon bridge."

"Yes, Boss."

"You know I'm right."

"I do. I already scouted out two big fir trees tall enough to span the creek. They'll be plenty stout for stringers. And they stand side by side. We can fall them across the creek, and the boys and I can plank them…put some rails in place. I'll have to bring in some fill rock for ramps on either end, but it's a natural place for a road. And it should be above the meanest flood we're likely to see on Abiqua Creek."

"You already planned this?"

"I did. You do know I was once a hard-working farmer."

"I heard rumors about that."

Bitter was startled when brother Luke pulled the buggy to a stop. It wasn't seeing Luke that startled him. It was the sight of Abigail Simmons, looking prim and proper…and proud.

"Holy smokes," he said under his breath.

Luke helped Abigail down from the buggy as both Morgan and Bitter walked down the steps to the yard. Luke pulled a leather case from the back of the buggy, grinned and said, "Howdy. We bring tidings. Morgan, this is Miss Abigail Simmons. She is my business partner."

And much more, unless I miss my guess, Morgan thought. But she held out her hand and said, "Welcome. You picked a warm day for a ride."

Abigail smiled and then said, "It is such a beautiful valley. I love seeing it. But that brute of an animal in your pasture startled the devil out of me."

Morgan chuckled and said, "That's Lucifer."

"He's huge. I've never seen a mule that big."

"He's a Missouri Mammoth Mule."

"Well, I'm glad he's fenced in."

"Oh, he just likes to make a fuss. Show the world who's boss. Why don't you come on in. I have some fresh coffee on the stove."

Sarah was telling the world all about something from her crib when they walked into the kitchen. Bitter said, "Have a chair," and then went to the bedroom for Sarah.

When he set her down on the floor, she stared at Luke and Abigail, a finger in the corner of her mouth. And then she smiled and walked to Abigail with her arms out. Abigail picked her up. "And, who are you, little one?"

The toddler smiled and said, "Sarah." A garbled "Sarah," but clear enough for social purposes.

"And you can talk already."

"Uh-huh."

Morgan poured coffee for the adults and set a glass of milk in front of Sarah, and then sat down. "So, Luke, what tidings do you have for us?"

Luke unbuckled the leather case and set three long envelopes on the table. He picked one up and handed it to his brother. "John, this is an adoption order making you and Morgan Thomas's legal parents. So, that should put an end to any claim the Dickson's make. And, by the way, Hezekiah Dickson, the one you wounded, has been sentenced to five years in the new prison in Salem."

Bitter shook his head. "Just five years?"

"The judge said he hadn't actually done anything to you. Just threatened to do something."

"What about all the cruel beatings he gave Thomas?"

"That never came up."

"Why wasn't I called to testify?"

"You've been gone a lot, and the judge didn't want to wait. So, the sheriff took your sworn statement to court and that seemed to be satisfactory."

"Unbelievable."

"I know, but at least justice was swift." Luke picked up another of the envelopes. "This is the deed for my old farm. It makes Ezra and Ruth Shipley joint owners. That might settle the dust a bit for them. This other is a new deed to this farm making you and Morgan joint owners." He smiled. "And, finally, I wanted to be the first to congratulate our newest State Representative."

"Well damn. I had hopes I'd lose."

"Not a prayer, little brother."

Morgan smiled at her husband, and said, "Congratulations. Remember, it's only sixty days every two years."

Bitter shook his head, but didn't say anything.

Morgan took Sarah from Abigail's lap and said, "Miss Abigail, would you like to take a walk with Sarah and me out to the orchard?"

Both men rose as the ladies left the house. When they were out of sight…and hopefully out of hearing, Bitter sat back down and said, "Okay, big brother, what's going on?"

"I don't know what you mean."

"Yes, you do. Here you are, a married man taking a long ride in the country with a very pretty young woman and introducing her to Morgan as though you had intentions of making her more than your 'business partner'."

"I do. I intend to marry her."

"What about Lydia?"

"Well, in one of her tirades, she slipped. I swear she mentioned a 'first' husband. So I contacted your man Nelson Goff. He started an investigation. It seems, if Goff is to be believed, she ran away with an older man when she was fifteen. A very rich older man, by the way. She was briefly married to him until he sent her back to her parents. That marriage was never dissolved."

"Holy smokes."

"Yes. My thoughts exactly. When I confronted her, she broke down and admitted it. Wanted me to forgive her because she was so young when it happened. She tried tears, and when that didn't work, her true nature came out. She said she'd kill me before giving up her house and her position in the community. Never said a word about Eloise.

"So…since we have never been legally married…I'm having my non-marriage dissolved."

"And then?"

"And then, I will marry Abby and get on with life. I will see that Lydia has sufficient funds to live comfortably, and I will have the right to see my darling child on a regular basis. Lydia will be free to remarry…as long as no one but you, me, Goff and Lydia know the truth. And, I can remarry in six months.

"By the way, I'm in a partnership with a lumberman named Simpson. He is building a mill just above the junction of Mary's River with the Willamette. He plans to bring log rafts to the mill from the McKenzie watershed, Mary's River, and the Coast Fork of the Willamette. We'll ship lumber from Corvallis by steamer for now. I'm holding a share for you."

"I don't have much spare money, Luke. Not more than about five hundred dollars. And we won't be bringing in much until after fall harvest."

"I'll put up your share, and you can repay me from the proceeds. There is going to be a great need for milled lumber. We'll need timbers for bridges, lots of bridges right down the middle of the Willamette Valley. And Portland is growing way beyond the original Stump Town. It's to be the commercial center of Oregon. And as the state capitol, Salem will have to grow. It's fast becoming a market center for farm produce."

"Is this another one of those times when I don't have a damned thing to say about it?"

Luke grinned and held out his hand. "Together, brother, together."

A blond head peeked around the door and Ethan said, "Hi, Uncle Luke."

"Ethan. Look at you. I swear you've grown a foot since I saw you last." Luke held out his hand and Ethan gave it a quick shake.

Mikey and Thomas edged into the room.

"Thomas," Luke said, "I brought the adoption papers with me. You are now Thomas Bitter. Welcome to the family."

Thomas nodded, his voice too choked to talk, and then turned and walked back out on the porch to hide the tears in his eyes.

Mikey said, "He likes it. He's my other brother, you know."

Bellamy

A DAY AFTER LUKE AND ABIGAIL'S VISIT, Bitter was down along the creek eyeballing two tall fir trees he planned to use as stringers for what he thought of as "Morgan's Bridge."

Bitter shook his head. "I don't like it," he said to the boys. "We need to get the bark off or the trees will rot and our bridge won't last long. That means falling them on the ground, rolling them over to peel the bark, and then rigging a block and tackle to get them across the creek." He paused, looked up at the tops of the trees and then said, "You know what?"

Thomas shook his head. Ethan and Mikey just waited.

"We need an engineer. Someone who knows how to build bridges. I think I'll go talk to the Scotts who helped me build the barn. If they don't want too much money, I think we'll hire this bridge built. What do you think?"

"Not as much fun," Mikey said.

"Okay. How about this: We get them to set the stringers and then we do the planking and the rails."

"Better, Pa," Ethan said.

"Okay. Let's go talk to your mama."

When Morgan heard the plan, she said, "Do it, John Bitter. Go see the Scotts and get a price. They can get it done a lot quicker than we can."

Bitter nodded. "I'll go see what they can do. I kept looking at those tall trees, thinking about how much they weigh. I'm not sure we have enough mules to pull them across the creek. This will be better."

He started for the barn and then heard Lucifer announce someone was coming. Bitter squinted, trying to see who was driving a spanking new buggy down his farm lane. And then he turned and trotted back toward the house. "Morgan!" he hollered. "It's Sergeant Bellamy and Wanda. They finally got here."

Morgan came out on the porch, drying her hands on her apron. "Oh, my. That's just wonderful! And I don't have a thing to serve them."

"Coffee or cider will do, love."

A big grin on his face, Sergeant Major Jack Bellamy, retired, pulled the nice bay mare hitched to the buggy to a stop and stepped down. He turned and gave Bitter a salute. "Captain Bitter. It's good to see you…even if we are a year late." Bellamy gave Wanda a hand down, and then Morgan was running across the yard, arms wide.

"Oh, Wanda. I thought we might never see you again, and here you are."

Bitter gave Bellamy a bear hug and said, "The last time I saw you, Sergeant Bellamy, you and your squad were following Blind Charlie who was tracking some ambushers. How did that turn out?"

"Ah, Captain. It was a fine chase, but we finally caught up with the outlaws. Seems their horses sort of bogged down in a slough they tried to cross. The were sitting in the saddles shooting black water moccasins who found their presence objectionable. Must have been a dozen of those ugly snakes swimming circles around them. They were out of ammunition by the time we got there, and glad to have us kill the surviving snakes.

"One of the outlaws wanted to know how we had tracked them, and Blind Charlie pointed to a buzzard in the sky. He said the buzzards knew it was just a matter of time before they had good horse meat and tender white flesh for dinner."

He laughed and pulled a wicker picnic basket from the back of the buggy. "Wanda baked you some pies."

Bitter said, "That will ease Morgan's sense of hospitality. Well, come on in. How was the trip?"

Bellamy said, "I'd rather ride a bucking horse than sail in a ship. We hit one storm coming up the California coast. The sailors paid it no mind, but I feared for our lives. Too rough for comfort, and my stomach never quite adjusted to the constant motion. Still, two months versus four or five months. I guess it was worth it. And not one single Indian tried to steal my horse."

Wanda said, "Sorry to just drop in, but we wanted to surprise you. We bought a small café in Salem…with living quarters in back…and it needed a little fixing up. Some paint, some curtains, a new stove. But the location is good and we should do just fine. We've been working on it for the past couple of weeks."

"What's the name of this place?"

Bellamy laughed. "Wanda's Eatery. What else?"

"That dust-up back in Marshall was a busy time. I've always been thankful you and Wanda were there." Bitter smiled and asked, "And how is Sheriff Tucker?"

"Oh, he still complains about Gertrude and swears he'd rather be fishing than wearing a badge. It might be true. The carpet baggers have been a pain in the behind."

Wanda looked around at the house and asked, "Where are the boys?"

Bitter laughed. "Out and about…probably down on the creek. They use these warm days as an excuse to duck work and go swimming." He paused. "We are officially the adoptive parents of Ethan and Mikey. And, we have also adopted a boy named Thomas. We sort of found him on our trip across the Oregon Trail."

Bellamy said, "I'd like to hear that story."

"Well, we were kegged up on the Little Blue River trying to figure out a way to keep the Cheyenne from killing us, when Ethan spotted what looked to be a couple of Indians hiding in the grass. They weren't really hiding from us but rather from the same Indians worrying us. And the boy wasn't Indian. He was a white boy old Owl had adopted. Owl was a Cheyenne medicine man. We sort of took them in."

A small cry from inside the house called Morgan into the bedroom.

Wanda held out her arms when Morgan carried Sarah to the kitchen. "What a darling little girl. The spitting image of her beautiful mother."

Sarah held back and then said something only a mother would understand. "She wants to know who you are. Sarah, this our good friend Wanda from Missouri and her husband Jack."

Sarah wiggled to be put down, stared at Wanda and then tottered over and held out her arms. Wanda had to hide a tear when she picked the little redhead up and held her in her arms.

"Oh my," was all she could say. Finally, emotions under control, she said, "Jack, why don't you set the pies out. We'll test a piece of apple pie on little Sarah."

The Ellis and O'Grady Wedding

LATE AUGUST BROUGHT A COOL SPELL for which a very pregnant Morgan Bitter was grateful. She felt guilty about wanting the wedding over so she could go home and be comfortable again.

Ellie Ellis and her mother planned a small garden wedding in the big grassy yard behind the Ellis house. Ellie's mother, Marie, had never warmed up to O'Grady, and she was not keen on seeing any of his friends at the wedding, but she held her peace. There was an even chance she would never warm up to him, but Ellie's father, Marvin, decided his daughter had made a good choice. And privately, he was relieved his headstrong daughter had even decided to marry at all. Marvin's sneaky trips to the O'Grady Pub, which he never admitted to Marie Ellis, convinced him O'Grady was a stayer, a quality Marvin looked for in horses and in men.

Tom Beecher wasn't having any of this "small" wedding nonsense. He provided roast pig and the fixings. And every farmer he knew and every hired hand on his three big farms was invited. He brought two kegs of beer from O'Grady's and four cases of imported whiskey which he openly "hid" in the back of his wagon, and from which he and Captain Kelly of riverboat fame supplied a very steady stream of freeloading customers in a prenuptial celebration. Those who knew Tom Beecher also knew he cried openly at every wedding.

"It's the strength of our fair state, and it brings me great joy," he lectured when anyone chided him for his tears.

At the appointed hour, John Bitter and Ezra Shipley mounted their horses and herded a very sober Liam O'Grady down the road from O'Grady's Pub, Liam proudly driving his new black buggy, the red spoked wheels picking up ribbons of dust. Ellie had assured Liam he would be sober at the wedding if he had any hope of enjoying a blissful wedding night. Regretfully, O'Grady believed her. Ezra and Bitter laughed when O'Grady complained about facing the music without a decent drink. "That's no fate for an Irishman," he said.

Owl, Woman, Morgan, and Ruth, followed by the boys, and little Sarah in a little wooden wagon pulled by Mikey, walked the short half mile from Woman and Owl's cabin to the Ellis place, keeping to the grass along the dusty road in a vain effort by the women to keep the hems of their long dresses clean. All three were obviously and happily pregnant.

They arrived in time to find sitting places on one of the benches lining the lawn. Morgan smiled to see John Bitter, uncomfortable in his new black broadcloth suit, and O'Grady, dressed in a dark brown linen suit, a bemused look on his face, line up beside the preacher. Both unconsciously rocked a bit from side to side as they waited. Tom Beecher flanked Bitter, and Ezra stood beside Beecher, waiting for the bride. No one said a word about a black man standing up for O'Grady. In truth, the settlers in French Prairie were an accepting lot.

Marie Ellis might not cotton to O'Grady, but she nevertheless wanted a nice wedding for her daughter. As she told her friend Edna Young, "You only get one wedding." So, when she discovered what Beecher was up to, she had the little organ moved from the house to the lawn where Edna, who played the piano for church service waited nervously to fumble her way through a version of Mendelssohn's "Wedding March."

At a nod from Marie, Edna pumped and played, and O'Grady took a deep breath at the sight of Ellie, dressed in a white gown, walking slowly on her father's arm across the lawn between rows of benches borrowed from the church while her friends and neighbors rose to honor the bride. Liam failed to notice the pretty little flower girl leading the way, scattering rose petals on the path.

The ceremony was longer than Bitter thought it should be, but preachers are preachers everywhere, and Reverend Ardmore was no different than the rest. Given a captive audience, Ardmore was bound to sermonize, be the occasion a funeral or a wedding. When he finished warning the soon-to-be-married couple about the sins and sinners waiting to ambush the unwary, Ardmore finally had them recite the wedding vows, waited patiently for Bitter to fumble the wedding ring from a vest pocket, and then pronounced them man and wife. A loud cheer erupted from some of the slightly inebriated. The rest settled for a more sedate clapping of hands.

Bitter pretended to not notice when Beecher's wife walked up and wiped the old man's eyes with a handkerchief.

"There you go again, Tom," she said, but she said it with obvious love.

After the cake-slicing ceremony, a round of dancing, and one, just one, celebratory drink, Liam and Ellie thanked the crowd of well-wishers. Under a rainstorm of rice, they climbed into the new buggy and trotted away.

The boys were given permission to run back to Woman's cabin to change clothes and hunt up their friend, Alex. Which they did.

Sarah had fallen asleep during the ceremony, so Morgan picked her up and carried her while Ruth pulled the wagon back to Woman and Owl's place.

The chivaree planned for that night was a bust. Liam and Ellie didn't go back to the living quarters in the back of the pub. They drove

instead to the Frazier home where Ellie's friend, Ellen, was waiting
with packed suitcases. The young couple quickly changed and headed
for Salem where they spent a blissful three days in a nice hotel.

Harley and Sarah McBeth-Eagen

ON A LATE SEPTEMBER EVENING, A warm breeze working hard to
suck the last drop of moisture from the fall leaves, Harley and
his wife, Sarah, walked down the lane, leading a pair of skinny gray
mules, each looking like it had just taken its last step as they pulled
a sun-bleached wagon into the yard. Rusty's bark brought Morgan to
the door.

"John!" she said, "Harley and Sarah just pulled up. Thank the Lord.
I've been praying for them."

The boys hurried from the supper table, and Bitter picked up Sarah
and carried her to the front porch. "By gollies, he said to Morgan, "I
wonder if we looked that worn out when we got here?"

"Probably." Then she shook her head. "No. I think they've had a
harder time."

Worried about what his reception might be, Harley stopped the
mules a good twenty-five yards short of the barn and just stood there,
big shoulders drooping. And then Morgan was off the porch and running to her brother.

"Oh, Harley! You made it. You made it." And then tears were
coursing down her cheeks and she hugged her red bearded brother so
hard it took his breath away.

Morgan released him and turned to Sarah McBeth Eagan, held
out her arms, and said, "Sarah, I'm so glad to see you."

Strong though Sarah Eagan might be, she could not hold the tears
back as she fell into Morgan's arms. Finally, she pulled loose and said,

"There were times when I thought we would not survive the trip, and yet here we are." She looked a bit embarrassed when she added, "And I'm afraid we are almost penniless."

Morgan smiled. "Don't worry. John will have a job for Harley. And we have a good house just across the creek for the two of you. It has a nice fireplace, a good cook stove, a table and chairs and a bed with a nice cotton tick. Ethan and Thomas have been camping out over there to keep squatters away. We'll get you settled, and then later, you and I will go shopping for all the other fixings. Now, I want you to meet the other Sarah, our little girl."

Sarah Eagen hugged Morgan and said, "I didn't think I was to ever sleep in a bed again. It's almost too much to believe we will actually have a house."

Harley was a bit wary of Bitter. "I thought you'd still be mad at me, John, from the time I shot at you."

Bitter wrapped his arms around Harley and pounded him on the back. "Harley, you old rascal, I never thought you were trying to shoot me. Scare me, maybe. But you're too handy with a rifle to miss me by much. No, I'm really glad to have you here. You and me, a couple of old Civil War brothers, have things to do.

"Morgan bought the farm across the creek. It has a nice log house and it's yours to live in while you help me train horses, cut hay, farm, and, by gollies, I don't know what else. Both Morgan and I have missed you. Now, you better introduce me to your wife. And I'll introduce you to our boys."

Harley looked at Bitter and asked, "Which one talks to animals? Morgan wrote us a letter about that. And who is that taller boy? She never mentioned him."

"His name is Thomas. Morgan and I found him on the Oregon Trail and just now adopted him. Shoot, old friend, I've got quite a family and I haven't been home much more than two years or so.

Morgan invited Sarah in while Bitter and the boys helped Harley unhitch the mules. Watered and grain fed, Harley's gaunt mules turned hungrily to eating the wild meadow grass in the upper pasture. The horses looked up to stare at the newcomers. When Rockford decided they weren't much of a threat, the other horses just went back to grazing. Bitter figured Harley's mules needed to gain their strength before facing Lucifer in what had become known as the mule pasture where old Lucifer reigned supreme.

Over a supper of fresh-caught trout, compliments of the boys, fried potatoes and turnip greens, Harley and Sarah slowly told a tale familiar to the Bitters. The Indians were still pestering travelers, and it was still dangerous to travel from army post to army post without an army escort.

Harley was still fussed about the squad of mounted troopers assigned to his group of wagons. "When the Indians stole my horse, the troopers would not help me track it. So, we had the choice of being left behind or trying to recover the horse."

Morgan nodded. "I don't think I slept an easy night until we made it to Fort Boise. And that long, dry stretch across Idaho…oh, my…so many grave markers."

Aunt Sarah, as she was to become known up and down the creek, looked at Harley with sorrow in her eyes. He nodded and she said, "One of the grave markers along that stretch is for our little boy. He just never flourished from birth until…" Sarah didn't cry, but she couldn't talk either. They waited, and they could see the anguish in her heart.

Finally, she blinked back her tears and said, "Well, then. I am so grateful to finally be here. And the thought of sleeping in a bed…I'm not sure I can remember what that's like." And then she laughed. "I don't suppose you could show us this Hill Farm you have been talking about. I'm about to fall asleep."

"Boys," Bitter said, "go get Windy and Star hitched to our wagon. We'll offload Harley and Sarah's belongings and take them to the farm." He grinned at Ethan and Thomas. "Guess you'll have to sleep in your tree fort tonight. Pretty tough, I reckon."

Thomas grinned back. "Oh, we'll make out."

On the roundabout way to the Hill farm, Bitter told Harley about his plans for a wagon bridge to join the two farms. "And, Harley, there is an unclaimed quarter-section right across the road from the Hill Farm. I'll back you if you want to homestead that piece. It's got a nice spring and some young fir for cabin building."

***

IT WASN'T TOO LONG BEFORE Uncle Harley had staked his claim to the property across the road from the Hill Farm that would be known for the next century as the Eagan Farm. And it wasn't too long after that before Uncle Harley had the boys busy spiking the planks down on the bridge stringers the Scotts had placed over the creek.

Mikey and Davey, Ezra's boy, had trouble driving the big spikes with a peen hammer, but Uncle Harley took care of that. He would drive the spike in a ways and say, "That one's yours, Mikey." And then he'd start another and say, "That one's yours, Davey," and the two little boys would each pick up a hammer in both hands and whack away, happy to have an uncle who understood little boys.

Ethan and Thomas moved into their tree fort with the scarred cougar hide, one that was sort of tanned, sort of. They knew as soon as school started, they would have to move back to the loft above the kitchen until the new bunkhouse was finished. They hoped the Scotts would hurry with the building. Ethan and Thomas did like their privacy.

A New Direction

AFTER A HARD BATTLE WITH MOTHER nature, Ruth Shipley gave birth to a baby girl she and Ezra named Rosemary, after Ezra's mother. Rosemary was a breech baby and Ruth was certain that without Morgan's help as mid-wife, she and Rosemary would not have survived. A little wan from the struggle, she held Rosemary to her breast and said, "Ezra, God and Morgan saved this little one. She somehow got the baby turned. God Bless Morgan Bitter."

Little did she know how frightened Morgan had been when confronted by her ignorance of things medical. A breech baby like little Rosemary taxed her knowledge and skill well beyond her comfort zone. Morgan nearly cried in frustration in her effort to turn the baby around so the head came first, key to a safe delivery for mother and child.

That first evening after Rosemary was born, Morgan sat with John before the fireplace sipping warm chocolate milk. The boys were in the new bunkhouse. Although Rusty was not allowed to sleep inside, Morgan and Bitter knew the boys sneaked him in after dark. His presence was a comfort to three boys who had been hard-battered by life, so John and Morgan ignored this small infraction of the rules.

"John, that was one of the most frightening things of my life. I was certain I was going to lose the baby and probably my best friend, all at the same time."

"But you didn't."

"It was more about luck and prayer than anything I did, John. I just feel like something…or someone…larger and smarter than I am guided my hands. It was like I wasn't in control."

Bitter studied her for a long thirty seconds. He knew his wife, and he knew when she saw a problem, she went immediately to working on a solution. Finally, he said, "And?"

She straightened up and looked him in the eye. "I want to study medicine. Willamette College in Salem trains doctors. I intend to become one."

"Oh. Most doctors are men. In fact, I don't know of a single woman who is a doctor."

"Well, then I'll be the first in Oregon. It's study here or go back east. There is a college back east that allows women."

He pointed at her enlarged abdomen. "I wouldn't like you to go east. And what about your pregnancy?"

"Indian women give birth and then go right back to whatever they were doing in the first place. I can do the same. It will mean living in Salem while I study, but I think I could live with Luke and Abigail. "

She handed him an envelope. "Ezra brought the mail today. Luke says your timber venture with Simpson is paying off. The letter says Luke has taken his share of what you owe him from the proceeds of last month, and you still netted over six-thousand dollars for the month of September. He says it could be double that next month.

"I think that means I can hire a nanny for little Sarah and the new one…whenever it gets here. I'm thinking I'll hire Aunt Sarah for that task. She and I will live in Salem during the week and come home weekends. What do you think?"

"Well, by gollies, Morgan sounds like you have it all worked out." He paused. "Six thousand dollars? Is that what I heard? And more to come? I don't know what we'll do with that much money." And then he grinned and patted her stomach. "Why, I think we can afford a whole passel of kids. What do you think?"

She smiled and said, "That might have to wait a bit."

"So…what will you do if you manage to become a doctor? I mean where will you practice medicine?"

"Why, right here. I'll open an office in Silverton and be available to the surrounding area."

"What if Willamette College won't let you in?"

"Then you, Tom Beecher and Representative Franklin will just have to put some pressure on them."

"The male students might make it rough for you."

Morgan smiled. "Rougher than sixty Indians charging our wagons?"

Bitter laughed. "And there you were, right beside me, firing that old carbine and then your pistol. Yep…I think you'll get it done."

He shook his head and said, "You know, I just get settled into the horse breeding and horse training business, and something comes along and boots me out of my rut. First it's the Pinkerton business. The money helped a lot. I'll admit that, but then it's politics. And now my wife wants to study medicine and become a doctor."

He reached for her hand. "Well, Doctor Bitter, you have my blessing. I don't know where it will take us, but I guess we don't ever know anyway. We just think we do. So, when will all this take place?"

"Not until next year." She placed her hands on her stomach. "I want this one to get a good start." She grinned and said, "You won't have to eat your own cooking until then."

October

A CRISP, CLEAR MONDAY MORNING SAW JOHN, Abigail, and Luke drinking coffee while they waited for the cook to bring breakfast to the table. When John told Luke he intended to rent a room at the Mill Creek Inn, Luke was offended. "No. We have lots of room. Seven bedrooms to be exact. And a water closet and a bath on the second floor. Nope. You stay with us. We can ride to work together. Talk over old times. And you can keep me posted on what the Legislature is up to."

John wasn't the least reluctant to give in to Luke's insistence. In fact, he hadn't looked forward to evenings in a small room. He wasn't much of a drinker or much of a socializer, so it could have been a lonely time.

John was uncomfortable in his new suit, compliments of Luke's tailor, but his reflection in the hallway mirror as he headed for breakfast, convinced him he at least looked the part of a state representative.

And Luke's barber had done a good job of getting the cowlicks under control.

"I hope the room was fine, John. How'd you sleep?" Luke asked his younger brother when he walked into the kitchen.

"Not well. I just couldn't relax. You know, I feel about like I did in the war when we were getting set for a big battle. I know the Democrats aren't going to shoot me, but the feeling is the same." He took a deep breath and then said, "Luke, I'm not sure I'm cut out for this politics business. I don't have any idea how business gets done."

Abigail laughed. "Why Captain Bitter, how can you have any doubts?"

Luke nodded. "She's right. For now, just follow Peter Franklin's lead until you learn the ropes."

Luke drove his buggy from his Mill Creek house to the Nesmith Building, temporary home of the Oregon State Capitol while the new one was under construction——a replacement for the one destroyed by fire.

Luke pulled the buggy to a stop and said, "Well, here you are, little brother." He held out his hand, "Good luck."

"I'll need it," Bitter growled.

Several well-dressed men were grouped near the entrance. When Bitter walked to the door, one of them rudely said, "And who might you be? I don't recognize you."

"I'm John Bitter." And without knowing exactly why, he added, "From Abiqua Creek."

The man frowned and glared. "Ah, the young upstart who knocked off our man. Well, you Republicans are still in the minority, and don't forget it. You'll do as we say."

Instinctively, Bitter patted the derringer in his vest pocket. He wasn't sure why he carried it, but habit and ingrained wariness made him feel better when he did.

He was rescued by Representative Peter Franklin who strode up the walk, followed by a law clerk carrying a box of papers. "Representative

Bitter. Good to see you. Ignore these malcontents. Come on in. I want to introduce you to some of our colleagues."

The first day was a blur of names. Only two stuck…Doctor Jasper Arthington, state representative from The Dalles, and Raymond Hill, who was to serve as John Bitter's aide. He was an energetic man, about six-foot four, thin as a rail, and highly intelligent. He didn't mention it on the first day, but Raymond Hill was studying for the law in Representative Franklin's law office.

Franklin said, "And this is Mister Hill. If he likes you, you may in time be permitted to call him Raymond. Isn't that right, Raymond? Oh, and one more thing. You pay his salary, so don't let him try to buffalo you. He thinks he's smarter than we are."

Hill just grinned and held out his hand, his blue eyes twinkling. "Right this way, Mister Bitter. Our desk is on the right-hand side. Near the back corner. You'll be sworn in shortly. You may, if you choose, tell the assembly how pleased you are to be welcomed as a member of this august body."

Bitter warmed to his aide, a man maybe a year or two older. He said, "And if I don't?"

Hill shook his head. "Don't pass. The opposition will think you are intimidated if you do. Always remember…you belong here because a majority of the people in your district elected you to represent them. You are a state representative."

"I think I'll need some help. Have you been doing this long?"

"Since I was fifteen. My father was a state senator a few years back."

"Why don't you run for office?"

Hill grinned and said, "Because I have more fun this way. And…I may have as much influence as those who vote. Besides, I'm looking forward to a nice quiet law practice in another year or two. By the way, my fee is twenty-five dollars a week."

Bitter laughed and said, "You know, I think you sound just like my son, Ethan. Charge the neighbors a penny for a fish and charge me a nickel."

Hill smiled and said, "The laborer is worthy of his hire."

⌇

A T THE END OF TWO weeks, Bitter had impressed most of the Republicans, and he was beginning to think he might actually be of use. His first speech, most of it written by Mister Hill, covered the issues facing Oregonians: roads, bridges, schools, police, and financing the Oregon Volunteers to help protect settlers and travelers once the U.S. Army pulled down the number of troopers assigned to the Oregon District. The sticking point was the question of finance. And it would be the major sticking point for the next century, a crude definition of the separation of one side from the other.

With December drawing near, the House voted to end the legislative session, not to reconvene for two years. Bitter thanked Mister Hill, who now allowed Bitter to call him Raymond, for his knowledge and his expert help. "Without the wording in the appropriations bill you suggested, we would not have funded the Oregon Volunteers, and I think the Indians are not going to go quietly. We'll need armed troops."

They shook hands. "I'm sure we'll meet again…Representative Bitter."

After the last day of the legislative session, Bitter left what he thought of as his "lawyer clothes" hanging in the closet of what Luke and Abigail thought of as John's room. He happily dressed in dark cotton trousers, a blue denim shirt a scuffed pair of riding boots, and a new fleeced lined jacket. He also owned a new hat, blue with crossed sabers on the peak. He strapped on his gun belt and felt normal again.

He thanked Abigail and Luke, and swung up into the saddle. Alamo bucked and crow hopped and then finally gave up the struggle. The tussle between rider and horse done, Bitter turned the horse and grinned at Luke and Abigail. "He missed me."

That night, Bitter rocked his new twin babies, a little girl they named Mary Beth, and a little boy they named Joseph after John and Luke's long dead father.

When the babies were asleep and tucked in, little Sarah walked across the floor, held her arms out and said, "Daddy." He grinned and picked her up. While they rocked, he said, "Little girl, it's nice to be home. And shut of politics."

Morgan smiled and said, "Not going back, are you?"

"Not if I can help it. I've done my civic duty. But…I just might have to study for the law. It isn't intuitive, but without the rule of law, we have no freedom or safety."

"And raise horses?"

"Yep. I can do both. Raymond Hill will open a law office in Salem. I can read there when he gets established."

"John, did you ever feel like we are part of something? Something important?"

He nodded, held Sarah out at arms-length and smiled. "I wonder what you'll think of your mother when she becomes a doctor?" Sarah gave him a smile before he sat her back on his lap.

He said, "I'd say raising kids is pretty important."

Morgan frowned. "We could do that anyplace. But this part of the country is so full of energy and ambition, I can't imagine living in Missouri again."

"Yep. I'd say Oregon is on the move and we are part of that, like it or not. Speaking of moving, I still want a ranch…call it a summer place…in Tygh Valley."

Epilogue

IT WOULD BE A RARE SUNNY day in March of the following year before Beecher and Franklin met at O'Grady's Pub to talk.

O'Grady said, "So, John Bitter did a good job. I'm not surprised."

Franklin nodded. "He delivers a good speech. Several Democrats voted with us on the bill to fund the Oregon Volunteers. We didn't get as much money as I think was needed, but John's speech helped turn the tide. Otherwise, we wouldn't have gotten any funding at all."

"But," Beecher said, "he says he isn't going to run again."

Franklin laughed, "You know, this political business has a way of grabbing you. You get so you can't stand the thought of somebody else holding office…especially if you think they won't vote your way."

Beecher nodded. "We'll let it rest for a year, but I'm inclined to run John Bitter again."

O'Grady shook his head. "He won't stand for it."

Franklin just nodded and said, "We'll see, won't we?"

———◆———

A T THE OUTSET OF THE Civil War in April of 1861, the citizens of Oregon were ambivalent about the war and ambivalent about slavery. Witness the 1862 Polk County Democrats stating, "We are in favor of prosecuting the war for the purpose of suppressing the rebellion, maintaining the Constitution and executing the laws; but we are opposed to any war for the abolition of slavery, or for any other purpose but for the maintenance of the Constitution and the Union."

Nonetheless, upon the withdrawal of Federal troops from the state, some citizen began to worry about Indian uprising, as well as the vague notion of invasion by Southern or British forces. Young men flocked to enlist in the Oregon Volunteers, only to be disappointed when the Civil War bypassed the Pacific Northwest altogether.

This in turn led a number of young men to travel east looking to join the Union forces in the fight to preserve the nation.

A good book on the subject is *The Enemy Never Came, The Civil War in the Pacific Northwest,* by Oregon historian Scott McArthur.

§

M ATTHEW PAUL DEADY WAS A federal judge who lived during this period. Cincinnatus Heine Miller later named himself Joaquin Miller, and become known as the "Poet of the Sierras." In the 1860s he served as judge in Canyon City, Oregon. This much known about Miller is true as he was known as "an incorrigible exaggerator" about everything else claimed. The Umatilla House existed as did Sherar's Bridge and a Jane Sherar. The towns, creeks, and places like Bake Oven, Dayville, Tygh Valley, and the Pudding River existed then and do so now.

Award-winning author Rod Collins has done a little of everything: teacher, newspaper editor, logger, truck driver, soda jerk, construction worker, wildland firefighter, fire lookout, aerial observer, and business consultant.

More important, he is a devoted husband, father, and grandfather. And, like Louis L'amour, he has walked the land his characters walk.

Bitter's Run and *Abiqua* are Rod's novels set in the post-Civil War era.

The high desert of Eastern Oregon is the setting for Rod's Sheriff Bud Blair series of contemporary crime-adventures: *Spider Silk, Stone Fly, Bloodstone, Mariah's Song,* and *Not Before Midnight.*

Rod is also the author of the award-winning business reference guide: *What Do I Do When I Get There? A New Manager's Guidebook.*

Books by Rod Collins

Fiction

The John Bitter Novels
Bitter's Run
Abiqua

The Bud Blair Novels
Spider Silk
Stone Fly
Bloodstone
Mariah's Song
Not Before Midnight

Non-Fiction

*What Do I Do When I Get There?: A New
Manager's Guidebook*

www.ingramcontent.com/pod-product-compliance
Lightning Source LLC
Chambersburg PA
CBHW020654120726
47906CB00001B/262